Isn't It Romantic?
by
Ronda Thompson

LionHearted Publishing, Inc.
Zephyr Cove, NV, USA

LionHearted Publishing, Inc.
P.O. Box 618
Zephyr Cove, NV 89448-0618
admin@LionHearted.com

Visit our website: **http://www.LionHearted.com**

Cover model Cherif Fortin
Cover photo by Lynn Sanders
Computer artist Julie Melton

ISBN: 1-57343-008-0

Printed in the U.S.A.

To Mike, my hero.

A special thanks

To Susan Collier Akers
for encouraging me to write this story.

To Kim Campbell
for helping me cut the word length.

To Jennifer Archer and Charolette Goebel
for their editing skills.

To my agent, Jean Price, and her
submissions director, DeWanna Pace,
for believing in me, and in my talent.

Chapter One

♥   ♥   ♥

"My mom sells sex for a living."

Katrine Summerville stumbled in the hallway and fell against the wall with a thud. The black pump she'd been trying to force on her foot dangled from a manicured nail, momentarily forgotten. Did Shelly just say what she thought she said?

"You have an impressive home," a masculine voice responded. "She must be good at it."

"Oh, she's talented all right. Mr. Martin says no one can hook better than my mom."

An uncomfortable silence followed. The voice obviously found the subject of greater interest.

"Who is Mr. Martin?"

"Craig Martin is mom's boss... so to speak. He thinks her ability is natural. You know, God given?"

"That's certainly mind stimulating."

To Katrine's ears, he sounded far from intrigued. Slipping the pump onto her foot, then smoothing a crepe creation over her hips, she emerged from the downstairs hallway. Later, Shelly would receive a lecture concerning her lack of aplomb and one about discussing her career with strangers. *That child was eleven going on thirty!*

Her date sat facing the opposite direction, not allowing her conclusive evidence he appeared as disinterested as he sounded. A thick abundance of dark hair brushed his shoulders. *Thank God he has hair.*

In all her thirty years, Katrine Summerville hadn't once been forced to embrace the humiliation of a blind date. Well, he wasn't even that. The man came with a price tag. A phone call from a friend who owned the Dating Service guaranteed a perfect escort would arrive for this evening's event.

"Mr. Westmoreland?"

When he rose, Katrine immediately noticed his height. Her escort stood over six feet, closer to six two. His tux strained at the shoulders—broad, powerful shoulders, her literary mind added. Before her gaze had time to examine the rest of his backside, the man turned and the fake smile pasted on her mouth faltered.

"He's a hunk, isn't he, Mom? Tall, dark, broad at the shoulders and narrow at the hips. Tight butt, too. He's perfect, isn't he?"

A sudden slackness to Katrine's jaw muscle suggested her mouth might be hanging open. She clamped her lips tight and pulled her stare from her escort's amused expression. "Shelly, run along," Katrine instructed through clenched teeth. "Thelma's in the kitchen. She said you wanted to bake cookies tonight."

Heaving a sigh of disappointment, her daughter moved toward a set of swinging doors. "It was nice to meet you, Mr. Westmoreland," she paused to dutifully reply.

"Your formality seems a little awkward after making mention of my, ah, attributes. Call me Trey."

His smile, albeit a sarcastic one, visibly improved Shelly's spirits. She smiled back at him. "Trey," she tasted the name. "I guess it's all right. I figured you for a Chance or a Devlin, something more romantic. It's better than John. Mom likes Johns because my father was one. It's common, you know?"

"I believe the term is slang, rather than common," he said dryly. "It was… interesting to meet you, too, Shelly."

While her daughter stood mesmerized by a man she hadn't met until twenty minutes ago, Katrine wondered what in the world he must be thinking. She supposed an explanation was in order. Shelly read the novels Katrine wrote even though she forbade her. The child understood things no eleven year old should.

Still, Katrine loathed the idea of spending the drive ahead answering questions about her career. It was a job, it paid the rent and she hated discussing her work with people who weren't literary. Trey Westmoreland struck her as the type who only read sports magazines. Her gift of perception encouraged Katrine to believe he spent all his time working out and chasing women. He was too good looking, too perfectly put together, too right to be anything but wrong for her.

Shallow, she added, conceited; the perfect doll for a top-selling romance author to dangle on her arm at an awards banquet. Good God, the man was a paid escort. She'd be disappointed had Cynthia sent anything less than a barbarian.

"I'll get my coat," Katrine said coolly, not offering an explanation concerning her daughter's brashness. "I expect you in bed by ten." She turned toward Shelly still poised by the kitchen doors.

Shelly, blonde straight hair hanging past her shoulders, pert nose and full lips—a small replica of her mother, nodded. "I promise to be asleep before you get home." She grinned. "You two might want privacy. Trey is definitely a rake. His blood is probably on fire with barely suppressed desire at this very moment. He's eyeing your breasts lustfully and no doubt his manhood is stiff—"

"Young lady!" Katrine squawked. Her blood was suddenly on fire, not with desire, but with embarrassment. "I want you to apologize to Mr. Westmoreland. You and I will talk about this, *later.*"

Temporarily contrite, or Katrine suspected, embarrassed for being chastised in front of 'the hunk', Shelly lowered her eyes demurely.

"Sorry, Mr. Westmoreland, I mean, Trey. I

hope you have a nice evening." She darted through swinging doors and disappeared.

"I–I don't know what to say." Katrine glanced up into a pair of thickly-lashed, blue eyes. "I've tried to keep my work hidden from Shelly, but—"

"Do you, ah, work here, at home?" Trey interrupted, helping her into a fake-fur jacket.

The warm pressure of his hands scattered her concentration for the briefest of seconds. His touch sent tiny shocks of pleasure racing up her spine. Impossible, she mentally chastised. This only happened in her imagination, to other people, characters of her creation, but never to her.

"Three years ago I had an addition built out back. I wanted to keep my profession separate from my private life. Besides, it was hard to concentrate in the house. You know, with Shelly underfoot?"

"I can see where that would cause problems." His condescending tone contradicted the frown shaping his lips. "You don't look like the type who does what you do for a living."

As she retrieved a beaded purse, Katrine interpreted the remark the same as she'd done countless times in the past. She supposed Cynthia told him about her profession. Most people assumed romance writers were blue-haired old ladies or oversexed, frustrated housewives. "At the risk of sounding clichéd, don't judge a book by its cover."

Her answer prompted a lift of his brow and

brought a slight smile to his lips. Katrine swallowed loudly. If she didn't fit the stereotype of a romance writer, Trey Westmoreland looked exactly as she envisioned a paid escort would. A thought struck her. Did he accept money for more than the service of a date?

"I guess we should go." Her voice sounded oddly breathless.

"Probably a smart idea." A flicker of heat ignited within the coolness of his gaze. "Before I ask to see where you do your work. You've made me curious about a profession I haven't given much thought. I suppose because you look remarkably innocent."

His suggestive undertones were confusing. Why would he want to see her office? What did innocence have to do with her writing? Suddenly, she understood. "While I'll admit there's a certain stigma attached to my profession, you shouldn't read too much into what's fact and what's fiction. My work is based strictly on fantasy. I offer escapism. A release from tension and everyday stress. Our professions might be the same in that aspect," she finished meaningfully.

He frowned while guiding her to the door. "Although most are allowed the pleasure of escape in what I do, I consider my profession more technical. To be honest, I stopped enjoying it a long time ago."

A man who didn't like sex? Katrine paused outside to key in her security code, mulling over his admission. Did the gigolo really consider sexual pleasure a technical undertaking? "Well," she sighed shakily. "I guess a person can get burned out on just about anything."

"Cynthia said she'd handle the normal fees. I assume any other arrangements are done in private?"

"Assume?" She glanced up, surprised. "Don't you know?" She thought he blushed.

"Actually, this is the first time I've done this. I mean, not had a date, but *this sort* of date. It was a desperate measure. I didn't have a choice."

Just her luck, an inexperienced gigolo. So much for using this date as research. Not that Katrine would have gone so far as to do what only a desperate, lonely woman would do—an interview would have satisfied her. The problem with being heralded the steamiest woman on paper was, she had little experience to back up her supposed expertise. How could she when her husband, the only man she had ever loved, died in a car crash six months after their marriage?

Katrine had been barely eighteen and two months pregnant. She and John were both virgins when they married. Six months together hadn't given them much time to learn about each other, much less their bodies. In short, she could hardly count herself worldly. To compensate her readers, Katrine simply took what little she knew on the subject of sex and greatly exaggerated.

"The standard fee will suffice," she bit out.

"There won't be any need for private compensation."

"No, there won't," he agreed defensively. "I'm not that desperate."

♥   ♥   ♥

Later, speeding down I-35, Katrine contemplated his destitution. He drove a red Jag. She wondered if the agency provided the car, but he seemed so comfortable behind the wheel, she discarded the notion. What measures forced Trey into the position of male for hire? He looked to be in his early thirties, possessed the body of an athlete and could have modeled for *GQ*, in her opinion.

"What made you turn to an escort service?" she questioned.

"It seemed the easiest choice." Trey maneuvered the Jag off the freeway. "I'm not interested in commitments. Ask a woman out a couple of times and she starts assuming things. I decided this might work for me. Companionship with no strings attached."

No, just a price tag, Katrine thought. His conceit set her teeth on edge. Not that she didn't imagine a man with his face had women more than eager to jump into bed with him, but to expect to be paid, to prey upon the loneliness of women! It was abhorrent.

"How about you?" he asked before she could

further interrogate him. "Why did you decide to go into your profession?"

She sighed. Katrine supposed this was inevitable. People were always curious about the life of an author. "After Shelly's father died, I had to do something. Up until that time, I'd always done it to relax or for my own personal pleasure, then I realized I didn't know how to do anything else."

"Shelly... you don't suffer any conscience for her sake?"

Since they were no longer on the freeway, Trey's face blended with the shadows, but his voice relayed a note of unmistakable censure. The matter wasn't his business, still, Katrine provided an explanation. "Actually, I didn't realize how much my career affected her until tonight. Tomorrow, I'll have a long talk with her about reality."

Whatever his response, it drowned within a loud knocking sound from the engine. "Great." He steered the Jag to a side road.

"What's wrong?" Katrine asked.

"It sounds like the pistons," he answered irritably. "What a place to have car trouble."

After she peered through the tinted glass, Katrine agreed. They were on a dark, deserted street. To her relief, he fumbled beneath the console and extracted a cellular phone. Switching off the ignition, Trey called AAA and ordered a wrecker and cab.

"Sorry." He turned to her after placing the phone under the console. "We'll be late."

Remembering the length of awards ceremonies past, and the fact she wasn't up for hers until the end, Katrine didn't find their circumstance distressing. Let her arrive late with such a gorgeous man. Perhaps someone would actually believe she lived a life comparable to one of her heroines. Her own story wasn't in any way romantic. There were no happily-ever-afters in real life.

"Should we lock the doors?" she asked nervously. Trey's scent did strange things to her. His body heat warmed her across the small, silent space separating them.

"Wise move." He pressed the door locks. "We can listen to music if you'd like. It won't matter if we run the battery down, anyway."

"That would be nice." She watched him from beneath her lashes. Did Trey's arrogant reference to sex being a technical undertaking suggest he considered himself an expert at stroking the flames of a woman's passion? It was silly to even imagine he could. Her heroines lost their minds over a kiss, shivered at a warm touch, melted with desire under a heated stare and felt their thighs quake at the deep huskiness of a voice. Katrine called it fiction.

Once, five years ago, she'd foolishly gotten involved in a relationship. Sex with Carl Thomas proved less exciting than it had with John. Carl actually admitted to being disappointed she wasn't as hot as her writing. The relationship ended badly and Katrine hadn't gotten involved with another man since. Put simply, Katrine Summerville didn't believe in romance.

"What kind of music do you like?"

"Country."

The sleeve of his jacket slid across her thighs as Trey reached for the glove compartment. He paused, glancing up. "You're kidding, right?"

"No, I'm not," she answered shortly. "I'm Texas born and raised."

"When in Rome." He shrugged, slamming the glove compartment. "I've been in Dallas for six years and never once felt the urge to cry in my beer."

"I didn't think your drawl was authentic."

"Philly," he answered before she asked. "Tell me when I find the right station. Wait, I hear a twang, this must be it."

Katrine laughed. "They don't call it twang anymore. I liked it even when they did. The music inspires me."

"How so?"

An unfamiliar sensation uncurled in the pit of her stomach. Trey's arm rested on the back of her seat. Given his height, his knees were almost brushing hers. Katrine found it suddenly difficult to swallow. What had he asked? A slow ballad began playing on the radio and she remembered. "Most country songs are only short love stories. They stimulate me. I mean my creative—"

"Speaking of stimulation," he cut her off, leaning toward her. "Shelly is remarkably perceptive. I've been wondering from the first moment I saw you if you'd taste as good as you look."

His lips against hers created a jolt Katrine felt certain wasn't a figment of her imagination. She began to protest his forwardness, then changed her mind, admitting to a certain curiosity over what Trey Westmoreland thought he possessed that was so wonderful. *Would this cost extra?*

While he kissed her, Katrine savored each feeling he stirred for future reference. His lips were firm, warm and definitely experienced, still, the uncontrollable urge to rip his clothes off hadn't overcome her. When he pulled away, she sighed with disappointment.

"I'm getting a crick in my neck," Trey complained. "Let's be more creative."

She found herself pulled halfway into his lap and pressed intimately against a broad chest, then his mouth was on hers again, hungrier than before. As his tongue inched between her lips, an involuntary moan left her throat. Odd, she thought. To her knowledge, a simple kiss had never elicited such a response from her. But then, she couldn't really count his talent as an elementary accomplishment. When his tongue moved inside her mouth with slow, steady strokes, Katrine's thighs went up in flames.

"Wait." She ended the kiss. "This wasn't part of the package."

"Ever the business woman," he said huskily, allowing her to scramble from his embrace. "I don't usually act this irrational. What's your name, anyway?"

Horror struck. She'd been lusting for a man who didn't remember her name. Now that she thought about it, Katrine couldn't recall introducing herself. Cynthia told her his name, she assumed he received the same consideration. "Katrine Summerville," she growled.

Stark brightness lit the Jag's interior, outlining the tense line of his jaw. "It sounds sort of Rebecca-of-Sunnybrook-Farmish. I expected something like Candi, Brandi or Bambi. There's the wrecker and the cab. Good thing I regained my senses. It might have been embarrassing."

"That's my real name!" Katrine's pen name was Kat Summers; damn if she'd bring that up at the moment. "And I promise, there wouldn't have been anything to be embarrassed over."

"Maybe not for you." His teeth flashed white in the glare of headlights as he pushed the lock release button. "It's been a few years since I've been caught in the front seat of a car with my pants down."

His assuming attitude added further degradation to an already humiliating circumstance. Angry over not only his conceit, but by her brazen behavior, Katrine shoved the door wide and climbed out, marching to the cab with long, unfeminine strides. A hand closed over hers as she placed her fingers on the door handle.

"Allow me," Trey said. "Just a suggestion, but I hope for the banquet we might act like we actually know each other. As if the night hasn't been paid for."

"Are you ashamed of yourself?"

"Only a little confused by my behavior tonight. You're definitely not my type."

When he turned and approached the wrecker, Katrine assured herself he wasn't her type, either. Not that she knew what sort of man interested her, but he certainly wasn't it. He fell into the outlaw category, dangerous to a woman's morality and peace of mind. Trouble.

"You want to get in and close the door?" the cabby questioned. "You're letting out all the warm air."

Shivering, aware of the cold only after having it brought to her attention, Katrine obeyed. The banquet should be well under way. If fate smiled down on her, she'd arrive in time to accept her award and put a fast end to the evening. Damn, she forgot. This year a new segment had been added.

Non-fiction, sports writing, reporting and outstanding work in the field of features and columns. Katrine inwardly groaned. The banquet promised to be boring and time consuming. A frigid blast reminded her of an added annoyance.

"Fairmont Hotel," Trey instructed.

The cab lurched forward. Katrine stared out the frosted window at the bleak winter night, still in shock over her out-of-character behavior. Her 'escort' hadn't donned a coat. Probably afraid to wrinkle his perfectly starched shirt, or... perhaps he had hot blood. She shifted against the seat, uneasy over the wicked thoughts running through her head.

"Cold?" He pulled her closer. "There seems to be a draft around the doors."

Dry air from the heater vents fanned her face. The warmth creeping into her bones at Trey's nearness might easily be rationalized as a result of the other. Both were man made.

"A–About the ceremony," she stuttered. "You're right, we should pretend to know each other."

"I've already explained about this being my first time. I'm curious to know why you want the charade and curious about something else, as well." His lips brushed her ear before he whispered, "Is sex better when the passion is paid for? When the pleasure's predicted? When there's no room for inhibition and no strings attached? Is it the simplicity of the concept that makes it so appealing? Lust, pure and simple... and paid for."

His mouth inched closer to her lips with every question. Perspiration broke out between Katrine's breasts. Visions flashed inside her mind. Scenes of steamy sex with Trey Westmoreland, imaginings of pleasure without the worry of where it might lead—what she might say to him in the morning. A business arrangement and nothing more. It couldn't appeal to Katrine, could it?

Assurances she wasn't the type who'd want sex without commitment refused to leave her lips in the form of a protest. Hesitation proved costly. Once again, his mouth fastened on hers. Desire immediately coursed through her veins.

Until tonight, Katrine had been a third party to lust. Her heroines lost their wills to the insistent throbbing in their lower regions, and felt their breasts swell with an aching need to be fondled. Her heroines, at least, had morals and an ability to tell the hero no before true love made surrender acceptable.

A suitable heroine, she was not. Katrine's fingers stole up his neck to tangle themselves in his hair. She wanted only a taste—a nibble of passion to help her understand the concept behind her writing.

She got more than she bargained for. Trey savored her lips, teasing and tormenting until he had her squirming against the seat. When the cold vinyl beneath her gave way to the warmth of soft, fine wool, she regained enough faculties to realize she'd crawled into his lap and now straddled him. His lap sported something that shocked Katrine right back into the twentieth century.

"We can't do this," she broke from him to whisper.

"I'm certain, as you can plainly feel beneath that nice round bottom of yours, we can."

He silenced the weak protest gathering on her tongue with the intrusion of his. This is wrong,

Katrine tried to reason. Terribly, indecently, deliciously, wrong. She moaned as Trey pushed the jacket from her shoulders and slid the straps of her dress down.

"You taste as sweet as you look," he said huskily, trailing a hot path from her neck to the valley of her breasts. "You're also a pro at making a man desperate. Name your price, and maybe I'll regain my senses."

"Do what?" Katrine's spine jerked ram-rod straight. "My price? You're the one with a price tag!"

His head lifted abruptly. The overhead light blinked on as the cab door opened.

"Didn't think I'd get you here in time," the man whispered, his face a bright red. "Lucky the two of you are at a hotel."

"Oh my God," Katrine croaked. She tried to disentangle herself from Trey's lap, but the pointed heel of her shoe lodged itself in the front seat's back. A ripping noise followed.

"My shoe's caught!" she shouted in panic.

"What did you mean by that?" he demanded.

"It's caught. You know? As in stuck—"

"No," he interrupted irritably. "About me being the one with a price tag?"

Katrine felt a more important matter should be addressed. She glanced toward the hotel lobby and groaned. Sure enough, a crowd had gathered. Those milling about were the smokers, the gossips, people totally bored by the ceremony who used any excuse to escape the tedious banquet hall. Elise Pennington, a woman Katrine recognized from awards ceremonies past, a woman who happened to work for one of the local gossip 'rags', actually had her nose pressed against the window. The reporter began fumbling in her purse and Katrine went into hysterics.

"Don't just sit there! Help me get my shoe loose! Pull up the straps of my dress. She's looking for her camera!"

Trey's eyes widened, his head turned and he cussed rather loudly. He lunged for the cab door, tumbling Katrine to the seat beneath him in the process. A bright flash, the sound of her shoe tearing free, and several colorful oaths from the gigolo's too-tempting lips preceded darkness.

Chapter Two

♥ ♥ ♥

The banquet room was a welcome sight. Tastefully decorated and dimly lit; the hum of conversation emitted a feeling of comfort Katrine had yet to experience since a paid escort darkened her door.

After entering the lobby, she'd bravely marched past the gaping mouths of those involved in one way or another with her profession, hoping to appear as if nothing out of the ordinary had just transpired. Clay Barns, director of the ceremony planning committee, greeted her and quickly escorted them to a table. Katrine had every intention of ignoring her 'date' for the remainder of the evening. What had he meant by 'name your price'? She started to turn and demand an explanation, but the sound of a loud voice booming around the room refocused her attention.

Jerry Caldwell, an editor for one of the area's top newspapers, stood at the podium on stage, hosting the event. Katrine resented the choice. Before this year, the award ceremony strictly paid homage to the fiction genre. As far as she was concerned, journalism didn't have anything to do with true literary art. Anyone could write the facts or express opinion. It didn't require talent.

"Due to a time problem, I'm afraid those honored for the remaining categories must share the lime-light," Caldwell announced. "I'll present two awards at once and help end what's become a long evening. Someone's got to keep the presses rolling."

Jerry's last comment generated the fake laughter Katrine imagined he anticipated. The editor wasn't one of her favorite people. Not that she disliked him so much, but rather, one of his prized possessions—a certain columnist who wrote a slam article on romance writers three years ago, her in particular.

Enraged over the columnist's callous remarks concerning the genre, Katrine contacted her attorney. Only a smooth-talking lawyer on the paper's behalf kept the incident from the media. The columnist paid through the teeth and Katrine received compensation for his over-rated opinion.

"I know this is boring you, but at least pretend to be interested."

When she glanced at her companion, Katrine found his gaze fastened on her mouth. She shifted uncomfortably in her chair. He smiled.

"You're the one who should be feigning an interest," she countered lowly.

"Oh, I'm interested." His gaze returned to her

lips. "Very interested."

He leaned closer. Their breaths almost mingled before the sound of her name being announced broke the spell.

"So with pleasure, I present the prestigious Silver Heart to Kat Summers and the coveted Golden Lion to T. West."

T. West? Katrine stiffened, narrowing her eyes in search of a man she'd never had the misfortune to meet, but whose name brought anger boiling to the surface. "Bastard," she mumbled just as she heard her escort growl, "Bitch."

Her startled gaze locked with Trey's. Slowly, he rose from his chair. Katrine did the same. A hush fell over the noisy crowd. The spotlight found them.

"Kat Summers as in Katrine Summerville," he accused.

"T. West as in Trey Westmoreland," she spat.

"I thought you were a whore."

"I thought you were a gigolo!"

"Cynthia Lane is a friend of mine," he defended.

"She's my *best* friend!"

"I'll kill her!" both promised in unison.

"T. West and Kat Summers, come on down." Jerry attempted a poor imitation of a game show host.

When Trey rudely walked away, Katrine had little choice but to follow him. She held her head high, despite the humiliation she felt over consorting with the enemy. How degrading that she'd been crawling all over his lap only minutes ago. T. West who claimed romance novels gave women a warped expectation of love—T. West who'd viciously demeaned her talent and cost her a loss of projected sales for the novel he reviewed.

After reading the review, Katrine had called her editor and asked if they could sue the columnist. In a private arrangement, the paper agreed to compensate her losses and T. West hadn't reviewed her since, an oddity that soon became a curiosity among the tight-knit group of authors in the Dallas-Fort Worth area.

If the paper managed to keep the episode hush-hush, Cynthia Lane knew the truth. Katrine made no secret of her dislike for the columnist, even if Cynthia considered him a friend. Dammit, she'd found the perfect opportunity to set them up.

"Don't they make a handsome couple?" Jerry gushed, placing his beefy arms around the award winners.

A splatter of applause followed. Trey glared and Katrine growled. The editor quickly released them.

"Are you a couple?" Elise Pennington asked, tapping her camera as if it held a treasure.

Quiet expectancy blanketed the room. "No," Katrine answered, a bit too loudly.

Elise lifted a brow. "You looked like a couple… earlier," the woman's voice trailed suggestively.

"Research," Trey supplied. "Ms. Summers and I were discussing the over-rated element of romance lacking in relationships between men and women of the twentieth century."

"Westmoreland," Caldwell warned under his breath. "We can't afford this."

When Trey stared straight ahead, a muscle beginning to twitch in his jaw, Katrine suspected Jerry was responsible for her generous settlement, and certainly not the columnist.

"Even an opinion can be expensive in this day and age," she said softly. "If I were you, I'd do what I do, listen to my editor."

"Craig Martin," Trey said with a laugh. "I should have recognized the name. He's your editor, not your pimp. Your daughter had me going. Do you think it's fair to give Shelly the same shallow expectations of love you give your readers? You've obviously taught her to judge a man by the tightness of his butt and the size of his—"

"How dare you!" Katrine interrupted. Slandering her writing abilities was one thing, attacking her ability to mother was another. "Only a shallow man would assume to know what I have or haven't given my daughter. Shelly is very well adjusted."

"Accept your awards and move on," Jerry said after clamping his hand over the microphone. "Don't speak to her, Westmoreland. Not another word."

Trey ignored his superior. "What you write is sexist against men," he argued quietly.

"Then it's about time something was," she hissed under her breath. "And in case you don't live in the real world, let me tell you something. Women deal with sexism on a daily basis. What do babes in bikinis have to do with beer? What sport does the swimsuit issue of Sports Illustrated promote? Men have butchered romance and the media has helped them do it. The message being sent is a disheartening one. If a woman isn't built, and beautiful, she doesn't deserve to be loved. I give women the romance they can't find in today's society, and I don't care what they look like, or what they do for a living!"

Jerry removed his hand from the microphone long enough to shout, "How about a round of applause for our winners!"

Applause did not follow, Katrine noted. She imagined if not all occupants of the room could hear what transpired on stage, most could tell by her and T. West's expressions, that all was not well.

"Are you implying that looks aren't important to you?" Trey asked, lifting a brow.

"Not particularly," she clipped.

"So, you didn't tell Cynthia to send someone tall, dark and handsome?"

"Of course not," she lied.

He laughed in response. "I'll at least be honest. Since I assumed Cynthia's agency employed either out-of-work models or prostitutes working under a legitimate guise, I asked for a slinky blonde with nothing between her ears and legs all the way up to her ass."

"And you call me sexist," she accused. "I'm sorry you didn't get what you requested."

His gaze travelled her slowly. "That's a matter of *opinion.*"

Before she could stop herself, Katrine slapped him. The collective gasp of the audience merged with her own. Horrified, she stared at the ugly, red imprint of her hand against his cheek. *What had she done?* Katrine Summerville didn't let passion rule her senses or anger cloud her judgement. My God, she'd reacted like one of her feisty heroines. Mortified, she snatched her award and ran off the stage.

Outside, the night swirled around her, freezing the teardrop perched on the edge of her cheek. Katrine breathed a sigh of relief when a cab pulled up, hurriedly wrenching open the door. She couldn't understand how one man could so easily crack her control and put her on the defense.

She had climbed on her soap box over something she no more believed in than did T. West. For a moment, she wanted to believe in unconditional love, in happily-ever-after. She wanted to, but life had stolen the ability from her years ago. Now, Katrine dreamed for others, but never for herself.

♥　　♥　　♥

Red taillights were swallowed by the mist. A chill cut through Trey's tuxedo and ruffled his dark hair. He stood before the hotel clutching his award in a white-knuckled grip, silently cursing the woman who sped away. Kat Summers—a thorn in his side since he wrote the review on her. She made him look like an idiot three years ago, and she'd done it again tonight. You deserved it, his conscience warned. At least this evening, he reluctantly agreed.

He couldn't conjure a single excuse for his behavior with her. A groan of more than embarrassment escaped him as sleet began to fall from the sky. Trey searched for any excuse that might explain his overactive hormones and his unnecessary insults. None occurred. None but one, and he hated to even acknowledge it. Chemistry, the cursed thought surfaced. Illogical, irrational, undeniable attraction. Lust at first sight. All the makings of a torrid romance novel. "Dammit," he swore, stomping his feet to keep his blood from freezing.

"You waiting on a cab or trying to catch frost-bite?"

Glancing up, he was surprised to find a cab sitting in front of him. Trey bent, squinting through the half-open window at the shadowy figure inside. "I've got a couple of stops to make. Is that all right?"

"Hey, if you've got the money, I've got the time."

Irony twisted his mouth into a semblance of a smile. It was something he might have wished to hear from a certain pair of mind-altering lips earlier. A fresh wave of humiliation washed over him as he got inside the cab. She'd cast a spell over him. There was no way he'd have even considered paying for sex, not in this day and age, not ever, he corrected. Not until tonight, his disgusted conscience spoke up.

"Where to?" the cabby asked.

"The nearest book store," he answered, distractedly brushing bits of sleet from his lapel. Earlier, he meant to pick up a novel for next week's review, but a last minute scramble to find a date took longer than he anticipated. The price of asking a woman out once or twice and failing to contact her again left him in a bind. Four of the women he phoned had actually gotten married since he last dialed their numbers. Cynthia Lane and her dating service were a last resort. A short vacation to hell, he mentally added.

"What kind of bookstore you looking for?"

Trey glanced toward the driver. The man needed a shave and wore a shapeless cowboy hat perched on his head. "How many kinds are there?"

The cabby shrugged. "Two. You prefer floors your feet stick to, or not?"

"Not," Trey assured him.

"Good, I can pick up something for my ol' lady."

"Good," he mimicked dryly. "You can turn off the meter while you browse."

"All right, but if I get back to the car before you, it starts ticking again." The man eyed Trey's award. "You a writer?"

"A journalist."

"Oh." The cabby frowned. "I thought you might be somebody."

"I'm T. West," Trey ground out.

No recognition lit the cabby's eyes. He turned, smiling broadly. "I'm Charlie Grimes. Pleased to meet you. Every year I work the awards ceremony. Nadine, that's my wife," he informed. "She reads a lot. Well, most all the time now. She's gonna have a baby soon and the doc said if she stayed off her feet, her ankles wouldn't swell up so bad. Nadine's home anxiously awaiting my return, hoping I might have picked up someone famous this year. Guess she'll be disappointed."

"Guess so," Trey said dryly. "A few minutes earlier, and you could have driven Kat Summers."

"Kat Summers!" Charlie exploded in disbelief. "She's my favorite! I mean, Nadine's favorite," he quickly amended. "My wife'll be down in the mouth when she hears I almost gave Kat Summers a ride. Hey, she wasn't that leggy blonde standing outside the hotel a few minutes before you came out, was she?"

"Unless you want your face slapped, I wouldn't describe her with those particular words, at least not in her presence. But yes, that was Kat Summers."

A low whistle slithered from the space between Charlie's teeth. "Figured her for some guy's plaything when she rushed out of the hotel. Hot damn, and she's talented, too?"

"A matter of opinion," Trey grumbled. Kat Summers did what any grandmother in America could do as far as he was concerned. She wove incredulous tales of adventure and expected the reader to identify with shallow, physically-flawless characters. The stories were always predictable —they always lived happily-ever-after.

"Bullshit," he mumbled.

"Wind's coming from the stockyards," Charlie agreed, drawing air into his lungs in a huge gulp. Slowly, he released his breath. "Smell that money."

Trey eyed the cabby darkly and refused to either comply or comment on his misinterpretation. His thoughts returned to Katrine Summerville. Her novels were pure fantasy. The hero certainly never came home to find his heroine's things missing and a note taped to the dresser mirror. That was reality. His reality.

Once upon a time, Trey might have believed in everlasting love. Once upon a time, he dreamed of writing the great American novel, but that was before Linda Tate stole his dreams. That was before his crash course in divorce.

Their story had not ended happily. In his quest to please Linda by following in the footsteps of her newspaper tycoon father, Trey lost his dreams and eventually the woman he tried to pacify. He worked long hours at the paper, trying to measure up to her expectations. If he wasn't exhausted from meeting a deadline, or Linda wasn't engrossed in a romance novel, they made love. For six years they pretended contentment with each other, then Trey came home to the note. Linda wanted a divorce. She'd met another man. A rock-and-roll singer for Christ's sake!

His wife had completely blind-sided him. Her note said he'd become too boring, too structured, and lacked imagination or spontaneity. In short, Linda molded him into what she thought she wanted, then decided she wanted something else—another man—another chance to fulfill her unrealistic expectations of love. His wife hadn't needed security, she longed for unbridled passion, brooding stares and whatever other mush she'd been filling her head with while he slaved for her. Romance had ruined their marriage, or at least her view of what she imagined true love to be. Trey hadn't fought the divorce. How could he compete with fantasy?

Disillusioned and suffering the sting of her rejection, he'd quit her father's paper and accepted an offer in Dallas as a book review columnist. Trey decided if he couldn't write his own novel, he'd review the efforts of those who could, or in some cases, thought they could.

Romance novelists being among the latter. Although he admitted the story sometimes started out believable enough—a woman attracted to the wrong man and vice versa, soon formula took over. Through a series of ridiculous trials and tribulations, the hero suddenly becomes everything the heroine wants him to be, and of course, this helps them to live happily-ever-after.

"Here we are," the cabby said, pulling the cab up to the curb.

Good, Trey thought. He wasn't wasting another thought on Katrine Summerville, or his illogical attraction to her. Talk about the wrong woman. Trey placed his award on the seat and exited the cab. The door locks clicked and Charlie raced ahead, cursing the cold.

Trey's steps were unhurried. He loved the cold. Hot blood, he guessed, for he seldom wore a coat. After he entered the establishment, he realized people obviously seldom wore a tuxedo to a book store. He received several curious glances while striding to the new release section. As he plucked a copy of *Robert Ludlum's* latest from the shelf, a conversation on the next row captured his attention.

"B—But I drove all the way over here for that book," a woman stammered. "I'm not leaving without it!"

"Then I guess you ain't leaving. Listen, Lady, I promised my wife I'd get this book for her the first opportunity I got. Sorry."

Charlie's apology didn't sound too sincere in Trey's opinion. He walked around the aisle.

"No, you listen, Mister! I'm a woman alone. I risked being sexually assaulted or worse by driving over here this time of night. If you were a gentleman, you'd let me have the last copy."

"I'm no gentleman," Charlie assured her. "Not

if it means facing a one-hundred-eighty pound pregnant woman with swollen ankles empty handed. These days, if Nadine ain't happy, ain't no one happy, understand?"

"Problem, Charlie?" Trey glanced between the cabby and the endangered woman. She was a healthy specimen he doubted any pervert in his right mind would mess with, and to add further discouragement, she sported a head full of curlers.

"This woman's mad because my hands are quicker than hers," Charlie explained. "I snatched the book first. It belongs to me."

"The smart—polite," Trey corrected, "thing to do would be to surrender the novel."

The cabby snorted in response. "Well, you ain't got to go home to Nadine tonight, so why don't you stay out of this, Mr. T. West."

"T. West." The curler woman gasped. "The columnist?"

He cast a dark look in Charlie's direction and nodded. The loose folds of skin around the woman's jaws began to quiver. When she removed the newspaper from beneath her beefy arm, he began to search his pockets for a pen. It was silly, but on occasion, only when someone realized Trey Westmoreland was in reality, T. West, he'd been asked to autograph his column. He wasn't prepared when the bulk of the paper swatted him on the head.

"How dare you show your face on this aisle!" she shouted. "I used to love your column until you attacked Kat Summers! No self-respecting romance reader would give you the time of day after that!"

Ducking another swat, Trey stumbled backwards and knocked over an empty cardboard display case. Charlie made a mad dash for the pay out counter.

"Come on!" he shouted. "I didn't know Nadine had a twin!"

With one eye trained on the threat guarding her sacred romance aisle, Trey slid the novel he held inside his jacket and bent to right the display case. Kat Summer's name loomed in large letters before his eyes. Her name and a cover depicting a steamy picture of a hunk with muscles and a woman with cleavage. His vision blurred, and for a moment, the couple more than strongly resembled him and Katrine Summerville.

He blinked. "I'm losing my mind."

"He's stealing a book!" the curler woman shouted.

Seemingly from nowhere, a clerk appeared. "Open your jacket, please," he instructed.

People seeped from the woodwork. Embarrassed, Trey complied. "This is all a misunderstanding," he said calmly. "I'm T. West, the columnist, and I don't have to steal books; the paper reimburses me once I provide them with a receipt."

"Meter's running!" Charlie's shout echoed around the silent book store. A buzzer announced his departure.

"Could I see some identification?" the clerk snootily responded.

Breathing a small sigh of relief, Trey retrieved his wallet and presented a driver's license. "Now, if I could just pay for the book and get the hell out of here, I'd appreciate it."

"Ah, this is not proper identification."

Trey glanced down and felt heat explode in his cheeks. He snatched a condom from the clerk's fingers, replacing the article with his license. "Now, as I was saying, if I could—"

"Hold on a minute." The clerk raised a hand. "This says you're Trey Westmoreland, not T. West."

Accusing silence followed. Trey mentally cursed his petulance for privacy. Surprisingly, a woman came to his defense.

"They're one and the same," a female employee provided. "My boy works in the mail room at the paper. I've seen that man at the restaurant down the street and my boy said his real name is Trey Westmoreland."

"Thank you," Trey said through clenched teeth. "I'll drop by the mail room and say hello to your son tomorrow."

"Don't go near my Jimmy," the woman warned. "Any man who'd viciously rip out the heart of romance isn't fit to speak to my son."

"Amen," the curler woman agreed.

"Maybe we should get you checked out so you can go," the clerk suggested nervously.

As the she-wolves began to gather around him, their eyes glittering and their teeth bared, a thirst for blood clearly stamped on their faces, Trey quickly followed the clerk to the pay out counter. The transaction seemed to take forever, but finally, he escaped.

"This has been a night in hell," he grumbled, settling into the cab.

Charlie had his nose buried in a book. He marked his place with one finger and glanced up. "What the heck was all that about?"

Trey sighed tiredly. "Don't you read my column, Charlie?"

The cabby frowned. "A newspaper column? Heck no. When I read, I do it strictly for enjoyment."

"Well, if you don't want to waste your time and money on a poor selection, you should research the choices. I have a knack for knowing what most people want and what they don't. Which reminds me, I need to stop by the paper and check on things for my editor before you take me home."

"Fine by me." Charlie handed him the book. "Keep my place."

Once the cabby shifted the car into gear, Trey glanced down. His gaze focused on a likeness of himself holding a half-naked Katrine Summerville in his arms. He swore loudly. "Is this what you took on a crazed woman in curlers over? Is this what got me beaten up and nearly accused of shoplifting?"

"You were shoplifting?" Charlie whispered, obviously shocked.

"Of course not," Trey defended. He rubbed his forehead. "I really don't want to talk about it right now. Just be quiet and drive."

Charlie managed to remain silent for a good two seconds. "If you don't feel like talking, maybe you'd switch on the overhead and read to me. That Kat Summers sure knows how to get a person hooked right from the beginning."

Shelly's sweet voice sounded in Trey's head. *No one can hook like my mom.* How could an innocent misunderstanding lead to such a complete disaster? Annoyed all over again, he reached up and switched on the light. His finger rested between page one and two. *"The wind whistled an eerie tune through the moors—"*

"I read that part," Charlie interrupted. "Start at the top of the next page."

"Sabrina unconsciously moistened her dry lips as his hands strayed to the fastenings of his breeches... and this is page two?" Trey asked, lifting a dark brow.

"It's a dream," Charlie explained. "If Kat starts right out with the hot stuff, it's usually a dream or a flashback."

"I thought you bought this for your wife."

"A man's got to read something while he's in the can," Charlie reasoned. "Go on."

Trey unconsciously moistened his dry lips. *"Sabrina knew she shouldn't be here, not like this, not with him. Rolf was her intended's brother. Still, she couldn't find the will to leave, to glance away from the mesmerizing tune his fingers played against the compliant fabric of his clothes. Slowly, he slid the coarse wool breeches down his muscled thighs*—why don't these men ever have flabby thighs, or skinny thighs, or—"

"You got muscled thighs?" Charlie asked irritably.

"I guess so."

"I don't, and it doesn't bother me none. Keep reading."

His passenger obeyed. Trey read until his throat ached, until his eyes stung, until he realized he was on chapter nineteen and he and Charlie were sitting in front of the paper with the meter running. "Are you charging me for this?"

The cabby looked insulted. "Hey, you could have stopped whenever you wanted."

A burst of anger caused Trey's already heated temperature to rise a notch. He cursed Katrine Summerville while trying to see through the fogged up windows. She had to but walk into his life, and suddenly, he couldn't seem to get a grip on reality. He'd read her silly book because he felt powerless to stop, as helpless as he'd been to resist her full, ripe lips. She was trouble for him since he first saw her name in print.

One night with her and he'd been publicly humiliated, not once, but twice, and now he owed a cabby a generous amount for reading a novel written by an author he'd sworn to never review again!

Charlie pointed to the meter and whistled. "Hope you have a credit card with you."

Trey's expression wasn't in the least amused while digging for his wallet. "I want a receipt. Jerry Caldwell can pick up the tab for my reading time..." An idea suddenly occurred to him. He could substitute tomorrow's column with a different one. He glanced down at the book in his lap and smiled. Katrine would pay, too. Fitting, that her latest novel was entitled *Passion's Price*.

Chapter Three

♥ ♥ ♥

The smell of caffeine roused Katrine from dreams she couldn't recall. The knot of discomfort in her stomach, the labored sound of her breath, and the pillow clutched to her chest suggested a lack of memory might be for the best. She hadn't been dreaming of him, Katrine assured herself. If Trey Westmoreland intruded into her sleep, a shrill scream of rage would have shattered the quiet of morning.

Had she really slapped him and marched offstage without so much as a backward glance? Had she really let passion rule her head in the arms of the infamous T. West? A man who once said she wrote mush?

"Coffee's ready, Mom!" Shelly's shout floated upstairs.

Thankful for the intrusion into her disquieting thoughts, a tender smile touched Katrine's mouth. She winced while rubbing fingers across a puffiness not present prior to last evening. The cause of her swollen lips hadn't bothered to follow her.

Katrine wondered if Trey felt as humiliated this morning as she, then refocused her attention on the reason she smiled to begin with. Shelly, the gift God sent when so much had been taken from her.

Devastated by John's death, Katrine had at first resented the life growing inside her. Eighteen and alone, she worried how she would properly care for a child. More disturbingly, how she could set herself up for the pain of loving again?

Without the support of parents or family members, she survived on John's small insurance policy and nurtured the only thing she truly had left of him. When Shelly came, Katrine realized she'd loved the baby all along. Someone finally needed her, and unlike the mother who had abandoned her at the age of five, this someone would never leave.

"Mom, get it in gear. You have company."

Her heart slammed traitorously against her chest. Trey Westmoreland wouldn't come crawling to beg forgiveness for his rude behavior, would he? Doubtful, she reasoned, but washed her face, combed her hair and brushed her teeth before slipping into a pair of jeans and a t-shirt, just in case.

Any disappointment she felt upon finding Cynthia Lane hunched over a paper with Shelly at the kitchen table, quickly turned to anger. "You!" Katrine pointed a finger at the woman who'd been placed on two people's hit list.

"Calm down." Cynthia turned the paper face down on the table. "I had your best interest at heart. It seemed so silly. He needed a date, you needed a date. You're both talented writers with great careers. You're both gorgeous. You're both... going to kill me, aren't you?"

"I'd prefer to deal with you in Apache fashion. A slow agonizing death, but I'll settle for a rope."

"Mom, why are you being so mean to Cynthia?" Shelly asked. "You liked him, didn't you?"

For the sake of her innocent daughter, Katrine brought her temper to a simmer. Not so innocent, she remembered. "Shelly, did you know about this?"

"No," Shelly answered, and the pout on her lips bespoke it as truth. "But I would have been all for it. It was nice to see you have a date for a change. Especially with a handsome, put-together—"

"Speaking of which," Katrine interrupted. "Your comments both shocked and embarrassed me. Why would you say such outrageous things? And to a perfect stranger?"

Shelly sighed. "He was perfect, wasn't he? I didn't lie about anything. I heard you tell Mr. Martin just the other day that your sex scenes sold your novels. Trey did have the kind of body you write about in your books, and he was lusting for you. Any idiot could see that."

Katrine opened her mouth to further scold her daughter, then remembered the presence of a third party. "Stay put," she warned Cynthia before snatching Shelly's hand. "Come with me, Young Lady."

As they entered the den, Katrine glanced approvingly around the living area. Scattered about were authentic relics of a bygone era. Wooden spoons, cast iron skillets, pots and copper kettles. A Navajo blanket lay spread across the terra cotta tile surrounding a stucco fireplace.

Antiques were her link to other worlds; the past where romance once existed, having died out with the Indians; the buffalo; the measure of a man and the strength of a woman. The twentieth century generated a population of weaklings. A spoiled, self-indulgent, throwaway, if-it's-too-hard-forget-it, society. Was it any wonder true love found few to bless?

"Don't be mad at Cynthia." Shelly turned a pleading look on her mother. "She's practically the only friend you have and besides, she just wants what I want, for you to be happy."

The child, so much like her mother in appearance, possessed a weapon Katrine had trouble battling. She'd inherited her father's big, brown eyes.

"I am happy." Katrine steered Shelly to the sofa. "I have you and a prosperous career, what else could I want?"

"A man," her daughter informed. "I don't want you to be alone."

Seating herself on a leather sofa, Katrine pulled Shelly down beside her. "A man isn't a necessity to make a woman's life complete. You've been reading my novels. I told you they're too old for you. It isn't real life."

"It was real to Janie Reardon," Shelly worried. "Her dad wanted a divorce and her mom went crazy."

"We talked about that, remember?" Katrine took Shelly's hand. "Mrs. Reardon just needs some time away from Janie to adjust. Once she gets her problems settled, she'll be back."

"Janie's afraid she won't ever come back." Shelly said. "Janie must not be enough to make her happy. I'm afraid for you. What if I'm not always enough? You won't go away will you, Mom?"

Katrine felt a pang of guilt her own fear of abandonment had spread to her daughter. She tried to overcome the insecurities planted inside her from an early age, but knew they held her prisoner, grew stronger as time passed, put down roots.

"Shelly, you're the most important person in the world to me. And you're too young to worry over these serious matters or to make comments like the ones you made to Mr. Westmoreland last night. You're growing up too fast as it is. Stay my little girl a while longer. I'm not going anywhere, and the love I write about is only fantasy. Like a fairy tale."

Obviously skeptical, Shelly settled deeper into the leather sofa and drew the sleeve of her robe across her nose. "I'm never growing up," she decided bravely. "I'll stay here with you forever so you won't be alone. Unless, of course, you marry Trey, then I'll be free to have a life of my own."

Slanting her gaze toward Shelly, Katrine tried to decipher if her daughter offered honest self-sacrifice or attempted childish manipulation. "I'll remind you of that promise when you turn sixteen, seventeen, eighteen, and as I hear the wedding march being played. As for Mr. Westmoreland, it's pretty safe to assume he won't be responsible for your future flight for independence. I can't stand... I didn't like him very much," she amended.

"I saw the paper Cynthia was reading, and in the picture, you seemed to like him a lot."

"The paper?" Katrine puzzled.

"She has a regular newspaper, and one of those you see in the check-out line at the grocery store stuck inside. I saw her staring at it, but don't get mad. She tried to hide it real fast."

A sinking feeling started in the pit of Katrine's stomach. *Texas Trash,* put out by an independent Dallas producer, prided itself on featuring gossip about its own first-and-foremost. The 'rag' only stooped to three-headed babies or alien sightings if the Dallas area proved too discreet in its offer of tidbits. Elise Pennington had obviously managed to get a snapshot of her and Trey. She rubbed her forehead. "How bad is it?"

"I couldn't see the picture very well, but the title was printed in big, black letters. It said, *Best-Selling Author and Well-Known Columnist Delve Deep For Research.*"

"Oh my word!" Katrine jumped up from the sofa and started to pace. "This could damage my reputation. I'm sure my readers remember the slam T. West did on me three years ago. They'll think I'm consorting with the enemy."

"He's not the enemy," Shelly argued. "He's the one."

"The one?"

"Mr. Right. Marriage. Remember?"

"Honey, I'm not even attracted to that arrogant, close-minded columnist. Marriage with him is the last thing on my mind."

Uncurling her body from the sofa, Shelly marched to her mother's side. "It's just like in your books. Lust comes first, then love. Give it time, Mom." She comforted Katrine with a pat before turning toward the stairs. "I'm going to my room where you're getting ready to send me anyway. Don't yell at Cynthia. She knows you like him, too. I'm not convinced you'll be all right once I've grown up. You might not believe in romance, but I do."

"Shelly," Katrine warned, then threw her hands up in frustration. The child had not only grown too worldly for her years, but she was evidently a hopeless romantic, as well. At least Shelly didn't have a warped expectation of what a woman should be looking for in a man as Trey suggested, Katrine soothed herself. Or did she?

"Why him?" She halted her mature daughter's progress. "Why should Trey Westmoreland be the one?"

Glancing heavenward, as if her mother lacked

the intellect of an eleven year old, Shelly said, "Because he's perfect. You know, tall, dark and handsome? I knew the moment I opened the door he was right for the part."

A groan left Katrine's lips. "Shelly, beauty is only skin deep. I don't want you believing a handsome face, or a beautiful one for that matter, reflects a person's character. It's discriminatory and shallow. The important part of a person develops from the inside out. Remember that."

Her advice drew Shelly's brows together. "Gosh, I hope Trey's insides are as nice as his outsides. I'll be awfully disappointed if they aren't."

As her daughter climbed the stairs, Katrine worried that Shelly was setting herself up for a future fall. She seemed to believe Trey Westmoreland would resurface in their lives. "He won't," Katrine vowed, then suddenly remembered her guest. Cynthia. *This was her fault!*

"Start talking." Katrine pushed the doors leading to the kitchen wide.

Cynthia Lane glanced up from her paper and lifted a dark brow. "Do I have ten minutes to get the hell out of Dodge before you draw down on me?"

Ignoring the reminder Cynthia thought the swinging doors leading to Katrine's kitchen resembled a saloon entrance, she crossed the mosaic tile to pour a cup of coffee.

"You're not going anywhere until you answer some questions. Why did you fix me up with Trey

Westmoreland? I've told you countless times I had no desire to meet him. I don't care if he is one of Harold's friends; I thought I made it clear unless a date with him included a cauldron of boiling water, a Colt 45, or the right to castrate him, I wasn't interested."

"The three c's," Cynthia countered slyly. "Instead, you got a cab, a camera and from what appearances suggest, an attempt at copul—"

"Let me see that picture." Katrine splashed coffee over the floor when she stormed to the table. "It couldn't be that bad."

"No." Cynthia shoved the 'rag' toward her. "I'd say it looks pretty good from where I'm sitting. All right, level-headed Katrine Summerville, pull an excuse from that creative mind of yours to explain this picture. Make it a good one, especially since you can't stand... didn't like him very much."

Katrine stilled her inclination to scold Cynthia for eavesdropping and glanced down at Trey's annoyed features. A dry sensation settled in her throat. She tried to swallow, then gasped with relief. Although the picture identified the columnist clearly, only a thick mass of blonde hair could be seen beneath him."

"Well?" Cynthia questioned.

"You can't tell it's me." Katrine seated herself because her knees were weak. "This cheap rag wouldn't dare mention my name without a clear shot of my face."

Her friend's gaze lowered to the newspaper. "They didn't actually name you, but—"

"But what?" Katrine demanded.

"They mentioned T. West."

"Oh." She understood. "You're right, I suppose it was obvious to everyone at the banquet we were together. Well, that isn't as bad as my readers catching wind of it. They'd feel betrayed."

"Your local readers are going to put two and two together and arrive at the correct conclusion over breakfast this morning."

"I'm not the only romance writer who attended the awards ceremony last night."

Cynthia tapped the newspaper as if it held a clue. "You're the only romance writer T. West reviewed in his column this morning."

A blonde brow lifted. "I didn't think he had the nerve," Katrine said, oddly pleased by the prospect of appearing in his column. Surely, he'd learned his lesson about slandering her talents.

"He's got courage all right," Cynthia agreed uncomfortably. "Trey isn't short on that, or I imagine anything else, except maybe tact. After his review caused so much trouble three years ago, his editor told him to steer clear of you and the genre. Since all hell is getting ready to break loose anyway, I'd like to know what happened in that cab Trey thought was worth risking his job over?"

The sinking feeling started again. "What did he say?"

Cynthia gathered the newspaper to her ample chest. "First things first. What happened between you two in that cab?"

"Temporary insanity," Katrine muttered darkly. She sighed. "All right, Trey thought I was hooker, and, well, I suspected he might be a gigolo."

A burst of raunchy laughter filled the room. "Oh, I see," Cynthia managed between chuckles. "Because of me, you both naturally assumed—"

"It had nothing to do with you," Katrine assured her. "Your past didn't even enter my mind. There was just something about him… something that made me think of sex."

Another giggle spilled from Cynthia's lips. "I think that's called chemistry, Katrine. It's perfectly natural."

"Not for me, it isn't," she muttered. "I'm so ashamed of myself. I acted like a floozy. No wonder he thought my name should be Bambi!"

Again, the brunette burst into laughter. She glanced down at the paper and sobered. "His is going to be Mud."

"Let me see that." Katrine held out her hand.

Reluctantly, Cynthia handed over the newspaper.

A few sentences later, Katrine's cheeks started to burn. A little farther, and she began to tremble. Finally, she slammed the paper down on the table.

"That… that," she struggled for a worthy description, but couldn't find one dirty enough. He's going to pay for this," she promised, beginning to pace. "T. West only thought I caused him grief the last time he messed with me. I'm going to—to—"

♥   ♥   ♥

"Serve your family jewels to you in a paper cup, Westmoreland!" Jerry Caldwell shouted. "That's what she's going to do." He snapped open the newspaper clutched in his trembling hands. "'If steamy sex appeals to you, Kat Summers takes a back seat to no one. She's hot, and this columnist means that literally. Thanks for the ride, Kat. For me, PASSION'S PRICE was worth the hundred bucks I spent for a night with you'." Jerry Caldwell slammed the paper down on Trey's desk. "You've really put your neck on the chopping block this time."

Rubbing his temples where a headache persisted, Trey wished Jerry would go ahead and lower the ax. He felt like hell and looked ridiculous sitting behind his desk in a wrinkled tux. After he settled the fare with Charlie in front of the newspaper, Trey had gone to work on his review. He sighed, then glanced up into Jerry's red face. "I don't know what you're so upset over, Caldwell. I thought my review was very complimentary."

"Complimentary my ass," Jerry grumbled. "Any person old enough to put sentences together will read that, then look at this," he held up a copy of *Texas Trash,* "and realize it isn't her writing skill you were referring to! The phones have been ringing all morning. Everyone wants to know what's going on between T. West and Kat Summers. Including me!" The wind left Jerry's sails as he crumpled into a leather wing-back chair. He lifted the front page of *Texas Trash* and eyed Trey expectantly.

"It began as a case of mistaken identity," Trey offered. "We didn't know each other's pen names until we arrived at the award ceremony. Cynthia Lane set us up."

His editor lowered the gossip rag. "Cynthia Lane? The restaurant-owner-down-the-street's wife?"

Trey nodded. "Harold's restaurant does a good business so he decided to invest in a new venture. Cynthia's running the escort service."

"Yeah, right." Jerry snorted. "Probably lining up some of her old running buddies so they can operate legit. I can't believe a man would marry a woman who used to hook for a living."

"Harold knew what he was getting," Trey countered coolly. "If it doesn't bother him, I don't see why it should bother anyone else. Fact is, I consider Cynthia a true friend. She judges a man by what he is, not by what she'd like him to be."

"I wonder," Jerry speculated, "what the sweet-faced Katrine Summerville and an ex-prostitute have to talk about when they get together. I heard Katrine used Cynthia for research a few years ago. Seems she was working on a novel where one of her secondary characters worked in a brothel. They met at Harold's for coffee. Guess that's how they became friends, and how Cynthia and Harold met."

'Used her' echoed around Trey's head. Maybe the gossip rag hit the nail right on the head. "Just how far would a writer go to expand her horizons?" he asked himself aloud.

"How far *did* she go?" Jerry questioned, wiggling his eyebrows suggestively.

Jerry's leer brought Trey from his personal musings. He cast a dark look the editor's direction. "I didn't kiss and tell at the age of sixteen. I don't see any reason to start doing it now. It's none of your business."

Color suffused Jerry's face. His grin did a reversal. "You've made it *everyone's* business. Your suggestive remarks concerning back seats, along with the cover on this excuse for a paper, planted a seed of speculation in the minds of her readers and ours. I told you to steer clear of Kat Summers."

Leather creaked as Trey rose, moving to stand beside a window. "Avoiding her would have been easier if I knew what she looked like. Why doesn't she put her picture on the back of her books the same as most authors?"

"She values her privacy, that's why. Most columnists place a picture of themselves in the corner of their column, too, but not T. West. You wanted to squeeze the melons in the grocery store without being recognized, remember?"

"This wouldn't have happened had you allowed me to attend the private proceedings with her and the lawyers three years ago. I should have been there."

"Why, so you could insult her again and up the settlement?"

Trey wheeled on him, past the limits of his patience. "I gave an opinion. Freedom of the press, freedom of speech. I told you then, and I'm telling you now, she couldn't have done a damn thing to us had you let her take us to court."

"That's beside the point," Jerry argued. "Kat Summers is a local girl who's done well for herself. She has thousands of adoring fans right here in the city. When you wrote that review on her three years ago, we lost a large portion of our female readership. Taking her to court would have only made matters worse. I want you to write a retraction in this Sunday's edition."

"No way." Trey moved toward his superior. "She publicly humiliated me last night. I'm not eating any more crow for Katrine Summerville and that's that."

"Mark my words, that isn't the end of it." Jerry had the sense to step backwards, but he fixed Trey with an unwavering stare. "You might have gotten away with this had *Texas Trash* not printed the picture. Now, I'm afraid if you don't print a retraction, she'll go for our throats."

"Let her." Trey shrugged as if unconcerned. "I've given authors with more clout than her a bad review, and they didn't try to sue us. Do you know why? Because a good author is secure in his or her talent. Deep down, Kat Summers must know all she does is prey on lonely women. She puts ideas in their heads—sends them out looking for something that doesn't exist. I'm damn sure not going to applaud her efforts, and from what I have read, she's truly talented at writing sabotage."

Jerry eyed him suspiciously. "Is this personal, Westmoreland? Have you got it in for Katrine Summerville because some babe from your past dealt your masculinity a blow? Maybe this babe said you weren't hero material, or maybe she didn't find you romantic. Is that what all this is about?"

A soft rap on the door saved Trey from providing an answer. Steve Boston, assistant editor, stuck his head inside the office.

"We've got trouble, Boss. Craig Martin's on the horn. He wants to talk to you."

"Her editor?" Jerry frowned. "I expected a call from her lawyer. This could be worse. Stay put, Westmoreland. We'll finish this conversation after I see just how much trouble Kat Summers isn't going to cause us."

After the door closed, Trey returned to the window. He glanced down at the busy streets, a brooding expression settling over his features. "It wasn't some *babe,* Caldwell. It was the woman who promised me forever and went back on the deal."

♥   ♥   ♥

Katrine stared at the phone, willing it to ring. It had been four hours since she'd called her editor and demanded he insist on a retraction. Cynthia had slithered away while shock still claimed Katrine, but the shock of Trey's blatant review would not soon fade. She was seething.

On a personal level, she'd found his suggestive remarks only embarrassing. *Texas Trash* saw to it that their relationship was no longer private. Katrine didn't want her readers believing she would have anything to do with T. West. Perhaps she'd been somewhat frantic when she called Craig. She could have sworn he covered the phone and laughed.

"This isn't funny," she grumbled, turning her gaze toward the computer screen. Trying to write had proven impossible. Katrine couldn't think of anything but Trey's review, his face plastered on the cover of the local gossip rag, and the circumstances that brought it all to pass. The feel of his hands on her, his lips....

"Mom? Are you okay in there? I brought lunch. You forgot again." Shelly entered, a tray balanced in one hand as she fumbled to close the door with the other. "I have a hot bowl of Thelma's homemade soup, a roll, and a tall glass of milk. Doesn't that sound yummy?"

Katrine curled her lip. "I hate milk."

"It's good for you." Shelly settled the tray on her mother's desk. She frowned while gathering a total of five coffee mugs. "You shouldn't drink so much caffeine. It keeps you awake at night and makes you edgy during the day."

"I'm not edgy!" Katrine snapped. "I… have writer's block," she explained in a gentler tone. "Thanks for bringing me lunch."

"You haven't heard from him, huh?"

The question confused Katrine. Shelly didn't know about her frantic call to Craig Martin. "How did you know I contacted my editor?"

"Editor?" Shelly asked. "I meant Trey. He hasn't called, has he? That's why you're bummed."

"No, Mr. Westmoreland hasn't called and I'm not in the least bummed about *that.*" Katrine thought to end the conversation by ladling a steaming spoonful into her mouth.

"Didn't figure him for a one-night stand. Maybe you were too easy, Mom."

"Shelly," Katrine choked. "I… we didn't, how do you know about one-night stands or being easy?"

Her daughter placed hands on her hips, presenting a confusing picture as to which person in the room was the adult. "Sex is everywhere, Mom. Eleven year olds know a lot more than they did when you were a kid. There's no reason to get bent about it. Considering the statistics on teen pregnancy, and now the AIDS issue, I've decided to stay a virgin until I get married. If I get married," she quickly added.

"Y–You have?" Katrine stammered. "I mean, yes, that's a very mature attitude. You should wait. And for the record, Mr. Westmoreland and I didn't—well, you know."

"Oh." Shelly gathered up the tray. "That explains the edginess. You're sexually frustrated."

As her daughter eased her way out, Katrine stared blankly at the empty doorway. *What would Shelly know about sexual frustration?* The child didn't even have hormones yet! What exactly was sexual frustration anyway? A tight feeling in your gut? The inability to concentrate on anything but blue eyes, broad shoulders, dark hair....

A jingling noise scattered her thoughts. Katrine forced herself to wait until the third ring before lifting the receiver. She answered with a calmness contradicting her shaking hands.

When a New York accent sounded in her ears, she ignored her immediate disappointment. She hadn't really expected it to be anyone but Craig. Certainly not a columnist who'd finally gone too far with his opinion. As always, it took her a few minutes to adjust to Craig's fast-paced dialogue. She wasn't certain, but she thought he said something about making an agreement with the paper that would be more profitable than a retraction. Something he believed would satisfy her readers as well as get her free press. Finally, his suggestion penetrated her understanding. Surely she hadn't heard him right.

"You want me to do what?"

Chapter Four

♥   ♥   ♥

"You want me to do what?" Trey bellowed in disbelief.

"Write a feature with her," Jerry Caldwell answered. "Hey, we got off easier than I thought we would. Kat Summers' readers might question her involvement with a man who doesn't respect romance. Craig Martin and I decided to go with the research thing. Although the picture is still incriminating, we hope to take everyone's mind off of what the two of you were really doing in that cab, and channel their interest toward the feature."

Trey walked away from the door, approaching Jerry with catlike grace. He'd been waiting for four hours to hear from Jerry. "Let me get this straight. First you crucify me for reviewing Kat Summers in my column again, but now you want me to generate interest for the paper with the very person I'm supposed to avoid? Give one good reason why I should team up with her on a feature?"

"Financial security," Jerry answered sternly.

"You can't afford to lose this job. You've got a loan in process on a house and I hear your Jag's in the shop. Besides, you owe it to the paper to boost our ratings. This whole affair is your fault."

It wasn't the first time Trey wanted to walk out on Jerry since coming to work for the paper. Caldwell was a typical businessman. If you made him money and provided subscribers, you were an asset. If you bucked the system, said the wrong thing, or did the wrong thing, you were a pain in the ass. Trey felt like being a pain.

"Don't threaten me," he warned softly. "I'll go back to editing copy in Philly before I submit to blackmail."

"Would you?" Jerry smiled his doubt. "You've made a name for yourself in Dallas. If you aren't too popular with a portion of our women readers, your honest approach at review is respected by most of our male subscribers. We might even get national exposure on this thing. That certainly wouldn't hurt your career."

"Not everything boils down to career," Trey countered. "A man should be allowed his pride even in the cut-throat business of ratings."

"Pride?" Jerry scoffed. "There's not a journalist alive who wouldn't send his mother down the river for a good story or to see his name in print. I bet your ex-father-in-law would be interested in carrying the story. If you consider him a part of the past, I keep up with any man who privately owns the largest newspaper in Philadelphia. I hear your ex-wife is single again. It might soothe your pride to show Linda Tate how far a Philly boy can travel on his own fuel. I'd be willing to bet she'd find a story about her ex and a romance novelist intriguing."

Jerry's news momentarily staggered Trey. He quickly recovered. "I'm not interested in impressing my ex-wife. I won't do the feature." He turned toward the door. "I'll quit before I let you fire me over Katrine Summerville. Consider this my resignation."

Jerry's smugness faded. "You can't quit! All right, that was uncalled for. I'm sorry."

Trey kept walking. He moved past secretaries who paused in their typing to watch him storm by, oblivious to their soft sighs of appreciation. Glass rattled as the door to his office slammed shut. He took deep steadying breaths to bring his anger under control.

Damn Jerry! Damn himself! For one irrational moment, Trey wished Linda could see how well he'd done for himself. He wanted her to regret leaving him. How ironic if Linda were to believe he'd become involved with a romance writer, especially since she'd claimed the man she left him for stepped right from the pages of a romance novel.

That was six years ago, and Trey admitted he hadn't gotten over the blow. His wounds were more easily irritated in the dark days when he'd done the review on Kat Summers. Maybe he hadn't been unbiased. When he spotted one of her novels, all he remembered envisioning was his wife with another man.

Linda surfaced inside his memory. Dark hair, velvet-brown eyes, small, petite figure. His thoughts shifted and the hair became blonde, the eyes green, the figure slender and tall. Before the ripe fullness of Katrine Summerville's lips took shape in his consciousness, Jerry barged into the office.

"At least listen to what we've got planned. Any journalist in the country would give his eye-teeth to do this article."

"I'm listening." Trey removed an original painting of a glorious Southwest sunset from the wall. "Talk away. It won't do any good."

"The feature is, of course, on romance."

"End of conversation."

"B–But, b–but," Jerry stammered, "the two of you get to spend four weeks on the town, *compliments of the paper.* All you have to do is write the realistic opinion of the date while she writes the romantic side. We're calling the feature; *Does Romance Still Exist In The Twentieth Century? A Date With Reality."*

Trey smiled. "I had the distinct impression my opinions were responsible for landing me in hot water to begin with, Caldwell."

"That was before the 'rag' picture and your suggestive review created a charged outbreak of curiosity concerning T. West and Kat Summers.

Craig Martin thought matching the two of you against each other would be good publicity for her. Rationality versus romance."

"Sounds too easy." Trey purposely narrowed his gaze on Jerry. "What's the catch?"

Caldwell began picking imaginary lint from his jacket. "You're supposed to gradually fall under the spell of romance, you know, become a believer? Craig thought it would be nice if you wrote something mushy in the last feature."

Silence for a moment while Trey tried to mentally count to ten. He only made it to seven. "I'm not believing this!" he exploded. "I told you I wouldn't back down. Find yourself another stool pigeon."

A whine escaped Jerry's throat. He blocked the door as Trey moved toward him. "Think of the publicity. Imagine spending four nights on the town with a knock-out like Katrine Summerville. Doing this article might set you up with babes for life, and all you've got to do is produce a little thrust and slobber of your own when it's all said and done. What's so bad about that?"

"First of all," Trey ground out, "I've learned my lesson about being set up. Secondly, but most importantly, I don't write gush. I'm a journalist! Gush is Katrine Summerville's department. Why did she agree to do the feature, anyway? I thought you said she'd go for our throats."

His editor flashed a lewd grin. "Play your cards right, and she might go for yours before the romancing is finished. Kat Summers can't do anything to us, not this time. Thanks to *Texas Trash,* and your steamy review, it would be her word against yours. I imagine she knows the cabby can testify to her being in that cab, and from all appearances, very willing to give you something to write about. She needs a way out."

The anger simmering in Trey's veins rose to the boiling point. "Dammit, Jerry! If she can't do anything to us, why are we messing with her? Why didn't you just tell Craig Martin to go to hell and forget the whole thing?"

"Forget it? Jerry echoed incredulously. "This feature could boost our ratings sky high. *Forget it?"*

It had come down to ratings. It always did when a man's pride tipped the scales against fame and fortune. "I see." Trey seated himself before snatching up his name plate. "I'm supposed to gallantly save her reputation? I'm supposed to let her spread ludicrous, flowery, nauseating nonsense around for the sake of romance? I'm..." Trey paused, his building outrage fading to a simmer while his mind snagged on a catch to trip up Katrine Summerville.

"Humph." Jerry reinstated his presence after a few moments of silence passed.

"What if she doesn't find anything romantic about our dates?"

Footsteps heralded Jerry's approach. "She's got to, that's her part of the bargain. Kat Summers is to write the romantic interpretation of your dates, and T. West is to write the realism. Hell, I'm giving you the key to the city. The opera, the finest restaurants—how could she find any of those places unromantic?"

A soft scraping noise filled the room as Trey unconsciously slid the smooth surface of his name plate along the length of his desk. Would getting even with Katrine Summerville be worth the humiliation of agreeing to do the feature? The possibility he'd like to see her again was cleverly rationalized as revenge. "All right, Caldwell." He smiled slightly. "Let the games begin."

♥   ♥   ♥

"Well, what do you think?" Katrine glanced past her reflection to ask.

Shelly, sitting Indian-style on her mother's rumpled bed, nodded. "You're a fox, Mom. Where's he taking you that you've got to get all dressed up?"

Unconsciously running a hand over her hair, Katrine leaned closer to the mirror, wondering if her lipstick might be a shade too dark. "I'm not sure, Honey. Dinner and drinks, but he didn't say where. Mr. Caldwell told Craig we have the key to the city. I assume we'll go to *Chez Fred's* and then maybe to *The Baron's.*"

"I knew you'd see him again," Shelly said with a satisfied smirk. "It's fate."

Her daughter became the subject of Katrine's reproachful glance. "It's business." She ignored the tattle-tale shake of her hands as she lifted a brush to her already perfect hair. She couldn't believe Craig got her into this mess. Her editor and Trey Westmoreland. "I told you about the article. This is nothing but an assignment for T. West and Kat Summers. Don't confuse the issue."

"Right." Shelly snorted. "It's taken you five hours to get ready for this *assignment*. I don't think I'm the confused one."

Katrine summoned an excuse for her meticulous preparation and came up void. The soft sound of chimes filled the air and saved her the unwanted bother.

"He's heeere," Shelly drew out in an eerie voice, mimicking the child in *Poltergeist*. "Want me to get it so you can make a grand entrance?"

"I want you to get it so I can find my shoes," Katrine said calmly. "Are your things packed to spend the night with Melissa?"

"Ready and waiting by the door. I'll get out of here just as soon as I see his mouth water."

"Young Lady," Katrine warned. "No references to any part of Mr. Westmoreland's anatomy."

"I'll keep my opinions to myself," Shelly conceded reluctantly. "Don't make me stand down there and suffer in silence too long. And, Mom, wear the red-sequined heels with that jumpsuit. Put on a little more perfume. After five hours, you're fading."

Once Shelly disappeared, Katrine scrambled toward her closet. The huge walk-in housed at least twenty pair of shoes, all bunched in a pile on the floor. That she wasn't the tidiest of people registered as her gaze roamed the cluttered confines of her closet.

Clothes hung, half on, half off hangers like a trapeze artist waiting to make the fatal plunge to the ground below. Her belts were all twisted together, forced to share one peg, some knotted beyond restoration. Purses, bulging with tissues, gum wrappers, and weighted with pennies, were thrown in one corner. "Someday," she promised for the tenth time in a month.

Locating the red-sequined heels beneath a wadded blouse she'd put out a search and rescue call on two years ago, Katrine emerged from the closet with a frustrated sigh of relief. Trey probably assumed, like any woman, she'd be up here primping for him. "Well, I'm *not,*" she assured her reflection, squeezing into the sparkling shoes, then unscrewing the lid of her favorite perfume.

"Mom! You can hold up on the primping and come down!" Shelly shouted with the healthy lung capacity of an eleven year old.

She jumped. The bottle slipped from Katrine's grasp and her efforts to catch it resulted in disaster. Hands held out in front of her like a zombie, she moved toward the bed. A towel received the wasted indulgence of a hundred-fifty-dollars an ounce perfume. The room reeked. She reeked!

Waving her arms wildly in hopes evaporation might render her only sweetly nauseating, Katrine left her room and walked across the landing. An unusual silence struck her immediately. Shelly wasn't babbling. *Something is wrong.*

The oddity so unsettled her, she forgot to cease the flapping of her arms while descending the stairs into the huge living area. Katrine suddenly found herself a prisoner of Trey Westmoreland's steely-blue stare.

"Is that a nervous condition, or are you planning to take off?"

Silk-clad arms fell limply against her sides. Heat suffused her face. Whether the reaction stemmed from embarrassment or anger, proved debatable. Standing before her was no tux-encased hunk, but a Levi-straining, leather jacket packing, T-shirt sporting, grubby tennis shoe wearing grease monkey! His hair, that glorious mane of ebony waves hanging to his shoulders, appeared as if it hadn't seen a comb for the better part of a week!

"Sorry," he said, glancing down at himself. "My mechanic and I were working on the Jag. The time got away from me."

"Did the grease gun overpower you as well?" Katrine mumbled the only question seemingly appropriate.

"Maybe you should change, Mom," Shelly said quietly from her station at the door, overnight bag slung across one shoulder.

"Unfortunately, all my dirty clothes are clean."

"I'll fix it so you won't be embarrassed to be seen with me." A smile touched Trey's lips. "Don't get your feathers in a ruffle."

Reference to her bird-like entrance inspired a giggle from Shelly. "He's witty, isn't he, Mom?"

"Witless," Katrine said under her breath. "Why don't you go home first and clean up, then come back for me?"

He frowned. "I live on the other side of the city. We're talking two hours if I drive over there and back again. It'll save time if you go with me now."

"Lighten up, Mom." Shelly opened the coat closet. "Where's your sense of adventure?"

"Maybe it flew out the window." Trey turned to Shelly and winked, procuring another laugh from her as she pulled a red, wool cape from the closet.

Katrine felt a slight resentment over their easy manner with each other. Shelly shouldn't feel comfortable around a man she hardly knew, especially since Katrine's senses went on the alert the moment her eyes met his. Grease monkey or not, Trey brought an overwhelming essence into her female-dominated home. Maleness.

Odd, Carl had spent time in her home, and yet, she never noticed a change in the very air around her. A charge of electricity that made her feel breathless and filled her with a sense of forewarning—an uneasy suspicion her previously mundane existence had just been threatened.

"Where's your purse?" Shelly asked.

"On the sofa." Katrine moved to the sofa and retrieved a leather shoulder-strap bag. "Run along, Shelly. I'll see you in the morning." She flinched when her daughter delivered the finest wool money could buy into the greasy hands of her date.

"Have fun, and don't do anything I wouldn't do." Shelly grinned before easing the front door open.

"Hold it." Trey stopped her. "Where's your coat? It's cold out there."

"I'm just going next door," Shelly explained.

"You might decide to play outside before it gets dark. Take a coat."

Her eyes travelled upward. "I'm eleven. I don't play outside. I don't play at all."

Draping the cape over his arm, Trey took it upon himself to open the coat closet. "When I was your age, there wasn't much I liked better than a game of stickball on a cold winter day."

"What's stickball?" Shelly sounded less mature than she had a moment earlier.

Trey mimicked her, rolling his gaze heavenward. "What's stickball? You poor, mistreated girl. Listen, wear a coat to go next door and I'll come over some morning and teach you."

"Promise?"

He shrugged before removing a small goose-down jacket from the closet. "Sure."

"All right." Shelly accepted the coat. "Mom,

have you got your key? I don't want you waking Melissa's mother up at two in the morning, asking for mine again."

Stunned at her daughter's curiosity over stick-ball, it took a moment for the question to register. "Y–Yes," Katrine stammered. "I checked before I put my purse on the sofa earlier. Besides, I haven't done that in a long time."

"You haven't had a date in a long time," Shelly reminded, much to her mother's embarrassment. "Don't forget to enter your code for the security system before you come inside and—"

"Good night, Shelly," Trey interrupted. "Your mom's in good hands. Take the evening off."

"Bye, Honey," Katrine said too loudly.

Shelly kept her gaze levelled on Trey. "We have a date, remember?"

"Wouldn't miss it." Trey messed her hair play-fully and shoved her out the door. He sauntered toward Katrine and drew up short. His eyes began to water. "What did you do, take a bath in that stuff?"

Katrine ruffled. "At least I took one," she ground through her teeth. "What's that fragrance you're wearing called? *Oily Sweat?*"

"I thought you might find it rugged. You know, manly?" He tossed her the cape.

Soft wool slapped her face before she brought the bulky cape under control. "Are you trying to impress me?" she asked sarcastically. "If so, you're off to a great start. Considering what I've got to work with, I'll be hard pressed to find anything remotely interesting about spending an evening with you."

A dark brow lifted. "I guess you can always steal subject matter from our first meeting." His gaze settled on Katrine's lips, and he smiled slightly. "You seemed eager to work with what I had in the back seat of the cab... hard pressed as you were and all."

Heat crept up Katrine's neck and exploded in her cheeks. She hoped they might forget what transpired between them before they arrived at the awards ceremony. All right, she mentally amended, she wished he'd suffer severe amnesia.

For over a week, she hadn't been able to con-centrate on anything other than the feel of his lips against hers, his touch. Lust ruled her senses for one brief night and the arrogant grease monkey standing before her obviously wasn't going to let the episode die anything but a slow death. Katrine searched her mind for a way to wipe the smug smile off his mouth.

"I was curious," she answered in bored fashion. "About how a gigolo made his move. I wanted to hear your pitch. You were research, and that's all you were. Now, could we get this first assignment over with as quickly as possible?"

She felt satisfaction when the smile he wore slid from his face. In answer, Trey walked to the door, opened it and in a gallant gesture, bowed to her.

"Madame, your carriage awaits."

♥   ♥   ♥

"I'm not getting on that." Katrine stared at the motorcycle. "I thought you said you were working on the Jag."

Trey removed two helmets from the sissy bar. "I didn't say we got it fixed. Sal, my mechanic, was kind enough to loan me his wheels. Put this on."

Mistrustfully viewing the helmet he thrust toward her, Katrine refused. "I'm not riding on a motorcycle."

The thin set of her lips worried Trey. He might be pushing her too far, too fast with the motorcycle. Katrine looked like she was about to bail out. She couldn't. He wasn't finished with her yet.

"Okay, we'll take your car."

"I don't have one," she informed him. "I don't drive."

Despite the seriousness to her voice, Trey found it hard to believe a successful woman didn't own a car. "You're kidding, right?"

"No. Once again, I'm not kidding. It's not that odd, you know? We have buses, cabs, trains, planes—"

"But why go through the hassle? And what do you mean 'I don't drive'?"

"I used to," Katrine admitted. "I haven't been behind the wheel since I was eighteen."

Although Trey found the oddity curious, he

used it to his advantage. "The bike will have to do then. Climb on."

Katrine held her ground. "I'll call us a cab."

Annoyance on her part had been anticipated. It was, after all, the point of paying Sal for letting him use his Harley. Trey didn't expect a flat out refusal with ultimatums.

"Fine." He slipped the helmet on his head. "Call yourself a cab and go on this date alone. You've got a feature due next week. My half will be easy. Kat Summers doesn't have the spirit of adventure her heroines do."

Throwing a long leg over the Harley, Trey gave the starter a kick. He purposely revved the gas, creating enough noise to insure her neighbors rushed to their windows or dialed 911.

If the rocks in her yard were larger, Katrine might have crawled beneath one. The subdivision she lived in was a quiet, orderly neighborhood where even the children were well behaved and seldom seen outside.

"Wanna see me pop a wheely?" Trey shouted over the noise. "Bet I can keep the front wheels up for at least half this block, maybe all the way to the end."

Frustrated, Katrine jerked on the helmet. She fumbled with the strap until the roaring ceased and his fingers grazed her throat. Despite the chilly wind, his hands were warm. She shivered. Trey obviously felt her response, he pulled the cape closer around her neck.

"Get on and wrap your arms around me," he instructed. "When I lean, lean with me. Put your pretty, red shoes on the inside of my feet."

Heart hammering, Katrine did as instructed and came up flush against his broad back. She would have positioned herself differently, were there anywhere to move. The situation seemed entirely too intimate.

"Place your arms around me." Trey zipped his jacket, then removed gloves from his pocket. He paused, turning his head slightly. "Do you have gloves with you?"

"No. I couldn't find a pair that matched."

"Put your hands under my jacket."

"I'd rather not."

"Suit yourself."

After they eased from the drive, Katrine glanced up at Melissa's window. Shelly grinned broadly and waved. Katrine didn't dare remove her hands to wave back. *What was she doing?* Cars scared her as it was, a motorcycle surely held greater odds for death.

As the bike wound through quiet suburban streets at a leisurely pace, Katrine admitted she found the ride somewhat enjoyable. In fact, she felt a certain sense of freedom with the sinking sun in her eyes and the breeze tugging at long strands hanging past her helmet. Trey's back blocked most of the wind. He seemed confident and in control.

"Do you like it?" His shout flew to her.

"Actually, it's rather soothing! I never imagined riding a motorcycle would be relaxing."

He nodded in answer, proceeding down a side road beside the freeway. When he took the on ramp, Katrine stiffened. *Surely he didn't plan to take the freeway!* Trey gave the bike more gas and it lurched forward. Katrine's arms, draped loosely around his waist, tightened in panic. He weaved into the flow of traffic at a speed that pulled the skin on her cheekbones tight.

"Bastard," she growled.

"What? Faster?" He twisted his wrist, giving the machine more gas.

"Nooooeekk!" Katrine fumbled with his jacket, shoving her shaking hands beneath to secure a tighter grip. After the maniac rode straight between two speeding cars, within hearing distance of the occupants' conversations, she squeezed her lids shut and rested her forehead against his back. Forcing herself to breathe slowly, Katrine tried to concentrate on something other than impending death.

The heat rolling off the flat planes of Trey's stomach became the illogical choice. He had the body of an athlete, all muscle and bone. *Did he have hair on his chest? Where had that thought come from?* It stood to reason that he would. Most men with such an abundance of dark hair on their heads surely had hairy bodies to match.

She preferred smooth skin on the chest. Or so Katrine supposed, considering her limited experience. Carl had been extremely hairy, which repulsed her slightly. John was blonde like herself with little hair on his chest, but then, he'd only been eighteen when he left this world, left her.

Trey's strong, steady heartbeat penetrated her musings. For some reason, her hands roamed up his sides to splay themselves across his chest. She couldn't feel any padding to indicate the muscled contours of his pectorals were clumped with hair. Curiously, his heart lurched. Not so curious, she corrected, then quickly moved her hands back to his middle. Thank heavens her thoughts had strayed upward instead of downward.

Her face grew hot when the visual entered her mind. In one of her historical novels, she'd written a scene where the heroine sat before the hero on a horse. The rake took advantage while the heroine, too terrified of falling off, for a time failed to notice his fondling. Katrine was the terrified one, but the concept of reversing the situation intrigued her.

Mental notes were made for future reference. She imagined the hero speeding through the streets on a motorcycle, the heroine's hand roaming at will as he tried to control both powerful machines between his legs. Once the heroine ventured bravely to the waistband of his jeans, the hero would find a place to pull off the road and…

Reality shook her from the pages of fantasy. The roaring in her ears had ceased. Katrine lifted her head and opened her eyes. *Affordable Rooms* flashed brightly in the approaching dark. A seedy motel sat to her right, the parking lot crowded with rigs.

"Here we are," Trey said hoarsely.

"Here we are… where?"

"The restaurant."

"Restaurant?" Her confused gaze strayed to the left. An equally bright flash read; *Snotty's Truck Stop and Grill.*

"Snotty's?" she asked in disbelief.

"It's supposed to be Shotty's," he explained. "See, the light's broken on the 'h'."

"Oh, well that's different," she replied sarcastically. "Suppose you tell me what we're doing here?"

"Suppose you take your hands out of my pants so I can speak in a normal tone of voice?"

A tracer was dispatched from Katrine's brain to find her hands. They weren't really shoved down his pants, but rather, her thumbs were hooked on either side of the top fastening of his jeans. She snatched her fingers away. "I didn't realize, I mean, the ride, I was terrified and I guess…" her voice trailed away.

Removing his helmet, Trey turned sideways, allowing her a view of his strong jawline. "I thought you might be doing a little more research. If you're finished, I suggest we go into Snotty's, ah, I mean, Shotty's, and chow down. I'm starved."

"In there?" Katrine squawked. "It's a truck stop! You said you were going to clean up. You said you wouldn't embarrass me!"

A dimple appeared in his cheek. Although he wasn't smiling, Katrine had the distinct impression it took a great deal of discipline on his part not to.

"I said I'd fix it where you wouldn't be embarrassed to be seen with me. Most of the guys in this joint are dressed about the same as I am. You, on the other hand, might look somewhat conspicuous. You're definitely overdressed."

Anger began to thaw her frozen blood. *He planned this.* The greasy clothes. The motorcycle. The whole charade had been carefully plotted to humiliate her. "Here's a monkey wrench thrown into your clever scheme. I'm not going in there. Take me home."

Trey seemed to consider her request before he nodded thoughtfully. He didn't replace his helmet, but leaned to the side and slid off the bike. "I'd be happy to take you home. After I've eaten. Care to join me?"

"I do not," she growled.

"Fine."

In disbelief, she watched him walk away. "Fine," Katrine muttered. "He thinks I won't sit here and wait for him, he's wrong. I'll show him."

"Oh." He paused to turn around. "It's only fair to warn you that come dark in this neighborhood, any woman wearing sequined shoes is considered fair game by the truckers. Some of these boys have been on the road a long time…" his voice trailed suggestively.

Katrine's gaze moved from side to side. Another scheme, she assured herself. Trey wanted to frighten her. She refused to give him the satisfaction. Defiantly, she lifted her chin. Trey shook his head and continued onward. Without his body heat, the evening chill crept into her bones. She shivered as sirens blared an eerie song along the freeway. Her breath turned into steam and she shoved her freezing hands inside her cape pockets. This is certainly romantic, she thought with annoyance.

"Hey, Biker Mama!" a gruff voice shouted across the parking lot. "What ya doing out here all by your lonesome?"

Squinting through the gloom, Katrine made out the figure of a man standing beside a rig. She quickly averted her gaze, thinking if she ignored the trucker, he'd go away.

"Hey, Red-Riding-Hood. I'm talking to you."

Chapter Five

♥   ♥   ♥

The smell of unclean bodies assaulted her as Katrine entered the over-warm confines of Shotty's Truck Stop and Grill. Wolf whistles heralded the clicking of her red-sequined heels against the dull floor. She recognized a dark head bent over a menu in a booth by the front window. Her 'date' didn't glance up as she banged the helmet noisily on the tabletop and slid across crumb-covered vinyl to sit. A menu occupied the space before her, a cup of coffee and water-spotted silverware. Obviously, he anticipated her arrival.

A gum-popping waitress acknowledged Katrine's presence sooner than did the menu-enthralled man across from her. "I was hoping you were a no show, Babe," the waitress said between smacks. "Thought I might console him after my shift ends."

"After *my* shift ends, he's all yours… Babe," she added irritably. "I'll need a moment to glance over the menu."

"Mountain Oysters are tonight's special." The

waitress winked. "They're fresh."

Katrine winced, then watched the waitress take herself off, the deliberate swish of her hips wasted on Trey. "Thank's for sitting by the window in case I needed a witness to rape," she said with polite sarcasm.

"Sal would slit my throat if anything happened to his bike."

In a gesture depicting her annoyance, Katrine began drumming her fingernails against the formica tabletop. "I'm surprised you didn't take the liberty of ordering the special for us."

"It's the cheapest," he agreed, never glancing up from his menu. "But I haven't got a clue as to what a Mountain Oyster is."

The drumming of her nails ceased. *Could it be?* Philly reared him, but he'd been in Dallas for at least six years to her knowledge. "Surely you've eaten Mountain Oysters?" She gave a half-laugh. "If not, you've missed out on a true Texas culinary delight."

"Really?" He lowered the menu and his gaze settled on the top of Katrine's head.

Her hand went automatically to her hair, but she couldn't get her fingers through the tangled mess. So what, she mentally scolded herself. It wasn't as if he didn't look every bit as wind beaten. Only... he still managed to exude a persona of masculine virility.

Dressed in a tux, Trey Westmoreland presented the perfect image of suave, sophisticated ladies' man. This greasy, grimier version, provoked an image of danger. He had a wild, untamed look about him with his tousled hair and the dark smudge of grease on his cheek. Sexy, she grudgingly admitted. Jerk, she added in defense of traitorous thoughts.

"What exactly is a Mountain Oyster and how could they be fresh?" Trey questioned. "Unless it's a well-kept secret, there aren't any mountains in Texas."

Katrine owed him a return on what he'd been dishing out all evening. She shrugged. "They bring them in from New Mexico. You have a smudge of grease on your cheek." The subject was artfully changed. "Why don't you clean up while I order."

Trey knew exactly where the smudge lay, he'd put it there himself. This date had been carefully planned to insure Kat Summers sweated blood over every word in her attempts to describe a romantic evening with him. A trucker on his way out when Trey entered, proved more than willing to come on to her for ten bucks. Trey didn't know a woman wearing high heels could run that fast.

"All right." He formulated his next romantic move. While she smiled in obvious relief, her gaze roaming the crowded room in search of the waitress, Trey proceeded to clean up.

Water being squeezed from a soggy napkin into her glass recaptured Katrine's wandering stare. The anticipation she'd felt building ebbed when Trey took the napkin to his cheek and scrubbed frantically. The greasy wad found its way into the ashtray as he reached to retrieve another napkin.

It was a small comfort, Katrine soothed herself, to know her eyes couldn't widen and her mouth couldn't gape like her heroines in her books. She was, after all, in her own point of view. Glancing toward her reflection in the window, she quickly closed her gaping mouth and narrowed her gaze. Trey Westmoreland had the manners of a wart hog!

"Well, what's it gonna be?" Smacking accompanied the question.

"Two specials," Trey ordered, then took the slim end of a spoon to the dirt beneath his fingernails.

"I—"

"Two specials!" the waitress bellowed, drowning out Katrine's protest.

"You said you'd allow me to place the order." Katrine fought a sudden queasiness in her stomach. She'd never partaken of Mountain Oysters and wondered who thought of eating them in the first place.

"Sorry." He glanced up from his digging to smile. "I assumed by the expectation mirrored on your face earlier, you had your mouth set for Mountain Mushrooms."

"Oysters," Katrine snarled. "They're Mountain Oysters."

Her sarcasm brought a pause to his manicure. Katrine quickly schooled her features into a mask of innocence. He studied her a moment, his gaze lingering over her lips before he casually wiped his spoon with a clean napkin and took a sip of coffee.

The cup Katrine lifted trembled slightly. She wished he wouldn't look at her like that. Did he remember? The way their mouths merged so perfectly together?

"Jerry gave me a line about your editor pressuring you into doing the feature. What's the real reason?"

Business, she reminded herself. Trey Westmoreland represented an unpleasant writing assignment and nothing more. "Craig didn't pressure me, but he strongly suggested I cooperate," Katrine admitted. "He thinks I've kept too much to myself. More publicity, more money. You know how it works?"

"Yeah, I know the rules. Odd, I imagined most novelists lived to bring their editors and agents grief. You could have refused."

And let her adoring fans harbor the misconception Kat Summers was a floozie who consorted with the enemy? "You left me little choice with your sordid reference to our first meeting, only slightly less appealing than this second one. Besides, I wanted a chance to remind my readers why they buy my books."

"Which is?" he questioned.

"For the romance."

"Woman call it romance, men call it sex. Here's a news flash, it's the same thing."

"It isn't," Katrine defended, moving into unfamiliar territory. "Romance is… well, it's a feeling, a state of mind. Women need more than… than what you said."

He leaned forward, placing his elbows on the table. A smile played at the corners of his mouth. "What you're saying is, if I whisper something about the moonlight dancing on a woman's hair, or the fire in her eyes while I'm… romancing her, the, let's see, what did you call it in *Learning to Love,* oh yes, the 'burst of ecstacy' is better?"

The warm restaurant grew warmer. Katrine didn't care to discuss the 'burst of ecstacy' with any man, much less this one. She couldn't relate. The earth had never moved for Katrine except in normal fashion. His confession gave her an opportunity to change the subject.

"You've read *Learning to Love?*"

His smile faded. "I found myself curious about you."

Trapped within the blue of his eyes, the loud buzzing of conversation dwindled to a soft hum. Her throat constricted. "Me?"

"About what you consider romantic in a man." A husky quality flavored his voice. "I want to know what attracts you."

"Why?" She cleared her throat.

"Isn't it obvious?" His fingertips brushed hers.

Katrine's heart slammed against her chest. The look on his face was blatantly sexual and she couldn't help but respond to him.

"I want to know what you find romantic, so I can try my hardest not to do it. You'll have to dig deep for flowery words and over-used adjectives when writing about our dates."

His blunt explanation, the noisy rattle of dishes, the popping of gum, and the strong smell of grease, aided her escape from attraction.

"Don't underestimate me. I'm good at making women fall in love with jerks. The hero always is at first, you know? But I find some deep dark secret that helps the reader understand his behavior, and why he resents the heroine. I'm willing to bet you don't have any excuses. This should prove to be my greatest attempt at fiction, but I'll manage."

He responded with a soft snort. "If you've finished bragging about a talent I argue as questionable, shall we dine?"

"Let's." Katrine popped a calf fry into her mouth. It sat there, heavy on her tongue before her brain made the connection.

"Moooo," Trey drawled out slowly.

The calf fry went down her throat with a loud gulp. "You knew!" she choked.

Trey merely shrugged. "I had that trick pulled on me my first week in Dallas and ate two helpings before our copy editor told me what they were. I don't know what made me sicker afterward, the fact that I liked them, or the fact that I supported what I consider cruel and inhuman punishment."

"I'm all for gelding," Katrine decided. "The phrase 'cruel and inhuman punishment' suddenly has a nice ring."

"Put your opinion where your mouth is," he dared, glancing down at her plate.

Katrine's gaze followed his to a heaping helping of steaming calf fries. The fluffy baked potato and an order of fried okra added a welcome respite. "It's your turn," she goaded.

Trey speared the tender morsel with a fork, drowned it in sauce, then placed the delicacy into his mouth. With a sigh, Katrine unfolded her napkin and took up the challenge. Truckers came, truckers went, the night became unbearably long, but she managed to almost clean her plate.

"I want to go home," Katrine announced. "I've had enough adventure for one night."

Digging in his pocket, Trey removed several bills and placed them on the table. "I need to drop off Sal's bike first. If he doesn't have my Jag fixed, I'll call a cab."

The bike, she'd forgotten. Katrine's unsettled stomach churned. "I think I'll call myself one from here."

"And cost the paper what may be an unnecessary expense? Come on, it's not far. I won't go near the freeway."

He appeared sincere. But then, she'd trusted him before and look where it landed her. "If you pull any Evil Knevil stunts, you won't appreciate what you'll be wearing on the back of that jacket."

"No more stunts," he agreed. "One last stop and then you're free to run home and write about our romantic evening together."

A flicker of mischief danced behind his eyes. *What did he mean by 'run home'?* "We're only taking the bike to Sal, right? No other stops?"

"Not unless you want to go somewhere else," he offered politely.

She reached for her helmet. "I won't. There's no place like home."

Twenty minutes later, loud music pounding in her ears, the sight of fifty motorcycles lined up before her eyes, and the recollection she'd never been, and the certainty she wasn't now, in Kansas, Trey turned to Katrine with a pitying expression.

"You forgot to click your heels together."

"What are we doing here?" she demanded.

"I told you, we're taking the bike to Sal. He's in there."

"In there?"

"Right."

"And you think I'm going inside a biker's bar?"

"If you'd rather stay here, in the dark, by yourself, I'll understand."

"I hate you."

"You're breaking my heart. Let's go, Dorothy."

They hadn't been carried over the rainbow by a twister, but a midget in leathers, a female, stood inside the doorway, smoke from her cigarette creating a low cloud above her.

"Is that the bouncer?" Katrine wondered.

"No, she's the entertainment," Trey explained. "They have mud wrestling in about an hour."

"We'll be long gone before then, right?"

"Depends." He moved into the doorway. "Sal might not be here yet. I told him I'd wait for him."

"How considerate." Her voice cracked. "I suppose you'll sign me up to take on the midget if he doesn't arrive before the show starts."

It was tempting to bait her, but Trey allowed his date a reprieve. Her eyes mirrored distress. Wetness shone brightly within their green depths, beautiful pools to drown inside and make a man forget his bad intentions.

"If it's any consolation, she only wrestles men. It's been said Texas hasn't made a woman who can beat Wanda in a vat of knee-deep mud."

"I guess it's some consolation to know you're acquainted with these people," Katrine said. "I understand they don't think much of strangers."

"Well," he began and thought better of telling her the truth. Which was, he'd only been inside the bar once. He knew a few of the faces, Wanda the midget included, because they came and went at Sal's shop, a block down the street. These were Sal's friends and Trey doubted anyone would remember him. He found himself hoping the burly mechanic had arrived. This might be a mistake.

His thoughts were confirmed when they stepped inside. Conversation came to a halt, the cracking of balls on the pool table stopped; the music, thankfully continued to blare as all heads, some male, some female, some questionable, turned toward the door. "Damn," Trey said softly.

"Thanks for getting us both killed this evening. No way could I come up with anything romantic about you. You've saved me the trouble of admitting defeat to my readers."

He studied her pale features. Her lips trembled. He'd gone too far. "Katrine, I—"

"Hey, ain't you the dude who drives the red Jag?"

The high-pitched voice came from the vicinity of his belt loops. Trey looked down into Wanda's small features.

"Yeah," he said in his most masculine voice, "I'm looking for Sal."

"Sal ain't here," a voice said from the vicinity of the ceiling.

A chest the width of a wheel barrel came into his eye span. Trey noted the tatoo of an eagle's wing visible beneath a muscle shirt before tilting his head back. A bald giant stood before him.

"We'll be going then," Trey decided, taking Katrine's hand. A strong slap on the shoulder suggested otherwise.

"But he said if a fancy-lookin' dude came in asking for him, not to rough you up too bad before he gets here. He said you could wait."

The emphasis put on the last instruction changed Trey's mind. He amended his earlier decision. "Guess we'll have a drink."

"Hold it." The giant clamped onto Trey's shoulder again. "Sal didn't say nothing about Goldilocks here, or is she Red-Riding-Hood?"

"I think she's that Dorothy chick, Elmo," Wanda said dryly. "Check out her shoes."

"She's with me," Trey stressed.

"Is she your ol' lady?" Wanda wanted to know, running a hot gaze over Trey.

"No—"

"Yes!" Katrine assured the little woman, eyeing her date in a threatening manner.

"I guess she is," Trey corrected.

"Too bad," Wanda pouted.

"I'll say." The giant grinned down at Katrine, then turned a hard look on Trey. "Okay, she's in, but I'll warn you, I might try to steal her away from you before the night's over."

"Please don't," Katrine whispered weakly. "I get motion sickness when I ride a motorcycle."

"Come on, Dorothy," Trey said quietly, pulling her toward the bar.

Katrine stumbled along behind him, mentally cursing the red, sequined heels on her feet and cursing Trey Westmoreland. "You're obviously overdressed, too, Fancy Man," she said, seating herself on a bar stool.

"Hey, I wore my leather," Trey defended.

"That's a five hundred dollar bomber jacket

even if it does have a smudge of grease on the shoulder. I don't think it qualifies!"

"Get you a drink?" the bartender demanded.

"A white wine." Katrine rubbed her forehead.

Silence followed her request.

"I don't imagine they serve wine," Trey said under his breath. "Order a beer."

She made a face. "I don't like beer."

"Then you'll have tequila!" the bartender barked. "It's beer or tequila. We don't serve sissy booze."

"Fine," Katrine conceded. "I've never had it, but it must be better than beer."

"I'll have a shot with a beer back," Trey ordered. He waited until the bartender left before swiveling his stool toward Katrine. "Tequila's a wise choice. Let's just get smashed so if Sal doesn't show, we won't feel the pain."

She returned his sarcastic smile. "The way Wanda's eating you up with her eyes, you won't have anything to worry about. Not unless she's into whips and chains along with mud wrestling."

Picturing himself with Wanda made Trey laugh. The bartender slammed a beer on the counter with enough force to splash half the contents over Trey's hand.

"You laughing at us, Fancy Man?"

"No. He's laughing at me," Katrine injected, much as she hated to protect the idiot.

"Should I hit him?" the bartender asked hopefully.

"Not yet," she answered with a smile. Katrine needed Trey until he proved otherwise. "Do you have a phone?"

When the bartender scratched his head, she covered her shot glass.

"We had one. I pulled it out of the wall so I could strangle some stranger with the cord. It doesn't work anymore. That dude's not laughing anymore, either."

She continued to smile at the bartender, hoping her face would crack and fall in pieces to the floor like a cartoon character. If she had no mouth, she couldn't scream. The bartender filled the shot glasses on the bar, placed two lime halves beside them, winked at her and walked away.

"Why the hell are you flirting with him?" Trey demanded softly. "Are you trying to work him into a fevered state of lust so he'll go looking for the damn phone cord to strangle me with?"

"I'll help him search," she said through her fake smile. "But first, I need a drink."

Trey snatched up a salt shaker. "Lick your hand."

"I beg your pardon?"

"Like this." He brought a hand to his mouth and ran his tongue along the area between thumb and first finger.

Katrine didn't know whether to be repulsed or turned on. Repulsed, she decided, ignoring a contradictory tingling in her veins. "I'm not licking my hand."

"Then I'll do it for you. Salt and lime are necessities, especially your first time."

A shiver raced up her spine when he took her hand in his. Without looking away from her eyes, he traced a slow path along the curve between her thumb and finger. He lingered there, long enough to wreak havoc with her senses, then shook salt over the wetness left behind.

"Lick the salt, bite the lime, then drink the shot. Fast."

"You mean, just gulp it down?"

He smiled. "Tequila isn't meant to be sipped. Ready?"

She studied the liquid skeptically, then shrugged. "Ready as I'll ever be."

"To old age." Trey clinked her glass against his. "May we live to see it."

Deciding the toast was an appropriate one, Katrine mimicked Trey's actions. She licked the salt, bit into the lime and took a drink. The tequila started down her throat, changed course, then came back up. She choked before spewing the liquor directly into Trey's face. "Oooh," she gasped. "My God! That's horrible!"

Her date blinked, a droplet of tequila perched on the end of his nose. "The trick is not to pause between swallows," Trey informed dryly, searching for a napkin. Ironically, there wasn't one to be found. The sleeve of his jacket substituted. "Try again, but this time, turn the other direction."

Eyes watering, throat raw, Katrine shook her

head. "I'm not putting that foul stuff in my mouth again. In Philly, it may be customary to torture oneself with repeated attempts at suicide, but in Texas, we know not to go too close to the water once we've fallen in."

"You call yourself a Texan?" Trey snorted. "You'd never tasted calf fries until tonight, you can't handle one tiny shot of tequila, and you don't even like beer. Hell, aren't enjoying all three with frequency a prerequisite for citizenship? I thought Texas women were tough as boot leather."

"I'll have you know, I've met Texas women who could out-ride, out-rope, out-cuss, out-eat and out-drink any man who had the nerve to take them on," Katrine defended proudly. "I'm a city girl. I, well, I don't have any roots."

"Roots? What has that got to do with anything?"

Katrine didn't exactly know, except she assumed because she'd never stayed in one place long enough to develop a sense of home, of belonging, it might be the reason she felt like an outsider in a town she'd lived in all her life. She learned early in life that foster parents kept themselves at a distance. To love brought hurt later, when parting was inevitable. "It means, I don't know how to do any of those things," she said softly.

"Too bad," Trey mumbled. "I think if we have a few more drinks and mind our own business, we might get out of here alive."

Allowing her gaze to wander, Katrine discovered that most of the dive's occupants were no longer gawking at them. The sounds of conversation resumed; a stick hitting a ball, an occasional outburst of raunchy laughter, the noisy jukebox screaming heavy metal music.

"I guess I can try again," she said reluctantly.

Trey lifted his shot glass and motioned for the bartender. The man scowled as if he found him a nuisance, then lumbered forward, tequila bottle in hand.

"I figure you're good for two more shots before you puke, Fancy Man," he grumbled while tilting the bottle. "Lose your dinner on my floor, and I'll clean it up with your face. Understand?"

When Trey didn't answer with a dutiful, 'Yes Sir', Katrine glanced his direction. The arrogant stare he leveled on the bartender turned her blood to ice. *What the heck did he think he was doing?* The brute outweighed him by at least sixty pounds.

Slowly, a grin spread over the bartender's mouth. "Oh, I see. You think you're a drinker."

"I can handle more than three shots," Trey assured him.

"Bet you can't handle seven," the bartender goaded.

"Make it ten, back it up with a fifty, and you've got a bet."

A groan interrupted the stare-down between both men. Katrine realized it belonged to her. "What is this macho crap?" she said under her breath. "If you feel a need to demonstrate your masculinity, or lack of it, stay sober so you can protect me if the need arises."

His steely stare never wavering from the bartender's, Trey mentally admitted she had a point. Still, a man could only take so much pushing before he pushed back. The bartender had been baiting him since he sat down. Trey knew from his college days, it took exactly twelve shots to make him vomit, fourteen to render his fists useless, and sixteen to make him pass out.

He seriously doubted any real trouble would break out. Sal once admitted these people liked to scare people more than hurt them. Besides, he had a feeling his Jag wouldn't be fixed tonight, which meant they'd be taking a cab home. So what if a tequila drinking contest wasn't proper etiquette for a first date? This was no ordinary date. This was perfect. "Well?" he goaded.

"You're on, Fancy Man."

When Katrine groaned again, Trey nodded toward her glass. "Pour her one, too."

It took two before Katrine began to relax. Trey had downed six shots. They no longer sat facing the mirrored wall behind the bar, but had turned on their stools to study lifestyles of the bold and beer-bellied. A pool game was in constant progress, a few couples on the dance floor appeared to be 'coupling' rather than dancing, and an occasional outburst of tempers gone too far with drink added to their enjoyment. Katrine felt almost content in her leather-dominated surroundings. In fact, she had to stifle the urge to giggle at the antics taking place around her. She suspected the tequila added greatly to her good humor, and wondered how Trey managed to appear sober.

"Do you need to use the rest room?" he asked.

Her brow creased. "I don't think that's any of your business."

Slight movement of his gaze toward the ceiling suggested annoyance. "I'm asking because I feel the call and thought we should go together. I mean, at the same time. Oh hell, you know what I mean."

"Are you afraid to go by yourself?" she asked in a concerned tone, then spoiled the effect with a giggle. "Want me to hold your hand?"

He smiled slightly. "I can think of something I'd rather you hold, but it's your safety I'm worried about. I don't want to leave you here alone."

His protectiveness brought a warm feeling to Katrine's insides. His bluntness did likewise. "Oddly enough, that's the first romantic thing you've said to me. I don't require use of the rest room at this time. It's sweet of you to worry, but I'll be fine until you get back."

Romantic? Sweet? Trey frowned. In the face of true threat, he'd almost forgotten his pledge to be repulsive. "The paper can't afford a law suit," he explained rationally. "I got you into this, I'll see that you get home. I'm responsible for you, so don't move."

Once on his feet, the liquor made him sway. The soft smile fading from Katrine's lips caused him a twinge of guilt. For a moment, her expression mirrored hurt. Had it been his reference to responsibility that shadowed her eyes with pain?

"Don't put yourself out," she rallied herself. "I can take care of myself."

An arguable assurance, Trey thought wryly. He imagined Katrine Summerville had been a spoiled little girl, twisting her doting parents around her little finger with pretty pouts and those jade-green eyes. Judging by the short time he'd spent in Shelly's company, the job now fell to someone else. Katrine seemed shallow and selfish. Very much like his ex-wife. "Stay put," he warned. He made it to the end of the bar before a voice halted him.

"Hey, Fancy Man, where you going?"

Turning, Trey fixed the bartender with an agitated expression. "To the head, if that's all right with you."

The man shrugged. "Depends on what you're going to do in there. If you puke, you owe me fifty bucks."

"I'm going for the usual reasons," Trey assured him.

"Just to make sure, I'm coming with you."

Katrine's solemn mood evaporated when Trey blushed brightly. She giggled, then laughed out loud after he cast her a dark look. He mumbled something about the man keeping his hands to himself before resuming his objective, the bartender following at a respectable distance.

After he disappeared, her mood shifted again. Katrine contemplated her resentment when Trey labeled her a responsibility. The past, she thought, could be forgotten, only his reference brought it painfully back. Shelly loved her, that was enough, Katrine told herself. Of course, children loved easily. Sometimes even when there wasn't just cause to do so. But John, what could he have been thinking? Driving a car that fast on a winding stretch of highway he knew was dangerous? Maybe he didn't want to come home to her that night so many years ago. Maybe he didn't want the responsibility of a wife and child.

Giving her blonde tresses a toss, Katrine dislodged the painful questions asked too many times when the dark evening hours crowded her. She didn't have a beer to cry into and the music was all wrong. The sudden lack of which, turned her attention toward the jukebox.

She didn't suppose for one instant, while making her way toward the brightly lit contraption, a country song could be found among the selections. Her fingers traced the glass, puzzling over the assortment until she found it—one song, the label almost unreadable.

Her hands groped inside her purse for the correct change, then dropped quarters down the slot and punched the correct buttons. When Katrine turned to make her way back to the bar, a huge figure blocked her path. The wings wide-spread beneath the muscle shirt identified him as the giant Wanda had earlier referred to as Elmo.

Chapter Six

♥   ♥   ♥

"Wanna dance?"

"Ah, n–no," Katrine stammered. "I don't know how." She thought her explanation would prompt him to move from her path, but the giant stood his ground, refusing to let her pass.

"I really don't—" Katrine began, then the loud blare of music drowned out her voice.

Elmo's leer faded with the twang of a steel guitar. His gaze widened in surprise. "You've got guts, Goldilocks. Playing Tammy Wynette in this place. Lucky for you, it's only on the box because I want it there. Nobody plays that song but me, or a chick if I give her permission. You'd better dance with me or you're liable to regret it."

Her gaze darted from right to left. The pool table, once again, stood silent. She'd become the object of everyone's attention. "But-I-really-don't-know-how," she managed in gathering panic.

"I'll show you." He pulled her onto a small dance floor.

The breath left her lungs with a loud whoosh as he drew her roughly against his broad chest. The giant didn't dance. He merely swayed to the beat. Katrine had little choice but to 'stand by her man' and sway with him.

When Elmo finally positioned her at a vantage point where she could see the bar, Katrine noticed Trey standing by his stool, scanning the area in obvious search of his missing date. Katrine willed him to find her on the dark dance floor. As if by telepathy, his gaze wandered in her direction, passed over her, then quickly returned.

The sudden scowl marring his handsome features, the movement of his lips, which she felt certain released an unrepeatable response, and the stiffening of his jaw muscle revealed his displeasure.

To insure he understood the circumstance wasn't pleasing to her either, Katrine made a not-so-subtle jerking motion with her head. Being that she was his unwanted responsibility, Katrine expected rescue. Instead, Trey slammed another shot of tequila down his throat and leaned against the bar. From all appearances, he meant to leave her at Elmo's mercy.

Hoping the giant hadn't noticed her appeal for intervention, she glanced up. Elmo's eyes were closed in blissful contentment. Tammy Wynette continued to whine on about the duties of womankind, and to Katrine's disbelief, a tear rolled from beneath Elmo's lashes, tracing a path down his cheek.

"Ah," she began hesitantly. "Are you all right?"

He sniffed and wiped a beefy arm across his face. "This song always gets to me. It's so... romantic."

An hysterical urge to giggle overtook her. For the sake of continued motherhood, Katrine held it in check. "Do you believe in romance?"

"Sure," he answered defensively. "When it's all said and done, what in this world's worth a damn besides a hot woman, a cold beer, and a bike that runs?"

"Mmnn," Katrine responded thoughtfully. "Do you mind if I use that sometime in one of my books?"

"Are you a writer?" He pulled back in surprise.

It was a long shot, but Katrine took a deep breath and plunged ahead. "I'm Kat Summers, the romance writer. I don't suppose you've read any of my novels?"

"No," he said in a rush, then shook his head. "I mean, no way could you be her. I mean, I've read all her books. Your books. Are you teasing me?"

Elmo, all two hundred and fifty pounds of him, Katrine approximated, was not a man to tease. Then again, any man who openly admitted to reading romance novels couldn't be all that bad. "Yes, and I'm thinking of writing a contemporary romance where the hero's a biker," she lied, then thought it wasn't such a bad idea. "You know, show the softer side of a misunderstood breed?"

"You won't make the guy look like a wimp, will you?" Elmo questioned with concern. "You won't make him say some of that flowery stuff your other heroes say?"

"Oh no, not a biker," Katrine assured, her thoughts formulating a scheme to get back at Trey for an evening in hell. "I'm conducting a little experiment tonight. It's a study on man's protective nature. Would you help me with the research?"

He lifted a brow as they side-stepped two burly men dragging a vat of mud into the middle of the dance floor. "Name it and I'll do it, Red-Riding-Hood. I'm a hopeless romantic."

Katrine tried not to smile too noticeably.

♥　　♥　　♥

One dance. Trey would allow the giant one dance as long as he kept his hands where they belonged. He'd resisted his first inclination to charge to Katrine's rescue. She deserved a little grief for obviously playing that whining song blaring in his head. He tried to relax. Having just finished his ninth tequila shot aided his efforts tremendously. One more, and the bartender owed him fifty dollars.

Not enough to suffer the embarrassment of being watched while he attended to personal matters, but a bet Trey intended to collect. After the song ended, he and Katrine were leaving. Period. Whatever it took, they were getting out of this place before the evening got any worse.

The natives were growing restless. The bartender wasn't grinning at him anymore. Wanda stood by the door, cracking her knuckles while running her hot little eyes over Trey as if contemplating a tasty meal. Nervously, he glanced toward the dance floor and felt his defense mechanism kick in. Elmo had pulled Katrine closer. It looked as if things might get out of hand.

Even in the dim light of the dance floor, Trey saw the roundness of her eyes, the unnatural flush to her face. Of course, the silly cape she refused to shed couldn't help matters, he reasoned. It was easily eighty degrees in the crowded establishment. He'd once considered removing his own jacket, but the lack of ink design on his biceps suggested he keep his oddity hidden.

When Katrine's head turned his direction, her plea for intervention obvious to Trey, he couldn't continue his charade of indifference. He had hoped it wouldn't come to this, getting himself beat to a pulp over a woman. It sounded sickeningly romantic. Nevertheless, he pushed away from the bar and approached the dance floor, questioning his sanity, preparing his body for pain, and cursing himself for bringing her to a place as rough as this one.

"Let go of her," he said in his most macho voice, addressing a broad back. "The dance is over."

Steely muscle wrapped in thin cotton turned to

face him. "No, it ain't," Elmo countered with a leer. "I like the way she smells, the way she feels all snuggled up against me. When anything's over between me and Goldilocks, I'll say so."

Despite the tequila rolling around in Trey's stomach, Katrine's wide-eyed stare spurred him into action. Suicidal as it seemed, he drew back his fist and landed a solid blow to an equally solid jaw. Pain exploded in his knuckles. More distressing than the possibility of a broken hand was the understanding he'd dug his own grave. The giant's head never snapped with the punch. He smiled at Trey now, the promise of a slow death shining in his narrowed gaze.

"You wanna fight for her, Fancy Man?"

"Not particularly." Trey brought his stinging knuckles to his mouth. "You wanna back off so it doesn't come to that?"

"Not particularly," the giant mimicked Trey's dry tone. "But I will even the odds a little."

Before Trey figured out what form equalization might take, the giant grabbed him by the collar and lifted him off the floor. The next moment he felt himself falling. His landing was cushioned by the soft, oozy feel of mud.

"If you wanna fight for her, fight Wanda. Beat her, and you and Goldilocks are free to go."

The mud weighed Trey down, sucking at his legs and arms. "I can't fight a woman." He attempted to gain his feet, only to fall back into the clinging ooze. "I damn sure can't hit one!"

"Well." The giant's grin broadened. "I guess that's why she's never been beat. Come get it, Wanda!" he shouted.

A shrill shriek split the bar's sudden silence. The pitter-patter of small feet preceded Trey being attacked by a midget. Wanda, hair flying and teeth bared, landed directly on top of him. As the air left his lungs in a whoosh, his gaze sought Katrine. She stood beside the giant with a peculiar expression on her face. The strain had become too much for her, Trey decided. Her lips were twitching. She was obviously on the verge of hysterics.

"Fight or drown, Handsome," Wanda said, recapturing his attention.

"I can't hit you. You can't fight a man who won't fight back."

To prove otherwise, Wanda grabbed him by the throat and shoved his head under the mud. Trey fought his way up, gasping for breath.

"I could have already beat you," the small woman said. "Ten seconds under the mud is all it takes to win."

"Give her a fair fight, or I'm taking your woman home with me," the giant warned.

Wiping gook from his eyes, Trey didn't dare glance at Katrine. Could she sue him for mental anguish? Ten seconds, surely he could hold a woman half his size under the mud for that long without hurting her. Elmo's challenging stare said he had no choice.

Quickly, Trey clasped Wanda's shoulders and

tried to throw her to the side. A chorus of loud cheers followed his maneuver, momentarily startling Trey, and warning Wanda that he'd lowered himself to mud-wrestling a woman. With a whoop of excitement, she slid from his grasp and gained her feet.

"Get up," she instructed. "We start on equal footing."

The mud put extra pounds on Trey's tall frame. With difficulty, he lumbered to his feet, then lunged for Wanda. She ducked, took his arm and twisted it painfully behind his back, forcing him to his knees. The absurdity of his situation struck. A female—a midget—was about to whip his butt.

"That's it," he ground out. "No more Mr. Nice Guy. Consider yourself warned."

Wanda laughed in his ear. Her tongue followed. Trey jerked in surprise over the defilement.

"There's nothing that turns me on like a good wallow in the mud," she whispered in his ear. "Give me all you got."

With a weary sigh, Trey complied. Releasing himself from her stronghold nearly wrenched his arm from the socket, but he managed, then went for Wanda in earnest. After the woman slipped through his hands several times, Trey realized she was cheating. Wanda had coated herself in oil, reminding him of a rodeo event he attended his second week in Dallas. A greased pig grab.

Finally, he managed to sweep her legs and land her in the mud. Trey pounced. As he and Wanda rolled beneath the surface, a faded memory from his youth resurfaced. The problem being, it wasn't Tarzan The Ape Man wrestling an alligator under water, but Trey Westmoreland, a once respected columnist, trying to drown a woman half his size.

He broke the surface gasping for breath while holding a squirming Wanda under the muck. A chant went up. One, two, three. Trey expected lightning to strike him dead any minute, or his mother to show up with a willow switch. Only slightly worse, a small fist rose from the mud and hit him in the stomach. Hard.

Trey struggled to the vat's side, unloading nine shots of tequila and fifty bucks. A pair of red, sequined heels bounced off his head. He glanced up to see Katrine standing before him barefoot.

She smiled, then linked her arm in the giant's. "Elmo has been kind enough to offer me a ride home. He's such a sweetie." Katrine tweaked the giant's cheek.

Elmo blushed. "I do have a soft spot for you, Goldilocks," he admitted. "Feel free to contact me anytime you need help in your research. I guess you were right tonight. Most men will make a complete ass out of themselves over a woman."

Shocked, Trey watched them walk away. Katrine only made it a few steps before she turned back, nodding toward the shoes. "Don't forget to click your heels together."

He glanced at the shoes, at the retreating couple, then reluctantly toward the small, mud-covered creature across from him. Wanda began to growl.

♥   ♥   ♥

Thirty minutes later, standing before a phone booth six blocks from the sight of his past humiliation, a pair of red, sequined heels stuffed inside his jacket, Trey waited for a cab. Not just any cab. A yellow and black number privately owned by Mr. Charlie Grimes.

It wasn't that Trey particularly wanted to see Charlie again, but all other cab services refused to drive the streets this side of town after dark. Charlie had also proved difficult, only agreeing after being sufficiently bribed.

"Hurry." He stomped his feet, leaving bits of dried mud in his wake. Thankfully, the outside layer had dried. His skin itched, and his pride had suffered immensely over being drowned by a person not even half his size. All this over a woman!

Of course, women had made men's lives miserable from the beginning. His mother and two sisters were no exceptions. All three gave torture their best shot when the subject of marriage came up. In their opinion, thirty-five was well past the age to have found a new wife. Also, at least six children should be stirred into the pot in case the second wife wasn't sadistic enough.

The Westmorelands were breeders. Both his brothers had four children each and one sister had five, the other six. Trey, in his barrenness, represented a black mark against an old family tradition. When he'd married Linda he'd naturally assumed she would want children someday. He'd thought wrong.

She believed children were only good for wrecking marriages and ruining a woman's figure. A thinking man would assume she'd change her mind as time passed, or rather, Trey had hoped she would. After the first couple of years, he realized his wife was more than serious.

Considering his family history, Linda not only took birth control pills religiously, but insisted he wear protection. Trey always felt as if he were preparing for battle before they made love. No wonder his wife found him boring. By the time he put on his armor, he wasn't much in the mood anymore.

The night he met Katrine, Trey hadn't acted responsibly. Despite the protection he kept in his wallet, the thought of being safe hadn't been uppermost on his mind. For some reason, Katrine Summerville drained his brain cells. He didn't think or act rationally when in her presence. His hormones went crazy.

Earlier, the feel of her hands roaming over him on the bike nearly drove him insane. Terrified as she was, her fingers seemed to know what they were searching for, even if she hadn't been mentally aware of her actions. He wondered what might have happened had he not reached the truck stop when they did.

Luckily, he didn't have to ponder the possibilities long. Headlights approached. Trey breathed a sigh of relief when Charlie's cab pulled up to the curb. He hurriedly opened the passenger door and slid inside. Charlie greeted him with a smile before his eyes grew huge.

"Good God, what happened to you?"

"It's a long story. I'd rather not talk about it."

The cabby ran a slow survey over him. "I agreed to take double the fare for coming over here, but I didn't know my cab would be too trashed to work the rest of the night. It'll cost you more than that now."

"How much?" Trey asked, picking dried mud from his face.

"Triple."

"That's robbery!"

"I've got a kid coming soon, and you'll have to pay someone else more than that to come get you. Take it or leave it."

"How are Nadine's ankles?"

"They look like overblown balloons," Charlie muttered. "Thanks for asking, but it'll still cost you triple."

"If you lower the price, I'll show you where Kat Summers lives. In fact, I might be able to get Nadine's copy of *Passion's Price* autographed."

Silence.

"Well?"

"Nothing for taking you to her house, double after that."

"Done."

"And," Charlie added, "You've got to tell me the story behind your sorry state."

"You can read it in this coming Sunday's addition. Kat Summers and I are doing a feature together."

A broad smile splashed across Charlie's face. "Hot damn, you finally get to work with someone famous."

Trey would have turned and given him a dirty look, but he didn't want to flake too much. Charlie might change his mind about the fee. "Yeah, lucky me," he grumbled.

Charlie pulled away from the curb. As usual, he couldn't keep silent for long. "First off, you'll have to tell me where she lives, then tell me about the article." Shortly thereafter, they coasted up to the curb of a neatly-trimmed town house. Trey suggested that Charlie cut the lights.

"She left with a man she didn't know. I want to be sure she got home all right," he explained their mission.

Charlie snorted. "I can't blame her much for running." He eyed him critically.

"She's the reason I look like this. Her and that teddy-bear biker with a cement jaw." A complaint concerning the country singer whose whining gave him a headache gathered on his tongue when he noticed Charlie wasn't listening.

"What are you gawking at?" Trey craned his neck.

A light was on in her upstairs window. Against that light, stood the silhouette of a woman. A very womanly woman. Trey swallowed loudly as the shadow slid, what he knew to be a red jumpsuit, off her shoulders. When she straightened, the outline of her breasts stood out clearly against a thin shade separating reality from the next best thing. Her arms went behind her back. Trey felt a sweat break out beneath the mud.

"Damn, she's having trouble with it."

"Yeah, damn," Trey mumbled before he found his way from a trance holding him a prisoner of lust. "Get your head in here!"

Charlie pulled his head back inside the cab. "Cut me some slack. I live with a woman who can't see past her belly to look at her swollen ankles."

"I imagine Nadine would cut more than slack if she knew you were sitting outside a woman's house watching her undress." He glanced around. "Doesn't Katrine realize there are perverts roaming the streets at night, just hoping to come upon a show like this?"

The cabby grinned. "You mean, like us?"

"I only wanted to make sure she got home." Trey felt embarrassed he'd stared at her as long as he had. "She's here, obviously safe. Let's go."

"Can't wait to read about this." Charlie smacked his lips. "It must have been one hell of a date."

"I'm sure she found it very entertaining," Trey said darkly. "I'll have to think of something equally amusing for our second date. Only next time, I won't let her turn the tables on me." Suddenly, his sour mood began to lift.

Chapter Seven

♥   ♥   ♥

Her portion of the feature was due in two days. Katrine stared at her notes with horror. "I'm not *that* creative."

Trey Westmoreland had made this assignment close to impossible. Worse, the jerk had the nerve to keep his promise to Shelly. The fact he arrived at nine o'clock to give her daughter a lesson in stickball, didn't aid Katrine's ability to buckle down and make something of the mess he claimed was a date.

He'd called last night and without more than a hello, asked to speak to Shelly. Much to her annoyance, her daughter had given him her private number and insisted he call her on that line. Acting very grown up about the call, Shelly later informed Katrine that he wanted to set up their 'date'.

A high-pitched squeal from Shelly caused Katrine's fingers to tighten around her empty coffee cup. Her first inclination this morning had been to dress nicely, put on her make-up and fix her hair. Katrine stifled her conceit, promising herself she wouldn't go anywhere near Trey.

Thelma would be working in the kitchen and able to oversee the lesson. After three days of reliving the horror of their evening together, she had no desire to see him again. Her gaze strayed unconsciously toward the door to her office. A small gravel yard separated her from the house. Many walls separated her from the street out front and… him.

"Coffee," she said under her breath. "I'm only going into the house to bring a thermos of coffee to the office. I won't go near the bay window. I won't," she assured herself.

Once in the kitchen, Katrine encountered Thelma on her way out. The woman had worked weekends for Katrine over the past five years, cleaning, doing the shopping, making casseroles to last them through the week, and baking. On occasion, Thelma stayed with Shelly if Katrine wanted to go out for the evening.

"I've got my list." Thelma waved a piece of paper. "I should be back in a couple of hours. Anything in particular you want me to fix this week?"

"Enchiladas," Katrine answered. "You make the best Mexican food I've ever eaten."

"I don't see how you could have much to compare them to." Thelma shook her graying head. "You should get out more. Shelly, too. Just listen to her. Have you ever heard such a truly childish laugh coming from that young miss?"

Katrine paused, coffee pot poised over the glass thermos while she listened. Silence for a moment, then the crystal clear pureness of a child's delight floating on the winter morning air. How long since she'd heard Shelly laugh like that? Never, she realized, a crease furrowing her brow. Shelly had always been a mature child. Even in infancy, she'd been rather serious.

Baffled, she moved toward the window. The sheers beneath the heavy curtains allowed her to peer out without pulling the drapes aside. Through a filmy haze, she saw Shelly, cheeks pink from the cold, positioned just before the curb, holding a large stick. Her daughter began to hop from foot to foot with excitement when Trey appeared. Katrine could hardly blame the child. It should be illegal for a man to look that good this hour of the day.

A breeze ruffled the feathered thickness of his dark hair as her fingers suddenly longed to do. His sweat shirt boasted the emblem of some college he wouldn't stand still long enough for Katrine to identify. The jeans hugging his slim hips were faded, a tear in one knee provided a glimpse of skin as he darted back and forth, controlling a ball with a stick.

He smiled when her daughter tried to steal the ball. Dimples, the kind that made long slashes in his cheeks, went unappreciated by Shelly as her gaze narrowed with determination.

"Get it," Katrine found herself whispering. "Take it away from him!"

"Oh, he'll let her have it in a minute," Thelma said at her back. "And when he does, hold your ears. I swear I've never heard a child yell that loud."

Although Katrine had heard Shelly's enthusiasm expressed throughout the morning, she wasn't prepared when the squeal hit her from so close a distance. She jumped back from the window, then groaned.

"Oh no, what will my neighbors think? This is a quiet subdivision. Shelly never even goes outside and now, there she is, scrambling down the street, hitting a ball with a stick and screaming at the top of her lungs."

"They'll think she's playing," Thelma said softly. "It's normal for children to have fun."

Katrine wheeled around in time to see the side door close. Had she detected a note of censure in Thelma's voice? Of course children played. True, Shelly wasn't the sort who cared much for dolls, or sports. True, she didn't have friends over often. In fact, she only had two that Katrine knew of, but Thelma hinted at oddness. Shelly was extremely intelligent. She made straight A's in school and never caused Katrine a moment of worry, except when she said something outrageously grown up.

There was nothing odd about Shelly's maturity, Katrine assured herself. She'd been the same way.

Katrine hadn't had many friends. Observing had been her strong suit, not participating. A coldness crept into Katrine's bones. She shivered, rubbing her hands briskly along her arms. All her life she'd stood at a window looking out at the world. Until John rescued her from the isolation she'd come to accept as normal.

He'd promised to love her, promised to be with her forever. He'd lied. Katrine retraced her steps to the coffee pot. She made it halfway, vowing to give the subject of Shelly's maturity more thought, when another scream sounded. Curious, she returned to the window.

Melissa from next door had joined the activities. Not only her, but two boys she'd seen on occasion from down the street, and three girls Katrine thought lived directly across from her. The children were enjoying the last vestige of Christmas vacation. They split, forming two teams. Boys against girls. Foreshadowing, Katrine thought with annoyance. What did Trey think he was doing? Turning a group of usually quiet, polite children into screaming, sweating hoodlums.

She had half a mind to go outside and tell him to leave her daughter—and the neighborhood— alone. The other parents were probably as agitated as she. Reasoning that the children would soon wear themselves out and Trey would leave, Katrine took her thermos and returned to the office. Her computer hummed a familiar song. Katrine sat down and tried to block out the noise. Thirty minutes later, as the voices grew more unrestrained, and she suspected greater in number, she ground her teeth in frustration. "What the hell—"

"What the hell is that?"

Glancing up with a start, Katrine met Trey's heated stare. "How did you get in h–here?" she stammered, realizing she'd been too busy fuming to notice his intrusion.

"I asked you a question first. What is that?" he repeated, glancing over his shoulder.

Katrine rose and moved to stand beside him. "That's my backyard."

"It's full of rocks."

"That's one of the reasons I bought the house. I don't have time to do yard work."

"Figures," he sneered, walking away.

"Wait just a minute!" Katrine shouted at his back. "What figures?"

He stopped and turned to face her. "It figures that you're too caught up in your silly stories to realize Shelly deserves more than this."

Confused and angry over his accusation, Katrine shut her office door and approached him. "How dare you invade my privacy, call my novels silly, berate me for having rocks in my backyard, accuse me of child abuse, then walk away! Who gave you permission to snoop around my house and poke your nose in my business?"

"Shelly gave me permission. Due to the number of children littering the street out front, I suggested we come back here to finish the game. Shelly's face turned red. Her friends snickered. She explained that we couldn't play in her backyard because it was full of rocks. I thought she might be exaggerating. She told me to see for myself, but to be quiet so I wouldn't disturb your work."

The way his lip curled over Shelly's reference to her writing made Katrine all the more angry. "Shelly's never complained about the backyard being graveled before. If she's respectful of my writing time, what of it? There's nothing wrong with my daughter!"

"I didn't say anything's wrong with Shelly," he said softly. "Nothing a little thing like childhood couldn't fix. You're the one with the problem. Can't you see what's wrong with this picture?" He indicated the vacant backyard with a sweep of his hand. "Where's the swing set? Where's the basketball goal out front in the drive? I told her stickball was like baseball, or hockey without the ice and she didn't make the connection. What do you do? Keep her locked up in the house every week-end?"

He'd gone too far. Katrine stomped her foot in a show of temper, then winced as a piece of gravel penetrated the flimsy sole of her shoe. "What I do and what Shelly does, for that matter, is none of your business. Leave her alone and get off my property!"

"Afraid she might accidentally have fun?" he goaded.

"I've seen your idea of a good time and I don't

think you could be trusted with my child. I told you to leave and I meant it!"

"You're beautiful when you're angry."

His compliment took her off guard. The hostility heating her veins ended up in her cheeks. Only when his gaze travelled from her head to her toes and his mouth twisted into a sarcastic smile, did Katrine recall how she looked. She controlled the urge to snatch the ugly pair of reading glasses off her nose.

"Just because you and I don't like each other doesn't mean Shelly should suffer." Trey still studied her with an intensity that made Katrine squirm. "I told her I'd take her ice skating next week. If you don't want her to go, you tell her. It's my opinion, every child should ice skate at least once before their eleventh year on this earth."

Katrine recovered long enough to glare at him. "I've never cared much for your opinions. Now, if you're finished advising me on what my child should or shouldn't do, I'd appreciate it if you'd leave. I'm busy."

Thinking she'd properly dismissed him, Katrine turned from Trey's embarrassing scrutiny. The wonderful thing about being a writer was that no one saw you while you worked. Katrine rarely bothered with fixing her hair or applying make-up before trudging out to the office each morning. Besides no make-up, her hair was pulled on top of her head in a pony tail. She wore a pair of old sweats and Big Bird house shoes. A geek, Katrine inwardly groaned. She looked like a geek.

"Another word of advice," he said at her back.

Refusing to face him again, Katrine kept walking until she reached the office.

"Don't undress in front of your window. There may be a mud-covered columnist and a nosey cab driver sitting on the street below. And, either get yourself a man, or a bra that hooks in the front."

It took her a few minutes to understand exactly why he'd give her such odd suggestions. When the realization hit, Katrine whirled around, her fists clenched at her sides. Trey was gone. Grasping the door handle, she shoved the door wide and stumbled inside, collapsing on a sofa situated across from her desk.

"That bastard," she whispered. "That pervert. He spied on me! He… he… wanted to make sure I got home all right," her voice trailed thoughtfully. A hot blush spread up her neck. She imagined Trey sitting out front, watching her undress. A fresh wave of mortification washed over her when Katrine remembered cursing a crooked hook on her bra she couldn't get undone. How much had he seen?

"Mom? Is something wrong? Are we making too much noise?" Shelly stood at the office door, a worried expression marring her young features.

"No," Katrine answered dully. "Nothing's wrong. Is it lunch time?"

Shelly glanced at her watch. "Oh, I guess it is. Mary Ellen from across the street wanted us to come over and play basketball. But, we'd better eat."

Guilt twisted Katrine's grumbling stomach. "Honey, why didn't you tell me you resented the gravel?"

"I don't resent it," Shelly assured her. "I... well, I know you're too busy with your writing to worry about yard work. Except, now that I'm older, I thought you might consider planting grass. I'd take care of the lawn and wouldn't let anyone come over and play. I only want to sit on it and maybe feel it under my bare feet in the summer."

"Of course," Katrine whispered. "Go to Mary Ellen's. We can forego lunch for another hour. I could use the time to get some work done."

"Thanks," Shelly said enthusiastically. "I'll tell them to be quiet, but well, it's hard. We get excited and all."

"It's all right." Katrine tried to sound calm. "I've never heard much noise around our house. It really doesn't bother me."

"There isn't much racket because they usually play down at Jimmy's. A couple of years ago I told them they couldn't come in my backyard or make any noise at our house so they quit coming over. Melissa's the only one who'd play with me after that. She understands. Her dad doesn't like noise either."

"Go on," Katrine instructed, turning her head away from Shelly. "I promise you'll have grass next summer and tell the kids the noise doesn't bother me."

"For real?" Shelly asked skeptically. "Did you hear Melissa screaming when Trey was here? I think she just wanted to get his attention. He's great, huh, Mom?"

She cleared her throat. "Yeah, great. Be back in an hour."

The sound of the door closing shattered the dam holding Katrine's emotions at bay. With a choked sob, she flung herself across the sofa. What kind of mother didn't think about having gravel in the backyard or putting a basketball goal in the drive? Because she'd never had a big backyard when she was a child, a basketball goal, a swing set, a dog, things normal children took for granted, she had forgotten the importance of providing those necessities for her own child.

Painful memories swam to the surface. When Katrine's mother abandoned her, she'd been placed in the care of a great aunt and uncle. They weren't cruel, but only old and barren of any children of their own. The small apartment they lived in wasn't meant to provide for the needs of a child, nor were they.

Great Aunt Jean did all that was required of a care-taker. Katrine had clothing, shelter and nourishment. Not once could she remember being held, loved, assured by her elderly guardians. She did remember constantly being told to be quiet because they lived in a retirement complex and noise wouldn't be tolerated by the other tenants.

Katrine suffered in silence, absorbing life with an intensity most children weren't capable of, because they were busy at play. She found school disturbing, subjected to roomfuls of noisy children when her upbringing had stifled Katrine's own verbal exuberance. But the wonder of learning how to quietly commit to paper her thoughts and feelings she embraced obsessively.

Later, after her great aunt became ill and Katrine was placed in a foster home, there were swing sets, grass, and the companionship of other children, but by then, another world had claimed her. The world of fantasy. A world where she could be loved, wanted, beautiful—a world where she could become all she wasn't.

Flood gates open, Katrine sobbed until the need for tissue sent her in search. Shelly thoughtfully left a box in the top of her desk drawer. Seating herself behind the computer, she lowered her head. The keyboard felt cold against the wetness of her cheeks, unmoved by the pleasure and pain it delivered. For the first time in her life, Katrine resented her writing. She begrudged no one the pleasure of escape into fantasy, but while her readers returned to real life after the story, Katrine had only found a new heroine to become, a different adventure to obsess her.

"I'll change," she vowed, lifting her head. "I'm going to become a mother. A real mother!"

Wiping the remaining tears from her cheeks,

she rose with the intention of fixing her daughter lunch. Not a sandwich or a can of soup. Not a frozen dinner Thelma had prepared, but an honest-to-God home cooked meal. The note pad laying on her desk caused her a moment's hesitation. The feature. Damn Trey Westmoreland.

How dare he be right about her neglect of Shelly! He seemed the type who proved annoyingly right about most things. Well, he was wrong about her lack of talent. Trey took her on the most unromantic date in the history of so-called courtship. His intentions were obvious, to make her half of the feature impossible. Katrine wouldn't fail Shelly, and she wouldn't allow the enemy to disarm her again.

"I'll give you romance, T. West," she promised. "You'll choke on it."

♥   ♥   ♥

Trey choked on the coffee sliding down his throat. Jerry Caldwell gave him a hardy slap on the back, then grinned like a Cheshire.

"She's good, isn't she?"

"Good at lying." Trey coughed again while staring at the newspaper clutched in his hands. "This garbage is so sugary sweet it makes my teeth hurt. Why didn't you let me edit it before you sent it to print?"

"*That garbage,*" Jerry stressed, "will make us number two before the week's out. After reading the sorry excuse of an article you submitted, I could only pray she, at least, wrote true to form."

"What's wrong with my feature?" Trey demanded. "I wrote the truth."

Jerry frowned at the article he held, his disappointment obvious. "You gave me one lousy paragraph. *'She was overdressed, complained about the restaurant, berated the meal, whined about the establishment I took her to for drinks, got me involved in a fight and left with another man.'* Period."

"That was pretty much the way it happened, in a nutshell."

"I don't want nutshells. I want details! Exactly what she wore, where you went, how she got you involved in a fight, why she left with another man."

The columnist slapped the paper on the edge of Jerry's desk. "I suppose if I went to bed with her, you'd expect me to give the public details on that, too?"

His editor's brow lifted with interest. "Did you?"

"I'm trying to make a point," Trey informed him, his expression one of disgust. "I'm a journalist. I write the facts and don't flower it up with muck. You've got your feature. The phones have been ringing all morning. We might make the national news. Don't tell me how to write my end of the bargain."

"Maybe you should study Kat Summer's style," Jerry suggested. "You could use a few lessons in creativity."

"Is that what this is?" With a crisp snap, Trey opened the paper. "'T. West arrived fashionably late, looking handsomely rugged,' I had on a pair of grease-covered Levis and a leather jacket," Trey explained. "'His comment regarding my perfume set my heart aflutter,' she was flapping her arms like a gull and even so, her perfume arrived downstairs long before she did. Oh, this is great. 'After helping me with my wrap,' which, by the way, is the same as slinging it in her face, 'We took an exuberant ride through the streets of our fair city, snuggled close together against the cold night,'."

He rose, carrying the paper with him while he paced. "We were on my mechanic's Harley, and she was so scared she didn't care what she grabbed hold of, which in my opinion, was the best part of the date. 'T. West, not a native of our great state, thoughtfully chose a cozy restaurant boasting true Texas cuisine', I took her to a truck stop and she barely choked those calf fries down. It was cozy all right, about a hundred degrees even without that silly red cape draped around her."

Lost in his own rambling, Trey failed to notice Jerry's gaping mouth. He continued, unmindful of his own confessions conflicting with the paper's thoughtful handing over of the key to the city.

"'After a satisfying dinner, laced with interesting conversation in which T. West expressed a desire to learn what I found most romantic in a man, we ventured into a colorful establishment I *can only describe as over the rainbow,'* we were arguing about sex and romance being the same thing," Trey pointed out. "She knows I only asked her what attracted her so I'd be sure to not do anything she might label as heroic. The 'establishment' was out of this world all right. I took her to a biker's bar—"

"Westmoreland," Jerry interrupted, his tone bordering on disbelief. "Are you telling me that with a limo service at your disposal, an unlimited expense account allowing the two of you to dine at the finest restaurants and relax over drinks in the most exclusive night clubs, you took her to a truck stop on a motorcycle and then to a biker's bar?"

A guilty flush of heat spread up Trey's neck. "You gave me the key, you didn't say I had to use it."

"B–But why wouldn't you?" Jerry stammered. "Why make this harder than it has to be?"

"Why make it easy for her?" Trey countered. "Most of the readers out there, hers and ours, don't spend their evenings doing the town in style. Let her find the romance in reality, that was the deal."

"It was supposed to work the other way, also." Jerry scratched his head thoughtfully. "You were supposed to find the realism in romance. It seems one-sided to let you make all the date choices. I'll call and give her the option of choosing the setting for half the dates, that's fair."

"Fair?" Trey grumbled. "Since when does Jerry Caldwell care about fairness?"

"Since I'm interested to see how you'll avoid finding anything romantic about a candle-lit restaurant or whatever she chooses for her dates. I should chew you out for this little piece of sabotage, but in all honesty, it gives the feature an intriguing twist. Exactly what sort of manly joust were you involved with?"

"I mud wrestled a midget," Trey answered flatly.

"And the age-old tradition of honoring a knight with her favor?"

"She threw her shoes at me."

Jerry crumpled into a chair, engaging in a fit of deep belly laughter. "This is what I want, Westmoreland. Her interpretation, then yours intermingled. Damn, I wish we'd have formatted it that way on this one."

"I thought I was to gradually fall under the spell of romance," Trey reminded, his disgusted tone proof he didn't like the bargain at all.

"You are." Jerry sobered. "But it should be very subtle at first. In the next feature, you might admit to finding at least one thing romantic about your date. Each article after should depict a decline in skepticism. I want my readers to believe in your surrender. I need our female following back, understand?"

"Yeah, I get it. You want me to sell my beliefs for the sake of ratings. Pretend this relationship represents something more than monetary gain and seduce our readers into feeling as if they've been given a satisfactory conclusion to the end of a fairy tale."

The editor sighed. "I don't know why you can't just sit back and enjoy this, Westmoreland. Why do have to make everything so difficult?"

"Life is difficult," Trey countered. "Katrine Summerville uses her talent to white wash it. She makes women forget the truly attractive attributes in a man such as; hard-working, dependable, committed to providing a secure future for his wife and family, and brain washes them into wanting unpredictable, spontaneous, dangerous—"

"Hold it," Jerry interrupted. "I think you've forgotten we're talking fiction. Or are we? Does your attitude toward Katrine Summerville have anything to do with your ex-wife?"

Mention of the past doused Trey's temper like pouring baking soda over a fire. "Of course not," he lied. "I just can't get too thrilled about being led around on a leash for the sake of ratings. I should have refused to do the feature."

Caldwell studied him a moment, then sighed again. "I don't understand you, Westmoreland. Hell, I'd like to be in your shoes. If I had your pretty-boy looks, I'd use them to get lucky every night. I'd take advantage of this opportunity and romance Katrine Summerville right out of her clothes. I'd see just how hot she is. I'd—"

"You'd end up in the hospital with a disease penicillin can't cure," Trey interrupted. "Be glad your mug resembles a bulldog, Jerry. With that attitude, you'll live longer."

"Don't play the saint with me," Jerry grumbled, opening a desk drawer. "I haven't forgotten how this whole business started. You aren't so level headed when it comes to a certain gorgeous romance author, are you?"

"No," Trey admitted. "That woman brings out the worst in me." He almost told Jerry about the real Katrine Summerville. The one who wore silly, red reading glasses on the end of her nose and Big Bird house slippers.

It was crazy, but he hadn't been joking when he'd said she looked beautiful that day. In truth, he'd been more attracted to her than when she'd been dressed to the teeth.

"I suppose you have a point about being cautious," Jerry said, studying his reflection in a hand-held mirror. The editor patted the extra skin under his jaws as if the action would eliminate the problem. "Only a man very secure in his masculinity would slip between the sheets with Kat Summers. If *you* have qualms about relating your personal life to the world, she wouldn't. You might not read about a steamy night between the two of you in the feature, but mark my words, someday you'd open one of her novels and there you'd be. Held up for inspection. Your sexual prowess judged by millions of women." Jerry shuddered. "Talk about measuring up."

"That's ridiculous," Trey argued. "She wouldn't

dare. I mean, I could sue her for something like that, couldn't I?"

Jerry shrugged. "I doubt she'd be foolish enough to use your full name but, 'Trey'… that's a sort of hero sounding name. If she used your first name, mentioned dark hair, blue eyes and dimples, well, considering it's more than common knowledge the two of you are acquainted—"

The sound of Jerry's office door slamming cut him off. The editor smiled at his reflection. "Chew on that worry bone for a while, Westmoreland." He laughed softly. "I'll teach you to call me a bulldog."

Chapter Eight

♥   ♥   ♥

"Mom, you really don't have to go skating with us," Shelly insisted as her mother dug around the bottom of her closet for a lost sweater. "Don't you need to write or something?"

Katrine glanced up, scrambling toward the open door on hands and knees. "That was the deal, remember? I can't just let you run around with a man I don't know all that well. You're the one who had a fit when I said you couldn't go. This is the compromise we agreed on."

"I know," Shelly grumbled. "But I thought you'd change your mind at the last minute and stay home. Trey doesn't know you're coming."

"He doesn't?" Katrine asked, surprised. "Why didn't you tell him?"

Shelly shrugged, plucking the fuzz balls off her sweater. "I kept thinking whatever's wrong with you would wear off."

"Motherhood doesn't just wear off," Katrine informed her daughter stiffly. "Run along and put on a shirt under that sweater. I imagine the rink will be cold."

"But Mom, he'll be here any minute."

"No arguments," Katrine warned. "Pull that hair back out of your face, too. You don't want it in your way."

An exasperated sigh followed as Shelly rose from the bed. "Funny," she said under her breath. "I remember a time when I knew what I wanted, and you minded your own business."

"What?"

"I said, the black sweater you're looking for is actually hanging up."

"Oh." Katrine struggled to her feet. She quickly snatched the sweater from its precarious position, then emerged from the closet. Once in the bright light of day, Katrine noticed the lint clinging to her black stirrup pants and groaned. *Couldn't she do anything right?* She'd done laundry by the tons before Mrs. Thelma Camp showed up five years ago to do it. Her pants must have come from the load she accidentally washed with a purse-size box of tissue.

"Where's the blasted tape?" she mumbled, pulling the sweater over her head. Her hair crackled with static. The door bell rang.

"You'll have to get it!" Shelly shouted. "I'm not dressed *again,* yet."

"He was late for our date, but he's right on time for Shelly," she grumbled. "'She complained about the restaurant, complained about the place I took her for drinks.' He made me sound like a whiner!"

The bell rang again.

"Mom!"

"I'm going!"

Taking the stairs two at a time, Katrine reached the front door. She paused to smooth her hair before fumbling for the knob. The bell persisted as the brass knob shocked the heck out of her. "Ouch!" she yelped.

"Hey, are you all right in there?"

She hesitantly touched the knob. Again, it shocked her. "Just come in," Katrine snapped. "It's not locked."

The door swung open. Trey stepped inside. He looked remarkably clean, indecently comfortable, and extremely annoyed.

"Why isn't it locked?"

Katrine raised her eyes from an unconscious survey of his attire to glare back at him. "Because I checked the mail thirty minutes ago and forgot when I came back inside."

"Ever heard of crime? Any weirdo off the street could walk right in here."

"Obviously," Katrine countered flatly. "Shelly should be down in a minute. Don't get too comfortable and shut the door."

"Bossy today, aren't we?" Trey mumbled, but did as he'd been instructed. His writing partner walked to an antique secretarial and began rummaging through the drawers. His gaze roamed her slender frame. He smiled at the shredded pieces of white clinging to her slacks. The oversized sweater hung below her hips. He wondered what she'd look like wearing nothing but the sweater. All legs. "What's your problem?" he asked casually.

"Motherhood," Shelly answered from the stairs.

The announcement received a dirty look from Katrine and an interested one from Trey.

"She's going with us," Shelly further complained, moving toward the coat closet next to Trey. She turned an expression half-irritated, half-pleading on him. "Tell her you're not a pervert and maybe she'll stay home."

"That does present a problem," Trey offered on Shelly's behalf, despite the part of him that wanted Katrine to come along. He knew which part responded to Katrine Summerville. The irrational, immoral part all men possessed. "I'm in the Jag," he finished when she paused in her digging to stare at him expectantly. "It's a two seater, remember?"

Her blush assured him she did. Nevertheless, Katrine appeared undaunted. She returned to her scavenging. "I'll call a cab," she decided. "My treat."

"Gosh, that's exciting," Trey said.

Shelly giggled.

"Give me a minute and I'll call."

"Allow me," Trey offered. "I owe a guy a favor. You wouldn't mind autographing your latest book for a devoted fan, would you?"

"Anything for a fan. Shelly, show Trey where the phone is in the kitchen."

Shelly took his hand. As they passed Katrine, a clean natural scent tickled Trey's senses. She stood bent over, going for the lint below her knees and providing him with a glimpse of her nice derriere. He tried not to laugh at her hair. Full of electricity, the fine strands stretched toward him as he moved past.

"What have you done to my mother?" Shelly whispered frantically after they entered the kitchen.

"Nothing," Trey said perhaps too defensively, considering what he'd been thinking he'd like to do to her two seconds earlier.

"She's changed. The day you came to teach me stickball, she became possessed."

"I think you mean obsessed," Trey corrected softly.

"No, I mean *possessed.*" Shelly peered through a small crack between the swinging doors. "Okay, she's gone back upstairs for something. What I'm trying to tell you is, she's become the mother from hell."

Trey opened his mouth to scold her for being disrespectful, then wondered if the mere mention of hell could cause him to detect a scorched odor. "Did Katrine burn something this morning?"

Shelly nodded enthusiastically. "This morning, yesterday morning, every morning, noon and night since you left that day. Look over there." She nodded toward the stove. "Your basic needs, salt, pepper, fire extinguisher. Now, what did you do to her?"

The situation might have been laughable had Shelly not appeared genuinely upset. "I merely suggested she wasn't doing her duty by you," Trey explained. "I thought you should have grass instead of rocks."

"Oh." Shelly calmed somewhat. "Well, you did good on that score. She promised me grass next summer. But you must have done more than that to turn her into... into... a mother!"

"Contradictory to what you've obviously been raised to believe, she *is* the mother, Shelly, not you." Trey helped himself to the phone. "The parent is supposed to take care of the child, not the other way around."

He watched her expression turn thoughtful as he dialed Charlie's mobile number. Had Katrine actually taken his opinion into account? The thought pleased him. Maybe she wasn't such a lost cause after all. Charlie's static-laced voice recaptured his attention.

"It's Trey, if you want to collect on that favor I owe you, get over to Kat Summers' house and give us a ride. No, I'm not joking." He sighed with annoyance. "No, I'm not covered in anything. No, you shouldn't bring binoculars, we're going to the Galleria to skate."

The phone slammed into its cradle with more force than he intended. Shelly lifted a brow.

"What was all that about?"

"We're supposed to have fun today." Trey avoided an answer. "No shop talk."

"All right," she agreed. "But about the other thing we were discussing, I see it differently than you. Mom and I compromise. She makes the money, I make sure she eats and takes halfway decent care of herself. She loses herself in her writing, and I go about my business. You've upset the whole balance. It's not supposed to work this way."

"What?" he asked, confused.

"You and Mom," Shelly answered impatiently. "I don't want you to change her, I want you to love her just the way she is, or was," she amended. "The same as I do."

The declaration so stunned Trey, he could only stare back at Shelly with disbelief. "I—" he began, then felt at a loss as how to proceed. "Shelly," he tried again. "I'm afraid it isn't that simple. People don't fall in love with each other because someone else wants them to. Your mother and I don't know each other well, and what we do know about each other doesn't look too promising for a serious relationship. I don't think it would ever work out."

"Why?" she demanded, her brown eyes full of hurt. "Why can't you love her?"

Her small face turned up at him with injured inquiry tugged at something dormant inside of Trey. He felt her pain within the erratic beating of his heart. Bending down, he tried to soothe the first of many lessons for Shelly regarding the reality of love.

"I'm flattered you want me to love your mother. Sometimes, I imagine children who've had a parent to themselves for a long time resent an intrusion."

"Do you have children?" Shelly suddenly thought to ask. "I mean, surely you've been married before. A hunk like you."

He smiled slightly over her compliment. "I've been married before, but no, I don't have any children." His own admission brought an empty feeling to his gut. As if he failed twice. "Your mother is very lucky."

Trey found his hand captured between two small hands. "I may not always be enough," she whispered. "Someday I'll be grown. I don't want my mom to be alone. It's horrible, being alone."

"It is." He nodded, recalling coming home to an empty apartment after Linda left him. He realized it wasn't only Katrine's future Shelly should worry over. A child should have brothers and sisters to fight with, to tell on, to share secrets with then use as blackmail against each other. The fear in her voice spoke of knowing.

"Your mother will find someone," he assured her. "Katrine is a beautiful woman."

"I guess she's right about beauty not counting for much when it's all said and done." Shelly sighed. "She can't seem to get a man no matter how good she looks."

"She told you that?" Trey asked, his tone skeptical. "The thing about beauty being only skin deep."

"Sure." Shelly shrugged. "Judging by the one man who ever spent any time with us, I've got to say she believes it."

"He couldn't have been all that bad?" Trey resented the hopeful note in his voice.

"No," Shelly admitted. "I was only six when he hung around here, but I remember he was hairy." She shuddered delicately. "And he wasn't funny like you."

"Maybe that's why she stopped seeing him. Hairy and dull in the bargain."

Shelly laughed, a delightful sound, Trey thought. Nothing seemed as pure as a child's laughter, a child's honesty, or a child's love.

"Mom's dull, too," she informed him. "That's why I didn't want her to come with us today."

Katrine dull? The panicked motorcyclist? The country-twang-playing, get-him-in-a-fight-with-a-midget-then-leave-with-a-biker, Katrine? "Your mother might be many things, but boring isn't one of them."

The lift of a perfectly arched brow indicated Shelly's misgivings. "She doesn't know how to have fun. I asked her to play with me once when I was seven. Being very immature at the time," Shelly was quick to point out. "She tried, but she wasn't good at it. I don't think she knows how."

"Everyone knows how to play," Trey argued. "I'm sure writers have a greater potential at playing pretend. Otherwise, they couldn't make up stories about people they haven't really met or places they haven't seen. I guess it takes at least a degree of imagination to write a romance novel."

"Oh, she has a great imagination. It's the real stuff she has trouble with. Wait and see. She won't have fun, I promise."

"And I promise she will." Trey got to his feet. "If there's one thing I can't resist, it's a challenge. I say your mother will laugh so hard her stomach will hurt and her eyes will water. Do you want me to show you how hard she'll laugh?"

Suddenly, he grabbed Shelly up, tucked her under his arm and began tickling. She squealed with delight.

"Kindly get your hands off my daughter," Katrine said from the doorway. "If the two of you weren't making so much racket, you'd have heard the cabby blaring his horn in the drive."

Frozen in place, Shelly a dead weight beneath his arm, Trey watched Katrine wheel around and stomp from the kitchen. He gently lowered Shelly to the floor, noting the smug expression on the girl's face.

"Is she having fun yet?" she asked dryly.

♥   ♥   ♥

The question was repeated an hour later at the Galleria.

"Well?" Shelly glanced toward her mother.

From their place on the rink, Trey followed her gaze. Katrine sat at a table, sipping coffee and watching the skaters with obvious interest. An 'observer' he noted with annoyance. He assumed she'd want to skate, but she refused.

"She's certainly having a blast," Shelly further goaded. "I haven't seen her laugh this much since the hot water heater busted and flooded the whole downstairs."

"Smart mouth," Trey mumbled. "She wears a seven and a half, right?"

A grin spread across Shelly's lips. "Oh, I see. You think you're going to *force* her to have fun. You can rent her skates, but you won't get them on her feet. Forget it, she's hopeless. Hey." Shelly's eyes narrowed with suspicion. "How'd you know what size shoe she wears?"

"Hay's for horses," Trey teased, ignoring the question. How many times had he picked up those sequined heels sitting on his dresser and thought about the woman they belonged to? Too many times to comfortably admit. He should have brought them back to her today.

The shoes looked totally out of place in the masculine decor of his bedroom. And yet… they added a touch of femininity and rekindled a remembrance of perfume bottles, pantyhose and jewelry. The annoying clutter of inanimate objects that meant nothing, until they were missing.

"Let's get her skates," he said abruptly, wanting to dismiss his thoughts before they settled on the day he found the clutter gone and only a note in its place. "I'll strike a bargain with you. If I get your mom to skate, you have to try it without clinging to my arm. Deal?"

"But I'll fall," Shelly whined.

"But I'll fall," he mimicked. "I thought Texas women cut their teeth on cactus. Of course you'll fall, that's how you learn."

"But, it'll hurt."

"Of course it hurts, that's what makes you try all the harder not to fall again."

"Does this conversation have a hidden proverb behind it?" Shelly questioned suspiciously.

Trey nodded. "Yeah, I guess it does. If you don't want bruises on your butt, learn to skate without falling down."

"Gosh, and you're deep, too."

In response, he flashed her his best smile.

Two women glancing back over their shoulders tripped over each other's skates and hit the ice. Trey, avoiding the pile of feminine limbs, took a firm hold on Shelly's arm and steered her toward the rental desk.

Chapter Nine

♥   ♥   ♥

"Creep," Katrine muttered. *Those dimples of his caused two women bodily harm and he just saunters off like nothing happened. He could have at least helped them up! And where does he get off having so much fun with my daughter? Who does he think he is? Tickling Shelly, making her laugh while she gazes up at him with adoring eyes! She's smitten. He'll break her heart!*

Keeping an eye trained on the child abductor, Katrine saw them head toward the skate rental desk. Good, she thought, they were turning in their skates. She'd had all she could take! Shelly hadn't acted like a child in what seemed ages. Katrine suddenly found herself wondering where the years had gone.

Why hadn't she thought to take Shelly ice skating before? Why hadn't she taken her to a rodeo, a state fair, any of those places denied her in her misguided youth?

Because, like her, Shelly had never asked. Like her, Shelly obviously didn't realize what she was missing. Not until *he* came along!

"I've got to stop being such a hermit," Katrine vowed softly, reaching for her purse. *I've got to learn how to have fun so Shelly will enjoy spending time with me the way she seems to enjoy spending time with him.*

"Your turn."

Katrine glanced up and met the steely blue challenge in Trey's eyes. Dangling from his fingers were a pair of skates. They appeared to be her size. "I–I–told you, I don't know how to skate," she stammered. "I thought we were leaving."

"What? And let you go home without joining in the fun? Shelly wants to see you skate."

"I don't know how," Katrine ground through her teeth.

"Shelly wants to see you *try.*"

"Forget it," Shelly said softly. "I told you she wouldn't."

The disappointment in her daughter's voice touched an exposed nerve. "All right!" Katrine grumbled. "Give me the damn things!"

"That's the spirit," Trey injected with enough fake aplomb to bring a smile to Shelly's lips. "File that away as a memorable quote from your mother. *'Give me the damn things!'*"

As Shelly broke into a full-fledged giggle, Katrine fought a smile traitorously finding its way to her face. The man was so annoyingly witty.

"Ready to fly solo, Kid?" At Shelly's nod, Trey took hold of her arm. "I'll help you get started."

With a glance over his shoulder, he instructed Katrine, "Lace up, I'll be back for you in a minute."

While slipping off her flats, Katrine watched her daughter's slow descent into the crowded rink. Trey had been nothing but patient with Shelly all morning, allowing her to cling to him while they moved around the rink at a snail's pace. It surprised her that he didn't skate well, but seemed to be a beginner himself.

She'd assumed, because of his athletic build and the natural grace with which he moved, anything requiring balance and strength would come easy. Anything that was, besides wrestling a woman in a vat of mud. She wondered what fate befell her red shoes. It had been childish to throw them at Trey.

Down right stupid, she later realized, when she arrived home with her feet nearly frost bitten. Elmo had graciously offered her his socks. Katrine had declined.

The giant turned out to be a gem. He proved nothing but gentlemanly, remaining in the drive until she made the safety of the house, but Katrine gave herself a good talking to the next morning. Her actions had been foolish. Anything could have happened to her. Why did she feel the need to so totally humiliate Trey that night, and why had she let him goad her into putting on a pair of ice skates? There was certainly no way she could balance herself on two thin steel blades, much less walk across ice.

"It's too late to back out."

Tilting her head, Katrine encountered his amused expression. "I suppose I'm committed," she agreed. "What do I do first?"

"Sling that saddle bag you carry over your shoulder and stand up."

The strap of her purse settled over her head, Katrine rose on wobbly knees. Her ankles immediately threatened to fold.

"Give me your hands," Trey ordered. The warmth of his fingers slid along the outside of her outstretched hands, securing a firm clasp. "I'll take you around nice and slow."

It wasn't that she trusted him, not after the 'date'. It was more a case of having the option removed once they stepped onto the ice. Her feet immediately went out from under her. "Whoa!" She frantically clutched his arm.

"You're too stiff," Trey warned. "I won't let you fall. Try to relax."

She took a steadying breath and willed her body to comply. Often, when a new book idea or a particularly brilliant plot twist concerning a work in progress left her too excited to sleep, she tried to mentally dissolve her bones in an effort to calm down. She blotted out the noise of the rink, imagining every muscle in her limbs beginning to loosen. Her next conscious thought was the realization she was falling.

The air left her lungs in a whoosh of surprise as her rear end met the ice. Trey landed beside her. He appeared to be as surprised as she.

"I didn't say turn into a rag doll! What happened?"

"I fell!" Katrine shouted back at him. "You told me to relax!"

"There's a vast difference between relaxation and a dead faint! Next time you fall, let go of me before you do it!"

"Hey, did you guys fall down?" Shelly slid ungracefully toward them. Her feet refused to stop and she tripped over Trey's outstretched legs.

He caught her, breaking her fall as a curse left his tight-stretched lips. "You two are an accident waiting to happen. I suggest we move before we cause a collision."

"How do you suggest we do that?" Katrine quipped with irritation.

"It's relatively simple," Trey returned in the same vein. "Roll over onto your knees, then get to your feet."

"A demonstration would be nice," Katrine decided.

Trey sighed, quickly doing as requested before helping Shelly up. Once he rescued Katrine, her feet went in opposite directions.

"Keep your legs together." He placed his arms around her waist. It dawned on him, while her body fit perfectly into the curve of his, that he'd never given a woman that particular advice before.

"Now what?" Katrine questioned.

"I'll do all the work, just lean back and enjoy

it." He smiled, admitting he'd probably given that instruction a time or two.

"My knees keep wanting to spread," Katrine complained.

His smile widened. "I suppose it's a natural response."

"What are you grinning at?" Shelly demanded beside them.

A guilty flood of heat surfaced in his face. "Nothing," he mumbled. "Let's go."

Shortly thereafter, Trey became uncomfortably aware of Katrine's bottom pressed intimately against him. The clean scent of her hair stirred his senses, the feel of her in his arms drove him crazy. *This was a mistake.* He tried to concentrate on putting one foot in front of the other. I'm not responding to her, he told himself. His feet weren't listening. Trey tripped.

"Ouch," Katrine yelped at the jarring feel of her knees hitting the ice. A softer yelp followed when Trey landed on top of her. She was on her hands and knees, and judging from the position of his arms along side hers, and his breath on her cheek, they didn't make a pretty picture.

"My gosh," Shelly ground in embarrassment, doing some odd thing with her feet to stop. "Hurry and get up before someone turns a water hose on you two."

"Shelly!" Katrine squawked.

The man indecently sprawled on top of her merely laughed. He struggled to his feet then helped Katrine up.

"Don't encourage her," she warned, managing an amazing turn to face him.

His gaze widened slightly over her accomplishment. "That was pretty good."

"Don't change the subject." Katrine cast a warning glance toward her daughter. "Shelly, the remark you just made was extremely crude. Suggesting we looked like a couple of dogs— well, where did you get such a comparison?"

"School," both Trey and Shelly answered flatly.

"School?"

"You know how dogs are," Trey said. "They only... ah, get together, in schoolyards, on church property or busy street corners. They have a wonderful sense of humor."

"Disgusting creatures," Katrine muttered.

"Melissa has a nice one," Shelly said softly.

"It barks morning, noon and night," her mother complained.

"Dogs and children come with a certain amount of noise factor filtered in," Trey said dryly. "Now, do we continue this abuse, or have your knees had enough?"

"I believe your knees are probably every bit as bruised as ours," Katrine pointed out. "You aren't any better at this than we are."

"No one can skate very well with another person constantly clinging to his arm."

"I don't see anyone clinging to your arm at present," she challenged. "Why don't you show us your stuff?"

"Unlike the obviously insecure heroes in your novels, I don't feel the need to prove my masculinity by strutting for females like some peacock. I can skate. We'll leave it at that."

"I want to see you strut," Shelly pouted.

"He probably skates as well as he mud wrestles," Katrine said under her breath.

His gaze shot her direction. "I heard that. All right. Prepare to be impressed."

After Trey escorted them to the side rail, he bent and began tightening the laces of his skates. "I could have taken Wanda," she heard him mutter.

Katrine smiled, her smile fading when he rose and dusted the ice from his knees. Trey Westmoreland was a man who'd always look good walking away.

"Here goes," he turned to say, then he was gone.

"Where is he?" Katrine craned her neck.

"There!" Shelly pointed. "Wow. Look how fast he's going!"

Tracking Trey wasn't easy. He sped along the ice, weaving in out of people the same as he'd done on the motorcycle. "Maniac," she whispered, but was impressed despite herself.

He passed them, turned and skated backwards, a cocky grin plastered on his face. Neither Katrine nor her daughter said a word to each other. *I can skate,* had been a ridiculous understatement.

After leaving them gaping while he shot around

the rink twice more, Trey skated toward the rail. He stopped abruptly, spraying Katrine and Shelly with ice shards.

Shelly laughed, clapping her hands with excitement.

"Where did you learn to skate like that?" she demanded.

Trey shrugged as if it were no great accomplishment. "I've been skating since I was a kid. I played hockey in college."

Hockey? Katrine's limited knowledge on the sport consisted of turning the channel when a game came on television. From what she could grasp of the sport, a bunch of men in stuffed shirts skated around trying to knock a small black thing into a net and usually knocking each other around more than the disk.

"Well?" Trey said.

She lifted a haughty brow. "I'm not familiar with the sport."

"And you're not impressed?" he goaded.

"Not very," she answered dully.

His grin stretched. "Maybe that's because you haven't had enough research in the area of speed skating. Come on, I'll give you a lesson."

Before she understood his intent, Katrine found herself pulled out onto the ice. Trey placed his hands on her waist and propelled them forward. "Wait! I thought we were leaving!" she shouted in panic.

"Can't," he said in an apologetic tone. "Not

until I make you laugh. Keep your knees bent and your feet straight. If we fall this time, it'll hurt like hell."

The word 'hurt' Katrine understood all too well. She couldn't tolerate pain, not physical or emotional. Since an argument seemed pointless, she did as Trey instructed.

"Here we go."

The floor rushed past her, filling Katrine's nose with the clean scent of cold. Trey's hands were secure on her waist, and after a few moments of fear-induced adrenaline being pumped through her system, she felt something she'd never experienced. A heady taste of recklessness. She had no time to think, to react, only to feel, and the pleasure of flying across the ice with Trey brought her such joy, she couldn't help but express it. Katrine began to laugh out loud.

Her eyes were stinging with unshed tears, her insides sore from laughing by the time Trey slowed, steering them toward the railing where Shelly stood wide-eyed.

"I don't believe it," she whispered. "You're laughing, just like he promised." The girl's gaze settled upon Trey with reverence. "You did it, Trey. And you didn't even have to tickle her."

Katrine glanced between the two of them in confusion. "What's this, a conspiracy going on behind my back?"

"Earlier, Shelly expressed a doubt you were capable of having fun," Trey explained. "Knowing

how much you like to be entertained, I told her
I'd prove her wrong."

"You are entertaining," Katrine admitted dryly,
then smiled at him. "And you skate better than
you…" She cut her eyes meaningfully at Shelly.
"Better than another sport I've seen you involve
yourself with."

"I want Trey to push me around the rink the
same as he did you," Shelly pleaded.

Trey looked to Katrine for permission.

"Only a couple of times, and not as fast," she
stressed.

"Why don't you get your skates off and meet
us by the rental desk."

She nodded, grasping the rail for support while
he took Shelly's hand and helped her onto the ice.
Once Katrine made the safety of a chair, she went
about removing her skates, watching the rink for
signs of Trey and Shelly while untying her laces.
When she spotted them, a strange feeling stole
over Katrine. They looked so natural together, and
she resented John all the more for not being there
to help her raise their daughter.

Her child drank up Trey's attention like a
thirsty flower. Katrine had told herself for years a
man wasn't a necessity to make a woman's life
complete, but what about Shelly? By denying
herself, had she also short-changed her daughter?
She suddenly wondered what her life would be
like if things had turned out differently, then
fought the picture forming in her imagination. A

picture of her, Trey and Shelly, together, as a family.

Don't, Katrine mentally warned herself. She was dreaming a very dangerous dream. On paper, Katrine knew how to make it turn out the way it should, but in real life, she knew the ending all to well. Nothing lasted forever. When she noticed Trey and Shelly headed toward the skate rental desk, she finished removing her skates and slipped into her flats.

Shelly's flushed face made her smile when she joined them.

"Did you see us, Mom? Weren't we great?"

"You were," she agreed. "Maybe we should check into some lessons for you."

"Really?"

Shelly seemed so excited, Katrine felt another twinge of guilt. Why hadn't she thought of doing this before? Beneath her lashes, she sought the source of her new-found enlightenment. Trey turned in their skates and cast her an approving glance. Katrine hated the pleasure it spread through her body. She shouldn't care about his approval. Still, as they headed down the mall toward an exit where they'd agreed to meet Charlie, Katrine felt obligated to express gratitude for her daughter's sake.

"Thank you for today. Shelly had a great time… and I did, too," she admitted softly. "I guess this goes to show we can spend more than a couple hours in each other's company without a major catastrophe occurring."

"Maybe we should take Shelly on all our dates," he suggested with a grin. "Has Jerry called you?"

"He has. Expect a limo at your apartment two nights from now. Jerry said he'd give the driver directions to your apartment and to my house, as well."

"I can't believe you want control of the next date," he said in a tone dripping with fake injury. "You couldn't possibly top the evening I had planned for us."

"Probably not," she said, enjoying the easy banter between them. "I'm insisting on formal attire. No grease," she added a warning.

His sexy smile dazzled her. Katrine took slow, deep breaths as they walked outside in an effort to clear her head. Trey Westmoreland was a dangerous man. If she didn't watch herself, she might start to like more about him than his looks.

"There's Charlie," Shelly said, running ahead toward the cab.

"I'll sit up front," Katrine decided.

"Afraid to get in the back with me?"

"Afraid you'll write something about it," she countered, walking around to the front passenger door. Thankfully, Shelly had already scrambled inside the back, saving Katrine the curiosity their conversation would have generated.

"I don't think I'd mind another round of research."

Hand poised on the door, Katrine stared over the top of the cab to meet his heated stare. Truth be known, she wouldn't mind another round, either.

"You two quit flapping your jaws!" Charlie rolled down his window to shout. "I've been sittin' out here for over fifteen minutes."

Trey opened his door and started to climb in before he realized Charlie had a passenger. Judging by the person's bulging belly, Trey suspected he knew who it was. "Nadine?"

"T. West," she snarled.

"Get in, Trey," Charlie instructed shortly. "I've got things to do."

Nadine shifted herself, grunting and groaning all the while. Shelly, not as mature as she sometimes seemed, ogled the woman's huge stomach from the other side of the car.

"Pumpkin, this is Kat Summers," Charlie beamed, turning to face his wife.

"I'm so h–happy to meet you," Nadine said.

"Nice to meet you, too." Katrine settled herself in the front seat, wondering why the woman's voice caught the way it did. Besides the fact she was obviously very pregnant, she looked odd. "Are you all right?" Katrine asked with concern.

"Not really." Nadine's face screwed up. She groaned. "I'm in labor."

Chapter Ten

♥   ♥   ♥

Trey gulped. "You're *what?*"

"I wasn't talkin' to you," Nadine snapped. "Now, Kat, as I was saying, I'm in labor and Charlie here thinks he's a doctor and knows we got time for one more fare before we go to the hospital. Since it was you, I unwisely agreed."

"Oh hell, Nadine," Charlie swore. "You know at them Lamaze classes they said the first baby takes hours. This kid's gonna cost me a fortune. I needed Trey's fare. It usually turns into an expensive one."

"I'm paying," Katrine reminded Charlie. "This was my treat, and I'm sure you're absolutely correct. I labored with Shelly off and on for two days before—"

"Do you think we can do something besides sit here and chit-chat?" the question barely made it through Trey's clenched teeth. "Hurry, before she… does whatever it is she's going to do!"

'She' turned a glare on Trey. "I won't make any bones about the fact I think you're about as sorry as a full tick on a starving dog. I didn't much care for your review on Kat three years ago. You'd best just sit there and keep your mouth shut, 'cause in case you ain't figured it out, *I'm not in a good mood.*"

"Sweet Cakes," Charlie warned. "Don't threaten my customers. I'll get you to the hospital in plenty of time."

The cabby took the car out of park and eased into the flow of traffic. Trey sat close to the door, his eyes trained on the back of Charlie's head. He knew plenty about kids, but had never witnessed a birth. Maybe if he ignored Nadine and the possibility she might deliver in the seat next to him, the situation wouldn't materialize. The feel of a strong hand taking his made detachment impossible.

Nadine gasped and dug her nails into Trey's palm. "Oooooh," she moaned, making small panting noises. "It hurts so bad, I just want to squeeze the life outta something!"

"How far apart are your contractions?" Katrine asked.

"They were ten minutes apart. Now five."

Katrine cast a worried glance the cabby's direction. "Charlie, I think you'd better forget about taking us home and go straight to the hospital."

"You sure?" he asked, as if being a romance writer qualified Katrine to know about such things as birthing babies.

"I can't remember how far apart they were when Shelly was born. They knocked me out and did a cesarean. Even so, I think you should hurry."

Trey wondered if the scar ran up and down or sideways. He wanted to think about anything but the woman crushing the bones in his hand. Since Shelly had been brought to attention, he turned to see how she was reacting to the circumstance. Her eyes were huge and kept darting to Nadine's stomach as if she expected something to pop out any minute. "Shelly, are you all right?" he thought to ask.

She nodded, but her face looked pale.

"Oh," Nadine whispered. "Either I just wet my pants or my water broke."

"Are you sure?" Charlie yelled.

"I'm sure it was one or the other!" she shouted back.

"Just drive, Charlie!" Trey ordered.

"Don't you yell at my Char—lie." Nadine bit down on her lip, squeezed her eyes shut and applied pressure to Trey's hand.

"She's having another contraction," Katrine fretted. "I don't think it's been five minutes. How long will it take to get to the hospital, Charlie?"

"In this traffic, maybe an hour. I know some short cuts, maybe I'd better take them."

Yes! Yes! Yes! Trey wanted to shout. He didn't dare, not with the future use of his fingers at Nadine's mercy. Progress of her contraction could be easily measured. The pressure to his hand started out gradual, increased, became unbearable, then declined. Trey tried to ease his hand from her hold. Nadine clamped down.

"Here comes another one," she moaned.

"It's only been two minutes," Katrine whispered.

"Breathe, Baby," Charlie called from the front seat. "That's what we paid all that money for, wasn't it? So you could learn to pant like a dog?"

"I'm gon-na kill you Char-lie Grimes." The contraction took Nadine's threat and turned it into a gasp of pain. "Oh, Oh, Ohhhh my Godddd!"

As numbness spread through Trey's imprisoned hand, he suspected he'd never hear a woman moan those three words again without seeing Nadine's sweat-beaded, twisted features in his mind. When Nadine increased the pressure on his fingers, he started to pant along with her.

"Quit that, Trey," Charlie grumbled. "You're fogging up the windows. I'm taking a dirt road, Nadine. It's rough. Hold on, Honey."

She did. To Trey. They bounced along a rutted road as Nadine grunted and groaned. "I need to lie down," she moaned. "I need to push!"

"No!" Charlie shouted. "It can't be time to push! You know what we learned in them classes? You can't push!"

His wife proved she could by bearing down with the next contraction. Trey bore down on his lip to keep from groaning out loud.

"Shelly, get up front with me," Katrine instructed.

Her daughter seemed eager to comply as she scrambled over the seat. Trey wanted to scramble up front with her. Nadine had other plans for him.

"Help me stretch out!" she barked, releasing his hand. The sudden blood rush to his fingers was close to orgasmic. Trey wiggled his fingers in bliss. Nadine grabbed hold of his collar.

"H-E-L-P M-E!"

Taking her beneath the arms, Trey tried to budge a one-hundred-eighty pound woman to the far edge of the seat. He felt the movement of her stomach against his. It didn't feel good. Nadine didn't look good. This wasn't good.

"How far are we from the hospital?" he croaked.

"Thirty minutes," Charlie answered. "How you holding up, Pumpkin?"

"Pull over," Nadine said. "I waited too long to call you. I'm gonna have this baby before we get to the hospital and I want you with me. So I can kill you afterwards," she added with a sob.

The cab skidded to a halt. Charlie almost wrenched the back door off its hinges. He poked his head inside. "Trey, don't look. I'm going to see what's going on down there."

Trey was all too willing to oblige. He had no desire to see what was going on 'down there'.

"Oh my gosh," Charlie whispered. "She's crowning."

"Crowning? What the hell does that mean?" Trey asked.

"It means he can see the top of the baby's head," Katrine explained.

Charlie nodded, turned white, then fainted

dead away.

When his body hit the frozen ground outside the car, Trey's panicked mind shifted into denial. *This can't be happening. Women don't really have babies in the back seats of cabs. This only happens in movies. A miracle would deliver them all, including Nadine. A doctor on the way to the hospital should pull up any minute and ask if they needed assistance.* His head swiveled from front view to back. Not a car in sight.

"What do we do, now?" Katrine choked, obviously on the verge of panic herself. "Trey, do you know anything about delivering babies?"

"Oh, sure," he snapped. "Not only did I major in Journalism and play hockey in college, I practiced obstetrics in my spare time! Hell no, I don't know anything about it!"

"I only asked!" she shouted back at him. "You don't have to bite my head off! If you hadn't taken Shelly ice skating today, we wouldn't be in this mess!"

"If you hadn't insisted on coming with us, we wouldn't have had to call a cab, and we wouldn't be here!"

"You are here," Nadine reminded weakly. "Someone's gonna have to help me."

Katrine began chewing her lip and Trey began glancing out the window again. In the front seat, Shelly snapped out of her fear-induced trance.

"I know, I'll use the mobile to call 911."

Both Trey and Katrine stared dumbly at her.

"The mobile?" they said in unison.

Shelly lifted the phone. "While I dial, Trey move Charlie up front with me, and Mom, you get in the back seat and help."

All occupants of the car shifted. After Trey and Katrine managed to settle Charlie in the front seat, they returned to the back and opened the door, bumping shoulders as they scrambled inside. Nadine was past the ability to make comments of her own, emitting only groans and pants while she labored with the burden of love.

"The lady on the phone wants to know where we are."

Glancing up, Katrine noted Shelly hanging halfway over the seat. It occurred to her, even in this mind-numbing circumstance, that an eleven year old had no business witnessing the miracle of birth. But then, maybe if young girls were forced to confront the results of passion, there might be less teen pregnancies.

Trey took the phone and gave directions as best he could. His tone was panicked and, reluctantly he handed the phone back to Shelly. "She said the level-headed kid who called should handle the instructions."

Shelly listened for a second, then asked Nadine if she could wait for the ambulance. A contraction gripped the panting woman and she shook her head to the negative.

"She can't wait," Shelly said calmly. After a short pause, she instructed her mother to get behind Nadine and lift the woman's shoulders when she pushed. "Trey." Shelly swallowed loudly. "The lady says you have to deliver the baby."

Katrine paused in her scramble to position herself behind Nadine and glanced at Trey. His face reflected sick horror. With trembling hands he gently pushed Nadine's dress up over her bent knees. The expression that crossed his face spoke volumes. *No way could that be possible!*

He took a deep breath. "Okay, tell me what to do."

"First, I think you should open your eyes," Katrine suggested.

"Oh. Right."

"The lady says when the head comes out, gently cup it with one hand and rotate the baby's shoulders to the side with the other," Shelly instructed.

Nadine began to pant again.

"Here we go," Katrine warned.

"Lift her shoulders, Mom."

"The head's coming," Trey announced. "That's it, Nadine. Just a little more. You're doing great. There," he breathed in relief.

"Quick, turn the baby before the next contraction," Shelly said.

Trey hesitated.

"Turn the baby." Katrine sounded frantic.

"It's so small. What if I hurt it?"

"Do what I said, Trey!" Shelly ordered.

He obeyed.

"Now, when the next contraction begins, the

lady says to be ready to catch the baby."

"It's starting." Katrine saw the muscles in Nadine's stomach begin to bunch.

"Push, Nadine," Trey instructed. "That's it! I have him! Shelly, what do I do?"

"What now?" she shouted into the phone, her calm obviously fading. "The lady says to use your finger to clean out the baby's mouth, then to gently wipe your hand across it's face to unblock the nose passage."

It took Trey a few seconds to complete the procedure. Nothing happened. "He's not breathing!"

"Help him," Nadine whispered. "Oh God, please help him!"

Shelly quickly relayed the frightening news. "Hold him up by his feet and give him a smack on the bottom!"

Fear shot through Katrine's body. She saw Trey lift the baby. It looked so small... so lifeless.

"My hands are too slippery," Trey ground out in frustration. "I'm afraid I'll drop him without both hands. Shelly, lean forward and give him a smack."

Without hesitation, Shelly complied. Silence, then a small chocking noise followed by a full-fledged wail of outrage, and life entered the cab. A miracle in the making.

"Ahhh," the air left Katrine's lungs in a relieved rush. Her eyes began to water. "Just listen to that, Nadine."

After gathering the squalling infant in his arms,

a look of pure wonder spreading over his tense features, Trey glanced up and smiled at Nadine. "He's perfect."

"Let me have him," the woman begged.

Trey leaned forward and placed the baby on her stomach. Katrine oohhed and awed with Nadine as they counted each tiny finger, each tiny toe.

"Have you ever seen anything so beautiful?" Katrine asked, meeting Trey's warm regard.

He shook his head slowly, his gaze never leaving her face. "No, I've never seen anything more beautiful."

Her pulse quickened. She and Trey shared something miraculous today. Could she look at him from this moment forward without remembering the tenderness in his eyes when he gazed down at Nadine and Charlie's baby? Judging from his easy mannerisms with Shelly, Katrine thought Trey Westmoreland would make a wonderful father. For only a moment, she resented the fact it wasn't their child he ogled with such… longing.

Yes, she assured herself, longing seemed to be the correct word. Would Trey want children of his own someday? Still captured by the warmth of his eyes, Katrine decided the beauty of what they'd just experienced had seduced her. Forget her earlier assurance that witnessing birth would douse the flames of passion. Something stirred in her veins, primal and instinctive. The need to mate.

"Ah, what?" Charlie muttered.

The spell held for a second longer. Katrine

recognized the answering spark in Trey's heated stare before he removed his jacket and covered Nadine. Their ordeal wasn't over. Sirens blared as the ambulance pulled up beside the cab. "Later?" he questioned softly.

Katrine felt her throat constrict. Did she dare agree to the blatant invitation in his eyes. "Yes, later."

Chapter Eleven

♥   ♥   ♥

As she fidgeted with the keys to the front door, a weary Trey, and a recently over-educated Shelly trudged along behind Katrine.

"The security system," Shelly warned.

"I remember," Katrine lied. She hadn't been able to think of anything but 'later' since leaving the hospital. She punched in the code and jiggled the key. Her hands shook. Warm fingers closed over hers.

"Let me," Trey suggested. "It's been a rough day."

"Next to delivering a baby, ice skating seemed boring," Shelly decided in a flat voice.

Trey laughed. "I believe you've found your calling, Doctor Shelly. You were great, Kid."

"Don't call me kid," Shelly grumbled.

"Why? You are one," Trey continued to tease. "You'd better get to bed before you drop where you stand."

Shelly nodded while he swung the door wide and handed the keys back to Katrine. "I could probably sleep through a tornado."

A pause followed her admission. One in which Katrine dropped her keys. She and Trey almost bumped heads as each bent to retrieve them.

"I'll just go," he said, the decision sounding more like a question than a statement. "I'm a mess," he indicated his clothing.

"You can take a shower here," Shelly politely offered. "Mom can wash your shirt and fix you a cup of coffee."

Meddling child. Katrine pasted a brave smile on her lips. "It's the least I can do for the hero of the day."

Her flattery caused a thoughtful frown to settle over his lips. The intensity of his gaze when he turned those too-blue eyes on her made Katrine's knees weak.

"Are you sure?"

Sure? No, she wasn't sure! If she let Trey inside the house, Katrine knew straight where it would lead. To bed. Her emotions had been batted around all day. She felt vulnerable, hungry for his touch, driven to bond with him. Inviting Trey in was emotional suicide.

"I'm sure," her voice cracked.

His smile suggested he doubted her sincerity. "I'll come inside for a while. But, I could use something stronger than coffee."

"I–I think I have a bottle of scotch in one of my cabinets. It belonged to… well, will that do?"

"That'll do," he answered. "For starters, anyway."

♥   ♥   ♥

Scotch splashed over the sides of her glass as Katrine hurriedly poured herself a drink. *What am I doing? I have a maniac in my shower! And worse, I'd like to be in there with him! I've definitely lost my head!* Taking a deep breath, she lifted her glass, snatched up the bottle and moved into the hallway where the lower level bathroom was located. Outside the door, on the knob, hung a shirt in dire need of a washing. She draped the shirt over one arm and tried to stare a hole through the door. Was he undressing?

Perhaps he'd already taken his clothes off. Katrine wished she had the nerve her heroines possessed. One in particular, would have simply placed her hand on the knob, twisted it, and found out.

♥   ♥   ♥

"That's it," Trey coaxed under his breath, watching the knob turn slowly. "Open the door and step inside. Prove I didn't imagine what your eyes were telling me earlier."

Jeans unfastened, chest bare, breathing labored, he waited. The turning ceased. Trey slowly let the air escape his lungs. "Tease," he accused softly, then walked to the shower, adjusted the water temperature to cold, slipped out of his jeans and stepped beneath the chilly spray.

A frigid blast of rationalism. *That's what I need.* He should have left when Katrine displayed misgivings concerning her earlier promise. Women like her always went back on the deal. So perfect on the outside, so shallow within. "No thank you," he mumbled, soaping his body.

He continued to mentally berate his irrational behavior while climbing out of the shower. *I might have done something really stupid tonight.* Something almost as crazy as glancing across that cab and wishing for one insane moment he'd see the wonder on Katrine's features again someday. Watch her face tilt up to his with the same awe-struck beauty while she nestled their child in her arms. It didn't make sense, and yet, it seemed so right at the time. He, Katrine, Shelly, together. A family.

Trey shook his head, scattering drops of water. "She's all wrong for you," he assured his reflection, grabbing up a towel. "You're thinking with the front of your pants. Do you think you can just hit and run so easy?" He didn't like the idea.

"Give in to her," he said, pointing a finger at his image, "and you're borrowing trouble. One night might not be enough. What if you want her again tomorrow night, the one after and the one after that? Next thing you know, you'll open a drawer in her bathroom, and there's your damn toothbrush!"

Opening a drawer, Trey noted a new toothbrush

lying beside a tube of toothpaste. He snatched it up. "This isn't mine," he assured his reflection before opening the box.

♥   ♥   ♥

He'd finished his shower, that much Katrine knew by the steady water pressure flowing into the washer. She shook soap into the machine and closed the lid. *What now?* Her gaze travelled upward. Maybe she could just hide down here in the basement until his shirt washed and dried, then extend it to him on a long stick. No, she worried. The shirt was white. It'd look like surrender.

"I should have let him leave," she repeated, unconsciously taking a sip of the scotch. The taste made her wince and she sat the glass down.

Carl had liked scotch. Boring, *hairy* Carl. It occurred to her the question of whether or not Trey had a hairy chest would soon be answered. Of course, accompanying that chest would be the hot look he turned on her countless times at the hospital. The one that made rational thought impossible.

"Are you down there?"

Oh no, he'd found her. "Y–yes," Katrine croaked.

Her eyes fastened on the stairs. His bare feet came into view, then thankfully jean-clad legs. *Uh-oh.* Skin. Flat corded stomach, broad shoulders, very little hair. She was in trouble.

"When I didn't find you in the kitchen..." Trey's voice trailed. He paused on the bottom step. "Why are you looking at me like that? What's wrong?"

"Nothing." She whirled around to face the washer. "Not one damn thing," she said under her breath. Katrine had seen that chest before in her dreams. In her novels, she covered it with dark hair because Craig Martin, her editor, insisted women liked a hairy-torsoed hero. Unfortunately, she didn't.

"Mind if I have a drink?" Trey walked toward a table obviously used for folding laundry where her glass and the bottle sat.

Katrine continued to study the knobs as if they held all the most renowned secrets of the world. "Go ahead. I–I only brought one glass."

"We'll share. That shirt's probably a lost cause," he said when the silence between them stretched.

Okay, I can't avoid looking at him any longer. Katrine turned. Muscles rippled when he lifted the glass. After taking a sip, he winced slightly the same as she'd done. "Charlie was certainly the proud father once he woke up, wasn't he?" she blurted.

"He acted like a total idiot." Trey laughed. "Cooing and clucking over the baby, then puffing up like a toad. You'd have thought Nadine didn't have a thing to do with the birth."

"Now, she was the strange one." Katrine

bravely placed herself beside him. "I thought Nadine wanted to kill Charlie while she was in labor, but after he regained consciousness, she gushed and cried all over him. 'Just look Charlie, look what we done'," she mimicked Nadine.

"Yeah, she was something," he said with a soft smile. "I guess she's forgiven me a little."

"I'd say she's forgiven you a lot," Katrine countered, taking the glass he offered her. "You puffed up nicely yourself when Charlie and Nadine decided to give the baby your name."

A tinge of red crept into his cheeks. "That kid owes me big time. 'Furguson' was their original choice. What kind of torture is that to inflict on anyone?"

"It isn't so bad," she admonished. "But, Trey, I think that's a sort of heroic sounding name."

"You do?"

"Umhum." She nodded while taking a drink.

He frowned. Katrine had the distinct impression he didn't feel as if she'd complimented him. She noted the smell of toothpaste on the glass in her hand.

"I guess you found a toothbrush?"

"Oh, yeah. Since there weren't any women's things scattered around, I assumed—"

"Don't worry about it," she interrupted. "Shelly showers in there sometimes, but we both have a private bath upstairs and plenty of toothbrushes. Consider that one yours."

"It's not mine," he barked, then immediately

wanted to smack himself on the forehead. He sounded so defensive, so paranoid. Her earlier admission she found his name heroic sounding rattled him, nor did he like the way he fought himself to keep his hands off her. Trey felt certain the talk he had with himself upstairs hadn't done a damn bit of good. "I meant, you can soak it in peroxide and use it again. I'm sure I don't have anything contagious."

She sat the glass down. "I'm glad to know that."

The words hung between them. Glad as in 'good, now we can quit reminiscing and do what we've been thinking about doing all afternoon', Trey wondered. Or did she simply wish him good health? An awkward silence settled over the basement.

"Today must have brought back memories for you," he said, retreating to safer ground. "With Shelly," Trey clarified when her expression seemed blank. He expected a smile of remembrance to soften her features. To the contrary, she tensed, her eyes filled with tears.

"As I said earlier, I had a cesarean. When the monitor showed fetal distress, they knocked me out. I'd lost John only seven months before. Once I knew the baby was all right, I felt relieved I didn't have to experience a natural birth. I'd already been through so much pain. Today I saw what I missed by not being conscious to hear Shelly's first cry, to hold her in that glorious moment of discovery. I felt cheated. I wanted to snatch the moment back—to relive it again."

"Life's full of pain and unfairness," he said quietly, pulling Katrine into his arms. "I'm sorry for you, but more for John. He never met the daughter who carries his name. He'd be proud of her."

She lifted a tear-stained face to his. "He would, wouldn't he?"

Trey nodded, his gaze caressing her trembling lips before he bent to taste them.

♥　　♥　　♥

For Katrine, it seemed natural to come together in the sadness of loss and the celebration of life. Her fingers touched the smoothness of his chest, reveling in the warmth of his skin. When her nails grazed the circle of his nipple, he groaned. His response unleashed something dormant in her, a desire to test the boundaries of her own sensuality, a need to rekindle the flame he'd built between them the night they met. She wanted passion, irrational and overwhelming. Bravely, her tongue stole inside his mouth to explore, to taste him as he tasted her.

"Katrine," he warned hoarsely against her lips. "I don't know what you want from me, and as much as I hate to point this out, I don't think you know, either."

But she did know. "I only want this moment,"

Katrine whispered, trailing kisses down his neck. "I want you to set me on fire. I want to feel your skin next to mine and not just imagine what it would be like to make love with you."

"Dammit," he swore softly. "I can't think straight with your mouth on my throat, with your hands roaming all over me. Katrine, this isn't rational behavior."

She sighed impatiently. "I've never done anything impulsive or spontaneous in my life. Trey, do you want to be rational or do you want to make love to me?"

Her head tilted back, a result of his hands in her hair. Their eyes fused.

"To hell with logic." He crushed her lips with urgency. The sweater around her hips inched up her stomach until he pulled it over her head. Skin met skin. "Mmmm," they both sighed with pleasure. Trey lifted her from the floor, never surrendering her lips.

"Oh," she gasped over both the feel of his arousal pressed intimately against her and the jarring thud her bottom made when he deposited her on top of the washer. He cupped the fullness of her lace-clad breasts, his thumbs teasing her nipples erect through the thin fabric.

"You're beautiful, Katrine. You fit so perfectly in my hands," he whispered against her ear.

"Get it off," she pleaded, struggling with the straps of her bra. "I want to feel your hands on me, your mouth."

"What's wrong with this?" he asked after frantically fumbling with the hooks in the back to no avail.

"Oh great!" Katrine almost sobbed. "I'm wearing the one with a crooked hook. There's a pair of scissors on the shelf behind me. Cut it off!"

His gaze searched the shelves. Trey quickly snatched up a pair of scissors. He eyed her skeptically. "Are you sure you want me to—"

"Just do it!"

Katrine jumped when the cold steel of a blade slid between her breasts. She heard a clipping noise, felt the lace being peeled away, and saw the flare of heat in Trey's eyes when he looked at her. Slowly, his head lowered to her breasts.

She sighed, twisting her fingers in his hair. He flicked his tongue across her nipple before taking the crest inside his mouth. His soft sucking sent heat racing up her thighs. A warmth that spread to her lower regions where her quivering insides contracted with a need only he could fulfill. She wanted him desperately, and to prove it, Katrine bravely reached for the waistband of his jeans.

Trey sucked in his breath sharply at her boldness, straightening to afford her better access. "Remember the night on the bike?" he asked huskily. "I haven't been able to forget the feel of your hands on me. I've fantasized about it a time or two, about what would have happened if I hadn't reached the restaurant when I did."

Katrine smiled seductively at him. "I've thought about it, too," she admitted, struggling with the button due to the tightness of his jeans, a tightness brought about by what he had bulging inside. "At the time, I was thinking about a book."

"A book?" He took a step back. "You were thinking about a book?"

"Yes," she answered with a hint of annoyance, pulling him toward her with the pressure of her hands on his waistband. "I can't get this button undone."

"One you planned to write, or one you've already written?"

"One I've already written," she snapped. "Trey, if you don't get this button undone, I'm going to take the scissors to your fly."

"I'll do it," he quickly decided.

While he fumbled with the fastening, the washing machine went into the spin cycle. Katrine slammed up against him, almost smashing Trey's hands in the process. He grasped her hips.

"This thing's getting ready to rock like crazy with only one piece of clothing in it," she warned. "We'd better—"

Before her words of warning were completed, the ride began. The thin slacks she wore weren't much resistance against Trey's Levi-strained hardness. The machine bounced and bucked, creating a friction between them that was, to Katrine's way of thinking, better than it had a right to be.

"Damn," Trey swore softly, securing a stronger grasp on her hips. "Damn," he said again before capturing her lips.

He split her bottom lip with his teeth because of the bouncing, but Katrine hardly noticed the pain. The machine-made friction drove her to the brink of a world she'd never experienced. She felt a tightening sensation grip her.

"Oh," she moaned, "Ohh my—"

Visions of Nadine's red, panting face surfaced in Trey's mind. Suddenly, he felt a loss of interest overriding the stimulating feel of Katrine rubbing wildly against him. "Don't," he warned between labored breaths. "Don't say that. *Not now.*"

A hand clamping over Katrine's mouth brought her plummeting from her journey into another world. She crash landed into reality.

"Ouch!" Trey wrenched his hand from between her teeth. "You bit me!"

"I was this close," she panted, bringing up her fingers to measure out an inch. "This close to being somewhere I've never been before, and you ruined it!"

"Katrine, let's not argue. *Not now,*" he stressed.

"Oh no you don't." She reached behind her, turning the washer knob to 'off'.

The bucking came to an immediate halt. Trey gave the top of the washer a frustrated pound with his fist, then tried to bring his breathing back to normal. "All right, that was the weirdest foreplay

I've ever had, but now we'll have normal sex."

"Not now, we won't."

"You're not going to leave me this way?" he asked in disbelief. *"This* is cruel and inhuman punishment."

She smiled.

"I'm sorry." Trey ran a hand through his damp hair. "You're obviously angry because I ruined your 'burst of ecstasy'. Hell, I'll give you another one. I'll give you as many as you can handle. Be reasonable."

In answer, she lifted a brow, grabbed up her sweater and held it to her naked breasts. "I don't want another one. *I wanted that one.* You can leave now. I'm not drying your damn shirt, and I'll go back to my imagination where you were a considerate lover!"

"Like one of your heroes?" he snarled. "You know real sex is never that perfect or that ridiculous. I'm sure a virgin is going to orgasm ten times her first night with a man."

"Ten times, that's unreasonable," Katrine agreed stiffly. "Once her first night, that's logical. Once in a lifetime, I guess that's too much to ask!"

He blinked. "You mean, you haven't...? You're kidding, right?"

Her cheeks started to burn. "I thought with you... I wanted to understand, to experience what I've written about, but—"

"I'm research," he interrupted flatly. "You

wanted me to help you with the damn 'burst of ecstacy'. Does every man who ends up between your legs also end up between the pages of your next novel?"

The insulting question brought Katrine's temper to a rolling boil. The light in the basement seemed suddenly too stark, her behavior too embarrassing. There was nothing romantic about the interlude. The hero was no hero at all!

She jumped down from the washer, lifted the lid and threw his wet shirt at him. "Don't flatter yourself. You don't have to worry about reading this scene in one of my novels. I write historical romance, Westmoreland, not hysterical romance."

"I'm out of here," he assured her, struggling to force his arms into a clingy, wet shirt.

"Good," she quipped.

"It was at least that," he agreed, moving toward the stairs. "Had you managed to unfasten my jeans, it would have been even better."

"Conceited bastard," she accused at his back. "I've always heard it isn't quantity, but quality that counts most."

He laughed. "Right. I've noticed all your fantasy heroes have plenty of quantity."

"Well, yeah, they know what to do with it, too!"

Trey hesitated on the bottom step. He turned. "I assure you I know what to do. Are you trying to goad me into proving it? Do you want me to give you something to write about?"

In answer, she snatched the scotch bottle off

the table and held it menacingly, as if she planned to throw it at him. "What I want is to never see you again."

"Fine," he said through clenched teeth.

As he moved up the steps, Katrine felt an emptiness settle inside her. She didn't truly want him to leave. She wanted him to make good on his earlier promise. She wanted to start over.

"The limo will pick you up at seven on Friday night," she called weakly.

"Fine!"

The basement door slammed.

Chapter Twelve

♥   ♥   ♥

Trey lifted a glass of Perrier to his lips. He sipped while caressing the cover of a book. The raised print of the author's name caused him to smile slightly. "If this is what you want, Kat Summers, this is what you'll get." When the security buzzer sounded, he placed his glass aside, rose, and walked toward the speaker system.

"Katrine?"

"No. I'm Bob, the driver. She's waiting in the limo. You ready?"

"I'll be right out."

Moving into the bedroom, he snatched up his keys and frowned at a pair of red-sequined heels cluttering his immaculate dresser top. He lifted a shoe and caught the faded fragrance of her perfume. She'd obviously spilled a few drops on her shoes the night he took her to Shotty's.

He swore the scent became stronger at night, when sleep failed to claim him. He'd lie awake thinking of her, reliving the feel and taste of her skin, fighting his irrational attraction. Quickly, he replaced the shoe and steeled himself for the evening ahead. What he had planned should cool things down between them considerably. Among other things, Katrine Summerville certainly stimulated his creativity.

Bob, the uniformed limo driver, waited outside the security gate. The chauffeur tipped his hat and hastened to open the door for Trey. The overhead light blinked on, revealing a long leg. Trey swallowed loudly.

Bending slightly, his gaze ran the length of an aqua gown with a slit up the side and a body melted and poured into it. Trey coughed uncomfortably when the swell of bosom rising above the gown's low neckline shifted into view.

"Ah, Mr. Westmoreland? Would you care to get in?"

A voice inside his head issued a warning: *"Step into my parlor..."* At least Katrine wasn't wearing black, he consoled himself before taking the plunge.

"Care for a drink?"

The spider wasn't wasting time. Damn, why did she have to look that good? Her long blonde hair was piled attractively on top of her head, leaving the slim column of her throat exposed. She wore the same perfume, only a lot less of it. And her eyes—what had she done to make them so green? With effort, he pulled his gaze from the tantalizing sight of her.

"Sure." He shrugged, hoping to appear unmoved. "Scotch?"

Bitch. "That'll be fine."

"Straight up?"

The minute I laid eyes on you. "No, rocks off, I mean, on the rocks," he quickly corrected, running a hand over his forehead. The limo's elaborate back seat felt much too warm.

"I thought we'd go to Chez Fred's for dinner, then... well, we'll see."

See what? Trey wondered. If we can find an all night laundromat? Why was she using that soft, husky voice on him? Why wasn't she being her usual shrewish self? What was going on?

♥   ♥   ♥

Katrine smiled inwardly over his flustered expression. The sales lady at the trendy upscale store assured her this particular dress, with a figure like Katrine's stuffed inside, would turn a man's mind to mush. With mush being the purpose of this date, Katrine hadn't hesitated to purchase the daring gown.

It was worth the ridiculous price to see Trey's eyes bulge and his adam's apple bob. Good, her efforts were paying off. Romance was in the air. She meant to insure Trey had as much trouble writing his boring, rational side to this date as she'd had writing about their first one. That his well groomed, impressively dressed self affected her as well, Katrine wasn't above admitting. The man sitting next to her was the same suave paid escort who picked her up the night of the awards banquet. The one who had her squirming all over his lap in the degrading space of an hour.

"How's Shelly? I should have called her the last couple of days."

Yes, you should have, Katrine thought with annoyance. Shelly had been moping around because he hadn't. "Maybe you should just stay out of my daughter's life."

Her suggestion snapped his head her direction. "Why?"

"I don't want her to get hurt."

"I'd never hurt Shelly. I'm nuts about that kid."

"What happens when the feature ends?" Katrine asked. "When we're not forced to share each other's company anymore? You'll go on about your business and gradually the phone calls and outings will stop."

"I'll always have time for Shelly. She'll outgrow me long before I've outgrown her."

Trey hadn't thought about life beyond the feature or the consequences of giving his heart to a little girl with blonde hair and brown eyes. Could he continue a relationship with a child that forced him into constant contact with her mother? A mother about to spill out of the front of her dress—a mother who drove him totally insane?

"We shouldn't discuss Shelly on our dates," Katrine said softly. "We're on assignment, remember?"

Resenting the idea of Katrine and Shelly going about their lives without him once the assignment was over, Trey smothered his caring, his confusion, his emptiness by reminding himself he had a date to ruin. "Damned right," he agreed.

♥   ♥   ♥

The soft strains of a violin echoed around a room bathed in soft candlelight. Quality linen draped a table for two. Silverware gleamed and crystal goblets of water sat before them. A smartly attired waitress laid immaculate leather-bound menus on the table.

"Would either of you care for a before-dinner drink?" she questioned politely.

Trey looked toward Katrine with inquiry.

"I'll have a glass of white wine." She returned the waitress's smile.

"And you sir?"

"Hmmm," Trey said, glancing at the bar selection on the back of his menu.

While he deliberated, Katrine reached for her water glass. His response froze her fingers on the goblet's stem.

"Beg your pardon?" the waitress asked weakly.

"I said, I'll have a hearty ale, Wench, then later, I'll lift yer skirts and have me fill of ye."

The girl's face flushed scarlet. She glanced at Katrine, obviously unsure of the order or how the man's date would react to his forwardness.

"He'll have a glass of wine," she said stiffly.

As the waitress eagerly scrambled away, Katrine turned a glare on Trey. "What do you think you're doing?"

He shrugged. "I only ordered a drink."

"I'll have a hearty ale, Wench? You're lucky she didn't deck you. And that remark about lifting her skirts? She wasn't wearing a skirt, Trey. What sort of nonsense—" Katrine supposed the color drained from her face.

When he made the ridiculous remark, a certain feeling of déjà vu stole over her. She'd heard those words before, and oddly enough, even six years ago when she wrote them, it was Trey's voice she heard in her head.

"*Border Lord*?" she whispered.

"Bingo." A smile settled over his lips.

A groan left Katrine's. "Trey, don't do this to me."

"Do what?" he questioned innocently. "Isn't Sean McNeil one of your fantasy men?"

"He's a fictitious character for God's sake!"

"But he's romantic, at least in your opinion." His gaze lowered to the daring neckline of her dress, then slowly traced a path back up. "I want to please you."

His heated regard sent the blood coursing through her veins. Katrine refused to let him sidetrack her. "It would please me if you wouldn't quote Sean McNeil for the remainder of the evening.

His crude mannerisms were excusable. He lived two hundred years ago."

"I don't think rape was any more excusable then than it is today."

"He never raped anyone!" Katrine defended, then realized she'd spoken too loudly. Several heads turned their direction.

"Oh, excuse me, attempted rape," he corrected. "If you'll recall, he practically forced himself on the heroine in the first chapter."

"Sean mistook her for the serving wench… ah, woman who'd agreed to meet him upstairs. Once he realized he'd made a mistake—"

"He didn't act too sorry in my opinion," Trey interrupted. "'I'm tempted to pretend I dunna ken it's a lady's legs I've landed between'," he quoted gallantly, then fixed Katrine with a challenging stare.

"Here are your drinks," the waitress announced loudly.

That the girl heard Trey's excellent imitation of Sean McNeil was obvious by the color of her cheeks, and also by the fact she served their drinks from Katrine's side of the table.

"Could I take your dinner order now?"

"Oh." Katrine reached for her menu. "I haven't even looked."

"I'll have the Cornish hen on rice," Trey said. "I hear it's excellent."

"In that case, I'll have the same," Katrine decided.

After the waitress gathered their menus and

took herself off, Trey continued, "Does that sound like an apology to you?"

"Trey." Katrine sighed. "You're a man. You don't understand the female mind. In a fantasy situation some women are turned on by forceful men. Not in real life, but in a book, where it's safe to be attracted to a man who normally wouldn't appeal to them.

"Just because a person enjoys murder mysteries doesn't mean they want to murder anyone, so just because a woman enjoys romance novels where the hero gets somewhat out of line doesn't mean she wants to be raped."

"All right," he conceded, "But tell me this, Ms. Summers who gave such a pretty speech at the awards ceremony about beer commercials being sexist; why are all the heroines in your novels perfect in form and feature? Isn't your message the same thing?"

Katrine shook her head. "Not at all. When a woman escapes into a novel, she becomes the heroine. We all want to be beautiful, desirable, courageous and have perfect bodies. We all want to fall in love with a handsome, dangerous, dark haired, dimple—" Katrine quickly cut herself off, realizing the man she was describing sat across from her. She lifted her wine glass and took a sip.

"You were saying," he reminded.

"I'm saying, romance is a private relationship between reader and heroine. The reader shouldn't feel threatened. It's not the same as if she's sitting next to her husband or boyfriend through the beer commercials listening to comments like; what a great pair of—well you know? Or, I wish you had a body like that, or, I remember when you had a body like that."

"Sounds like a man she's better off without," Trey commented dryly. "I guess I understand. Still, why do romance writers create heroes no modern-day man could compete with? Why can't they be regular Joes? Why don't they ever have a normal job? Why aren't they ever too tired when they come home from raiding and pillaging to make love to the heroine? They always save the day—they never fail."

While he raged on, his usual mask of control slipped, and Katrine saw a side of him she wouldn't have expected existed. A vulnerable side. He'd obviously been hurt.

"Who did you fail?" she asked, resenting whoever the woman might be.

Quickly, his mask settled back into place. "Linda. My ex-wife. I didn't measure up to her grand expectations. Putting food on the table and busting my ass to become everything I thought she wanted left me a little too busy to slay any dragons for her. Linda didn't want reality, she wanted fantasy. We did not live happily-ever-after."

"No, there's no such thing as happily-ever-after," she agreed softly.

"You don't believe in romance. You don't

believe in everlasting love or a love that conquers all. You're a fake."

His accusation lifted her gaze. She met the challenge in his eyes. Did she dare confess? Did she dare tell him how desperately she wanted to believe? With a past littered with rejection, could she tell him how frightened she felt of committing her heart to anyone save Shelly again?

"A person can dream," she answered, shrugging. "Different things appeal to different women. I dream better in the past. History is romantic to me."

"And heroes like Sean McNeil more desirable than mere flesh and blood men?" he prompted.

"Yes," Katrine lied. In her opinion, Trey Westmoreland put the border lord to shame.

"We'll see." He shook out his napkin and stuffed one corner in the collar of his shirt.

"Trey," she warned. "The waitress is headed this way with our food. Promise me you won't quote a two-hundred-year-old fictitious character during dinner. You'll either get your face slapped or the both of us thrown out."

He considered her request long enough to add greater tension between them, then smiled. "All right. I promise not to quote Sean McNeil."

As a wary waitress settled their plates before them, Katrine breathed a sigh of relief and sipped her wine. Chez Fred's definitely reeked of romance. Compared to their first date, this article should be a snap.

"Will there be anything else?" The waitress fearfully met Trey's eyes.

With a flash of dimples, he melted her on the spot. "No, nothing right now."

The girl simply stared at him. "A–Are you sure?"

"We're sure," Katrine snapped. "Everything looks wonderful," she said more courteously. When the girl seemed to get control of herself and went about her business, Katrine snatched her napkin from the table and spread it across her lap. "That was disgusting," she muttered. "I'm surprised she didn't offer to cut your meat for you."

"That won't be necessary." He paused to remove his cuff links. "And, if she wanted to, well, as you said earlier, different things appeal to different women. Tonight I'm trying to appeal to you."

If that were so, he wouldn't have a napkin hanging out his shirt like a five year old, Katrine thought. If that were so, he wouldn't be shoving the sleeves of his jacket up to his forearms that very moment.

"Does the meal meet with your satisfaction?"

The fact that his inquiry had been stated with nothing but polite concern sent off warning bells in her head. "It smells delicious," she answered as the aroma of roasted Cornish hen drifted up from her plate.

"Then let us feast."

Staring curiously back at him, Katrine found nothing amiss in his expression. She lowered her gaze and picked up her silverware.

"Wench," he added.

Slowly, she lifted her head. Forewarning of doom shrouded the romantic atmosphere of Chez Fred's as Trey Westmoreland, respected columnist, proceeded to tear into a Cornish hen with his bare hands. Bone snapped as he wrenched a leg neatly off the bird. He gave a grunt of appreciation, sinking his teeth into the juicy meat.

Once again, Trey had managed to imitate Sean McNeil to perfection. "You promised," Katrine whispered.

"I said I wouldn't quote him," he reminded, not bothering to swallow or even chew his food before speaking. "I didn't say I wouldn't eat like him."

♥   ♥   ♥

Fifteen minutes later, Kat Summers and T. West were shown the door of Chez Fred's.

"I can't believe you did this to me," Katrine choked, stomping across the parking lot toward the waiting limo. "I've never been so embarrassed in my life!"

Trey strolled behind her at a leisurely pace, attempting to remove the grease from his face with a handkerchief. "Some people just don't appreciate a romantic man."

Katrine whirled on him. "You hit a customer in the head with a bone!"

"The guy shouldn't have been sitting so close

to the hearth," Trey defended. "My aim's not as good as it used to be."

"It wasn't a hearth," she ground out. "It was a fireplace and it was a good ten feet from where you were sitting, or more exactly where you were growling like a dog while devouring a Cornish hen!"

"McNeil growled," he reminded. "I thought it might turn you on."

"Sean was an uncivilized border lord who had the manners of a pig!" Katrine shouted, unconcerned over the curious looks they received from couples coming and going from Chez Fred's. "If you'd read further, you would have realized I gave him that disgusting fault so the heroine, who was a grand lady, could teach him etiquette."

"I did read on," Trey admitted. "I liked him better before she civilized him. It stands to reason, if the man had been a jerk for thirty years, no 'slip of a duchess from England' would change him."

"It's fiction," Katrine pointed out tensely. "In reality, you've more than proven, once a jerk, always a jerk."

"I take it I won't be lifting your skirts later?"

His question drew her up short. Unfortunately, it also made Katrine see red. Trey transformed what might have passed for a romantic evening into the most humiliating experience of her life. She began to swing her beaded purse on its dainty chain.

♥   ♥   ♥

The dull security lights made her eyes glitter like a cat in the dark. Trey watched her purse swing back and forth, back and forth until he almost felt hypnotized by the motion. She was bluffing, he assured himself. Katrine Summerville wasn't the type to totally lose control of her emotions.

"You're making a spectacle of yourself," he said.

Her purse hit him in the head. A few chuckles from a crowd gathering on the parking lot added to his embarrassment.

"Kat—"

Again, she swung. The small purse couldn't hurt him, still, he wasn't going to stand in a parking lot full of people and continue to let her humiliate him.

"That does it." He rushed her, hefting Katrine over his shoulder. "Sean McNeil wouldn't take this off a woman."

The crowd applauded. A camera flashed to his left and Trey strode purposely toward the waiting limo.

When her fists began to pummel his back, he slapped his captive lightly on the rear. "Behave yourself, Wench. Action, reaction. Remember the first rule of writing."

"S–Should I get the door," the limo driver stammered.

"I'd appreciate it, Bob. I have my hands full at the moment."

Depositing Katrine into the limo proved difficult. As soon as Trey lowered her to the back seat, she tried to kick him. He clasped her ankles to keep from being injured, taking a moment to admire the length of her legs.

"Don't even think about it," she said softly.

He wondered if she referred to positioning himself within purse swatting distance, or what he was really thinking about—climbing between those long legs and having his way with her.

His gaze travelled upward, past her slim hips, snagged on her heaving breasts and finally found her face. If looks could kill, he'd be more than dead, he'd be viciously mutilated, as well.

"I'm warning you, Trey. If you climb back here, I won't be held accountable for my actions!"

"That makes two of us," he said, eyeing her exposed flesh without shame, then releasing her ankles to quickly shut the door. Taking a deep breath of cold air in an attempt to lower his libido, Trey walked around the limo and got in the front.

"Has the evening come to an end?" Bob asked hopefully.

"I think it's safe to assume Ms. Summerville has had all the romance she can handle for one night." He smiled. "The past finally caught up with her."

Katrine, still seething in the back seat, tried to

rearrange herself inside a dress that didn't compensate her sudden need for modesty. The moment her purse hit Trey's head, she knew she'd lost control. Realizing she'd gone off the deep end hadn't stopped her from swinging at him again. The man drove her crazy. She couldn't be in his company for longer than ten minutes without wanting to either kiss him or kill him. More often the latter.

He certainly met a challenge head on, she grudgingly admitted. Once again, she'd have a hell of a time writing about this date. The past had caught up with her all right, however, Sean McNeil would have done more about the fire burning in his eyes a moment ago than Trey had done. Not that Katrine wanted him to run his hands up her legs or kiss her into submission, but if he planned on competing against heroes from a bygone era…

An idea suddenly occurred to her. A wonderful idea. She had another favorite era in history and wondered if Trey could step into that role as easily.

"Bob, do you know where a place called The Watering Hole is?"

"I know where it is, Miss Summers," he answered nervously. "But I don't think the two of you—"

"Take us there," Katrine demanded. "This is my date, I'll decide when it's over. Cynthia told me about this establishment. She highly recommended the entertainment." When Trey's shoulders stiffened, the smile threatening Katrine's lips surrendered. "Don't worry, Trey. To my knowledge, this place doesn't have any mud-wrestling midgets."

What The Watering Hole did have was a planked sidewalk, swinging doors, and cowboys. A room full of seasoned ranch veterans lined up and waiting for a chance to prove their grit on a contraption fondly named 'Ball Buster'.

These hired hands had their own code of the west. No greenhorn who entered their domain, much less one who'd brought a beautiful filly with him, could leave unless he'd gone eight seconds on the mechanical bull. Ten if he was wearing a monkey suit.

Chapter Thirteen

♥   ♥   ♥

"About time you came in," Jerry Caldwell glanced up from his desk to complain. "Never late one single day in six years and you pick today. We went nation wide. Hell, we made the front page of *Texas Trash* and… what's wrong with you? Why are you walking like that?"

Trying to stifle a grimace of pain, Trey continued toward the wing-backed chair across from his editor. "I'm walking like this because, thanks to Katrine Summerville, I'm sore in a place a man doesn't like to get sore in."

A wide leer spread across Jerry's features. "Did she do that to you?"

Trey's gaze rolled heavenward. "Not in the way you think, but she's responsible. Katrine and a mechanical bull."

A shrill whistle escaped Jerry's teeth. "You climbed on one of those contraptions?"

Flinching as he shifted his weight, Trey refused to meet Jerry's eyes. "With encouragement from a room full of cowboys who didn't think a filly almost wearing an aqua dress should leave with a man in a monkey suit. At least, not until he proved himself worthy."

"I saw that dress she was almost wearing." Jerry nodded. "I don't know what is really happening between you two, but *Texas Trash* got a shot of you in the parking lot of Chez Fred's that did modern-man proud."

"What are you talking about?"

"This." Jerry handed him the rag's weekly edition.

When Trey unfolded the paper, he wasn't prepared for the eight by ten on the front page. His vision blurred. He felt a strangling sensation in his throat. Crumpling the paper in his fist, he left Jerry's office and hobbled to his own. Once there, he allowed himself the right to be enraged. "Head over heels." He snorted with contempt. "Not likely."

He shifted uncomfortably in his chair, wondering why that conclusion brought an empty feeling to his insides, or why he wasn't flying high over making the national news. A bright future loomed ahead, and no one to share it with. His feelings for Katrine were changing, growing and he feared failure. What could be more disastrous to his future than getting emotionally involved with her?

"Trey?"

He glanced up and came face to face with the answer.

♥ ♥ ♥

"My gosh," Cynthia Lane gasped. "It looks just like a cover from one of your books."

Katrine might have smiled at the irony of it all had the picture not brought about a case of hysteria. A hunk, a woman with cleavage and a headline that read: *Romance Writer Head over Heels about Columnist,* sent her running from the grocery store with Shelly, her basket of food forgotten and the copy of *Texas Trash* clutched in her trembling hands. Charlie Grimes had shown up at her doorstep early that morning. The man brought pictures of little Trey and wanted to discuss his every expression, his belches, his gas, all the things that make babies so precious. Katrine finally used the excuse of needing to shop in order to get rid of him. He thoughtfully offered his cab, free of charge, on account he owed them. After seeing the picture, Katrine needed a friendly face. She only had one friend.

"My, my, my," Cynthia drawled. "I never realized Trey was such a barbarian. This picture makes my thighs quake."

"Mine were quaking at the time," Katrine grumbled. "I wanted to kill him."

Unusual silence from the other side of the table brought Katrine's gaze up to meet Cynthia's knowing smile. "What?"

"You." Cynthia laughed. "I've never seen you this way. Sitting in a public restaurant with your sweats on, your hair in a pony tail and hardly any make-up on—talking about killing a man. You're never this animated when discussing anyone except a character in your books. You're falling for him, aren't you?"

"I most certainly am not!" Katrine argued. "Trey Westmoreland makes me crazy! He's too perfect and too flawed and—"

"And the same man you've loved in your imagination for years," Cynthia interrupted. "Katrine, you've found your hero. Admit it."

"No." Katrine shook her head. "He's real, I can't get close to him, I—"

"Can't control his every thought, his emotions, or the end of the story," Cynthia finished for her. "Look Kat, I know you won't talk about your past, but you can't live there. You've got to move forward and take chances. I took a chance on Harold. He's not much to look at, but he's my Prince Charming. There's one out there for every woman, but only a few know what they're looking at when they see it. Open your eyes, open your heart."

Did Katrine dare admit to possibly being in love with him? "All right, just say I'm interested in having a serious relationship with Trey. What makes you think he'd be interested? I mean, with those dimples, I imagine he has women falling all over themselves to go out with him."

"That's true enough," Cynthia agreed. "Picky boy, Trey Westmoreland. You know in the six years he's been coming here for lunch, I've only seen him with a date maybe four or five times. Never the same person. I'm inclined to believe he has a habit of taking a woman out once or twice, then never calling her again. At least I assumed that's the reason he approached me about finding him a date for the awards banquet. He said something about burning all his bridges."

"Yeah, I bet he burned them all right," Katrine muttered with annoyance. "He probably only wants one thing, just like every other jerk we're stuck with in the twentieth century."

"Hey, watch who you call what," Cynthia blustered. "Harold isn't a jerk. I don't believe Trey's a loser, or I wouldn't have set you up with him. He's too smart to sleep with every woman who'd go to bed with him. He wants a serious relationship, but just hasn't found the right... he's a jerk."

Katrine's head automatically began to turn, searching for the source of Cynthia's wide-eyed stare.

"Don't turn around. Speak of the Devil."

"Trey's here?" Realizing what a slob she looked like, Katrine instinctively slumped lower in the booth.

"Worse, he's with a woman."

"A woman? Is she pretty?" As soon as the question left Katrine's lips, she resented asking.

"Only drop-dead gorgeous," Cynthia unkindly provided. A flush of embarrassment bespoke her regret. "That is, if perfection appeals to you. Still, she has a sort of, I don't know, plastic look about her. Surely she's had surgery."

"Oh, that makes me feel better," Katrine bit out. "How am I going to get out of here without being seen?"

"You can either get down on your hands and knees and crawl out, or stay for lunch. Why not let them leave first?"

"Neither choice is too appealing," Katrine complained. "I don't want to be forced to sit here while he's with another woman. And, oh, Shelly!" Katrine sat up straight. "Too late." Cynthia sighed. "She's spotted him."

♥   ♥   ♥

Trey glanced away from his companion when Harold called a greeting. He nodded politely then noticed a familiar face seated on a stool next to Harold's cash register. Rather impolitely, he walked away from his date. "What are you doing here, Shelly?"

"Mom's having coffee with Cynthia," she answered, eyeing Trey's companion. "As for what I'm doing here, I'm allowed out in public once in a while, you know? What are you doing here? With her?"

Her displeased expression made him smile. Children were at least honest with their jealousy. "She's an old acquaintance of mine," he explained. "I haven't seen her in a long time and she just happened to be in Dallas—" Trey quickly closed his mouth. He sounded like a husband caught in the act.

"She doesn't look all that old to me." Shelly studied the woman. "What kind of acquaintance?"

"Trey, Darling, do you think we could find a table?"

"Ah, yeah," he answered when his companion joined them. "Linda, this is Shelly. Shelly, this is Linda."

Shelly impolitely ignored the introduction. "I thought your last name was Westmoreland."

"Oh, how cute," Linda laughed. "'Darling' is simply a form of affectionate address," she explained.

When Shelly's eyes narrowed, Trey thought it best to end the introductions. "It was nice to see you again, Shelly. We need to find a seat before the lunch rush arrives."

"But I'll talk to you *later*, right?"

"Right," he answered.

Her blonde head nodded. Shelly turned to retake her place next to Harold at the cash register. She paused as if suddenly remembering something. "Oh." She turned back. "It was nice to meet you, Linda. And by the way, you look great to be such an old acquaintance of Trey's."

Linda lifted a perfectly arched brow. "Is that what he called me?" She laughed. "We're more than that." Her dark eyes shifted to Trey. "We spent six years together. Trey and I used to be married. It was nice to meet you, too. Do your parents own the restaurant?"

The little vixen seemed at a loss for sarcasm, he noted, watching Shelly's face pale. "No," she answered, somewhat dazed. "The Lanes are friends of ours. My mom's and mine," she specified.

"So, how did you and Trey become acquainted?"

Color returned to Shelly's cheeks. Her eyes began to twinkle mischievously. "Acquainted?" She lifted a brow in mimic of Linda's earlier reaction. "Oh, we're more than that." She gave a fake little laugh. "My mom and Trey had a baby together."

♥   ♥   ♥

"I don't know what Shelly just said, but it made Ms. Perfect's mouth fall open," Cynthia informed her lunch partner.

Katrine fought the urge to turn her head in their direction. Unfortunately, she'd lost the battle a moment ago and snuck a peek at Trey and his date. The woman, whoever she was, could have stepped off the cover of Vogue. Katrine suddenly felt very tall, very gangly, and very ugly.

"Shelly is headed this way. Sit up and try to act unaffected."

"Why should I?" Katrine wanted to know. "I am affected. Extremely affected!"

"This could very well be a business lunch or she could be an old friend. You shouldn't jump to conclusions. You want to act grown up about it and set a good example for Shelly, don't you?"

"Not really," Katrine grumbled. "But you're right." She sat up straighter and tried to school her features into a mask of control.

"Guess who she is?" Shelly didn't waste any time as she slid in next to her mother.

"An old friend?" Katrine asked weakly.

"That's what *he* said, but *Linda* said she's his ex-wife."

"His ex-wife?" A lump formed in Katrine's throat. *That beautiful creature used to be married to Trey? That walking advertisement for Glamour Magazine once shared his life, his bed?* "Oh." She cleared her throat and turned a look of helpless appeal on Cynthia.

"Well, she's probably just in town for the day and they accidentally ran into each other," Cynthia reasoned. "Now, what would you like for lunch, Shelly?"

"I'd like a spaceship to set down outside and for aliens to abduct Trey's ex-wife for scientific research," she answered seriously. "I saw the way she looked at him. She's not here for the day. She's here to sink her teeth into him."

Shelly turned toward Katrine, her lower lip trembling slightly. "Mom, you're not going to let her have him, are you?"

The desperate look on her daughter's face broke Katrine's heart. "Honey, whoever Trey chooses to see is none of our concern. I told you from the beginning, our relationship is strictly business. I can't control—well, you shouldn't have expected—"

"You're not going to fight for him," Shelly interrupted in a stunned whisper. "Not even for me."

Again, Katrine felt her heart constrict. "You can't always have everything the way you want it to be, Honey. In real life—"

"I don't want real life!" Shelly said passionately. "I've never asked you for a puppy. I've never asked you to be a Girl Scout leader. I've never asked you for anything, but I want Trey. First, I wanted him for you, then something happened… in here." She placed a small hand against her chest. "Now I want him for me, too."

Shelly stood up abruptly, glancing toward a certain table. "If you don't do something about her," she nodded in the couple's direction. "That isn't going to happen."

Katrine was too stunned to respond as Shelly stormed away. She watched her shove two doors leading to the kitchen open and disappear. When Cynthia remained uncharacteristically silent, Katrine picked up a menu and glanced across the table. Her friend's frown put Katrine on the defense.

"What am I supposed to do?" she demanded. "Go over there, hit him over the head with a club and drag him out of here?"

Cynthia lifted a brow. "You might try a more

subtle approach. Surely you can think of a more creative way to catch him."

"You make him sound like a fish," Katrine grumbled. "I don't know the first thing about 'catching' a man."

Cynthia began to chuckle softly, then laughed out loud.

"What's so funny?"

"Come on, Katrine. You wrote the book, or at least a dozen, on the subject. If you don't know, who the hell does?"

♥   ♥   ♥

"So, you and Kat Summers delivered a baby together?" Linda mused for the third time. "That must have been an absolutely grotesque experience."

Trey watched her lips move. Perfect white teeth flashed behind the dark red of her mouth. "Actually, it was wonderful." He lifted his gaze to a pair of velvet-brown eyes. "Charlie, the cab driver, named the baby after me."

Linda wrinkled her nose. "How flattering. A cabby's baby being given your name."

"Well, at least someone's son has my name," he stated with annoyance. "Tell me again why you're in Dallas?"

"Shopping," she answered evasively.

"And why did you come to the paper?"

"To see you, of course." Linda swatted his arm

playfully, then forgot to remove her hand. "I'm here, you're here. It seemed odd to be in Dallas and not pay a visit to my ex-husband."

"You ended our marriage with a note six years ago. Didn't you find that odd?"

Her eyes lowered at his accusation. "You're angry with me."

The assumption was so ridiculous, Trey laughed. "I don't care enough to be angry with you anymore, Linda. But for a while, yes, I was damned mad."

When her gaze lifted, just the proper amount of pain shone in her eyes. "I thought you'd come after me. I–I thought you'd realize how you'd neglected me and come charging forward to reclaim the woman you loved."

Despite Trey's inner assurance he no longer cared for Linda, he felt the need to kill her at this moment. Did she suggest his devastation was all a game to her? "Why would I? You said it was over. You called me boring. You said you wanted another man. Why would I come after you?"

"Because, I wanted you to," Linda answered, her lips puckering into a pout. "It never occurred to me you wouldn't. Not until it was too late. You just ran off to Dallas and what else could I do but marry Stone?"

"I'm sorry I put you in such an awkward circumstance, Linda. I'm even sorrier for *Stone,*" he said, stressing what he considered the stupidest name he'd ever heard. "Did you leave him a note, too?"

Linda flushed becomingly. "No. He didn't deserve one. I caught him with another woman. I just left; a note wasn't necessary. He understood my reasons."

"I guess he would. I'm sorry," Trey said with more control. He knew how she must have felt. The thought of Linda cheating on him had torn at his insides. He'd taken it as a personal affront to his ability to please a woman and for a couple of years after their divorce, proved himself proficient with a number of one-night-stands. It was a stupid reaction, even though he'd been choosy about his women and careful, he hadn't proven anything except for being an insecure, insensitive jerk.

"I didn't blame him too much." Linda twirled a straw in her diet soda. "We didn't have a good relationship. Besides," she stared directly into Trey's eyes before wetting her lips with the tip of her tongue. "He didn't do anything for me, not like you do."

Trey couldn't believe the absurdity of the situation; the woman who turned his life upside down six years ago and admitted to playing some sort of game by doing it, was actually sitting across from him, wearing that 'come-on' look in her eyes. The one, he recalled, that had been few and far between after about the third year of marriage. Unconsciously, his gaze travelled to the front booth and a blonde ponytail. It was an effort to ignore Katrine, but after the humiliation she caused him last night, and because he didn't want to merge the past with the present, he thought it best to get lunch over with and Linda out of Harold's.

"Are you seriously involved with anyone?" Linda asked bravely. "Daddy says this assignment with Kat Summers is only a publicity stunt to help both your careers. Is that true? The picture on the cover of that dirty little gossip rag this morning was staged, wasn't it?"

The volley of questions brought his attention back to Linda. "I don't believe you have the right to delve in either my personal or professional life."

"You don't have to tell me," Linda decided smugly. "The man I married wouldn't lose his control to the point of hefting a woman over his shoulder and carrying her across a parking lot in front of witnesses. It's too out of character for your rational behavior. After all, if I couldn't force a spontaneous reaction from you, I'm sure a blonde romance writer whose dress clearly labeled her, *hussy,* couldn't."

"Katrine isn't a hussy," Trey defended without thought. "I liked that dress and—" He quickly closed his mouth. "It was interesting to see you again, Linda, but I should get back."

"You're in love with her," she accused.

"Don't be ridiculous," he blustered. "Falling in love with her would be like asking someone to shoot bamboo under my fingernails. The same—"

"I've never seen that look in your eyes." Linda

thrust out her bottom lip. "I've never heard that impassioned denial in your voice. At least you saw the logical side to falling in love with me. I come from a respected journalistic family. That woman is nothing but a romance writer—"

"Katrine Summerville probably makes more in a year than I do," Trey informed her stiffly. "She's very respected in her genre."

"Well, if you didn't charge to my rescue, you've certainly charged to hers," Linda quipped. "But then, Kat Summers, or Katrine Summerville, whichever you prefer, is obviously an expert at manipulating men. It's basically what she does for a living."

Displeased by the turn of conversation, mostly because he felt confused about, 'charging to Katrine's rescue', he snatched up the bill, indicating lunch had ended. "I've always suspected the two of you were a lot alike. Why don't you tell me the real reason you're in Dallas."

"Daddy said you'd be suspicious. At least she hasn't robbed you of all your rational logic." Linda rewarded him with a dazzling smile. "I wanted to see you." At his skeptical expression, she batted her lashes. "And, because Daddy wanted to know if you were happy here, or if you'd be interested in coming back. Your family is in Philly. I'm in Philly. This feature will make you a hot commodity."

"Funny, how everything seems to boil down to business. I've got a deal on a house that's supposed to close in two weeks. Does it sound as if I'm interested in moving?"

"A house?" Linda's eyes rounded in surprise. "Why would a bachelor want the hassle of becoming a homeowner? Unless…" Her gaze narrowed suspiciously. "Does this house by chance have a big yard for a blonde-headed girl to romp around in?"

"It has a huge back yard so my brother's and sister's broods can romp around," Trey answered. "My family rarely comes for a visit due to the space problem. I've had this deal in the works much longer than I've known Katrine and Shelly."

"Oh," Linda sighed with relief. She promptly returned to bargaining. "You could get out of it if you really wanted. I'm just asking you to consider coming back. I realize as far as the two of us are concerned, we need to spend time together before you'd be willing to give me a second chance. Is that so much to ask?"

Anything Linda asked was too much in Trey's opinion. After what she'd done to him six years ago, he found it amazing he'd kept a civil tongue in his head while talking with her. "Go home and tell Sam I'm not interested at the moment. As for us, I don't make the same mistake twice. I'm still the hard-working, boring man you married the first time, Linda."

"Are you?" She smiled slightly, just enough to be sexy. "I'm beginning to wonder after seeing that copy of *Texas Trash* this morning. I wish you'd lift me over your shoulder and carry me off somewhere this very minute. Would you make mad, passionate love to me? Did you with her?"

Trey painfully gained his feet, moving around to help Linda with her chair. It was a natural gesture he'd tried to break himself of with Katrine. "No." His simple answer left her to wonder which part of the question he referred to. "I hope you enjoy the rest of your stay in Dallas. Tell Sam I said thanks, but no thanks."

Reluctantly, Linda rose. "Trey, you just have to see me again so we can discuss this further."

"I don't have time," he said, clearly frustrated. "I'm working on a feature, remember?" Unconsciously, he glanced toward the front booth where Katrine and Cynthia sat.

"Oh, her," Linda huffed. "Oh... her," she repeated, her gaze darting from him to the front booth. "But of course. It stands to reason if the brat is running wild around the place, the mother is most-likely close by."

"Watch what you say about Shelly," Trey warned. "She's an exceptional child. I'm fond of her."

"I want to meet her mother," Linda decided. "If there's nothing serious going on between the two of you, it won't cause any riffs in your relationship by introducing us."

Trey frowned. "I don't see any point. It would be awkward."

"Just say I'm a fan and wanted to meet her," Linda persisted. "If you refuse, I'll simply go over and do it myself while you pay the check. I assume the blonde ponytail in the front booth belongs to Kat Summers?"

He sighed.

"You know I always get my way. I always get what I want."

The hot gaze his ex-wife ran down the length of him left Trey little doubt as to what Linda wanted, or more precisely, what she thought she wanted. He wondered why he'd ever found her little pouts cute. Trey wasn't conceited enough to believe Linda truly desired him. He was simply a toy she feared someone else wanted to play with. A toy who'd now become her favorite one.

"All right. But this had better be brief. I need to get back to work." He stepped aside to allow her to move in front of him. "And Linda, there's no reason to bring up the past."

"No." She sounded sadly resigned. "I don't suppose so."

Trey politely let the woman who once broke his heart lead the way.

Chapter Fourteen

♥   ♥   ♥

"They're leaving," Cynthia whispered. "You've given me a perfect excuse to watch Trey walk away, not that any woman with eyes in her head needs much of one," she added with a wicked grin. "I can't believe he rode one of those contraptions. Bet that was something to see."

Katrine smiled. "Actually, he did pretty well considering he'd never been on a mechanical bull. Those seasoned ranch hands gave him hell about the tux, but before long, they were giving him pointers and cheering him on. I'll say one thing for Trey Westmoreland, he's persistent. He just kept doing it until he got it right."

Cynthia's dark brows lifted. "Sounds like my kind of man. Think about it."

Her friend's advice was unnecessary. Katrine had thought about it—thought about the way his body moved with the motion of the bull, how the muscles in his arms bulged after he shucked his jacket and rolled up his sleeves. She thought about the hot blood racing through her veins when he finally mastered the machine, and also about the way he walked afterwards. Although humor didn't seem appropriate under the circumstances, she laughed.

"Hello, Cynthia."

Both women glanced up into Trey's strained features. "Katrine." He nodded an acknowledgment. "I have a fan with me who'd like to meet you."

My fan or yours? Katrine tried to paste a smile on her mouth as fake as the brunette's, who ran a cool and somewhat dissecting survey over her. Trey's ex-wife stared down her perfectly straight nose, then her smile widened. Katrine's unthinking rush into the restaurant earlier came back to haunt her in that moment. The Barbie Doll was obviously not the least threatened by what she saw.

"Linda, this is Kat Summers, and Katrine, this is Linda…" He paused to glance at the brunette. "Sorry, what's your last name now?"

The woman's smile faltered. "Westmoreland," she answered, retrieving the smugness she'd wore a moment earlier. "I took Trey's last name back after my divorce. Foreshadowing, I guess." She cut her gaze at Katrine, then slid her arm possessively into his. "I love your books. Trey used to enjoy them, too—sort of secondhand. He didn't know a few of those late night encounters where we embraced unbridled passion were linked to your talent. Not that Trey wasn't an expert at—" She quickly closed her perfect mouth. Linda flushed, as if she'd only realized her lack of delicacy concerning her and Trey's past intimacy.

Words, those valuable entities that rarely deserted Katrine Summerville, had. Her mind, however, had no trouble conjuring a visual. A steamy, lust-riddled picture of Trey and Linda—Barbie and Ken—her mind searched for a proper adjective—'doing it' seemed appropriate.

"Linda, we should be going," Trey reminded darkly. "I've introduced you to Kat Summers, and this is Cynthia Lane, now let's leave them to their lunch."

"No need to rush off on our account," Cynthia said, eyeing the brunette clinging to Trey's arm. "And I thought I knew everything about T. West, Harold's favorite patron. In all this time, I've never once heard him mention, ah, oh yeah, Linda."

Cynthia's sly jab brought Katrine from her disturbing visions and added tension to an already tense situation. "It's always nice to meet a fan, Linda," she piped up. "You seem to have a way with words yourself. Unbridled passion. How... original."

"Do you think so?" Linda's brow furrowed. "Maybe I could write a romance novel. With the right inspiration, I suppose anything's possible." She ran a meaningful glance over Trey.

"Inspiration is highly overrated," Katrine countered. "Persistence and determination get a book written."

"Oh, I'm persistent," Linda assured her. "And very determined when I want something. Kat Summers isn't afraid of a little competition, is she?"

"Of course she isn't," Cynthia answered. "Many a woman's tried to compete with Kat in the bedroom, so to speak, but Katrine's still the steamiest woman on paper. She knows all the ins and outs of romance. Oh." Cynthia's eyes widened. "No pun intended."

As heat clawed a path up Katrine's neck, she tried not to glare at Cynthia. She knew the game in progress. Her friend obviously meant to imply Katrine's writing skills reflected her talent in related areas. Since it was evident she couldn't compete with Linda's outer beauty, especially not this particular afternoon, Cynthia tried to give the brunette something to worry about.

In an effort to hide her embarrassment, Katrine said, "Romance writers don't view their writing competitively. Fortunately, the varied taste of the reader allows room for many authors to successfully write in the same genre. It's simply a matter of preference and style."

Again, Linda summoned a perplexed expression. "Oh, you mean it's like comparing Quarter Horses to Thoroughbreds? One is bred for beauty and endurance, while the other's just a fast race down a short track."

"I wouldn't insult the Quarter horse too loudly if I were you," Trey warned his ex-wife softly. "Especially not in Dallas. We really should be going. I need to get back to work."

"Of course you do, Darling." Linda patted his arm affectionately and flashed Katrine a brilliant smile. "Trey pushes himself relentlessly when it comes to his work. A trait I'll admit I once found a little annoying. But later, when I had time to reflect on our life together, I realized living with a perfectionist had its advantages."

The sultry look she turned Trey's direction made Katrine want to arch her back and hiss. How dare the brunette insult her. How dare the woman act so nonthreatened by the female her ex-husband had slung over his shoulder in this morning's addition of *Texas Trash*. Worse than the affronts to her insecurity, how dare Linda discuss Trey as if he were some stud whose virility needed confirmation.

And Trey, Katrine thought, suddenly switching tracks. Why had he brought her over in the first place? To flaunt the fact he'd once been married to such a perfect specimen of feminine fluff? To mock Katrine for only having perfect men in her novels? Katrine had a good mind to give Linda the impression she was well aware of Trey's virility. She had an even better mind to cause Trey a little grief for having the bad manners to introduce them.

"Trey's competitive nature was the very thing Cynthia and I were just discussing." *Don't,* Katrine mentally warned herself. *Don't let them goad you into it.* She ignored her sane side and smiled up at the couple, her stare colliding with

Trey's. "How are your 'jewels' this afternoon, *Darling?*"

If Katrine's daring shocked her, it was worth climbing into the gutter to see the smug smile slide off Linda's lips. Doubly rewarding to see Trey's eyes widen slightly and his jaw muscle clench.

"They're black and blue," he answered irritably. "I'd pretty much already figured you for crazy. I didn't know you were sadistic until last night, or should I say, until I tried to get out of bed and walk this morning!"

Katrine shrugged. "You said you could handle it. Once you realized what you were up against, you should have admitted defeat and cried uncle. Ten times in one night would make any man walk funny the next day."

"Ten times?" Linda gasped. "That's... that's disgusting!"

Trey seemed to suddenly realize Linda didn't fully comprehend the conversation. "Let me explain," he offered politely. "Cynthia knows what we're talking about, but if a person didn't—"

"Sure I know," Cynthia interrupted. "You see, I used to be a hooker, and I gave Katrine some research material which included all the different... bars I used to frequent," her voice trailed as Linda stormed toward the door. "What'd I say?" she asked defensively when Trey glared at her.

"Do you always so proudly announce your past profession to perfect strangers?"

"I'm not proud of my past, but I'm not ashamed, either. I did what I had to do when my stepfather raped me when I was fifteen and my ma threw me out into the streets. Ms. Hoity Toity didn't have to get her panties in a bind. If she'd have let me finish, she would have realized—"

"I believe Ms. Summerville wanted her to get the wrong impression. Isn't that right, Katrine?"

Katrine felt like a naughty child called to account. "I, well, she made me mad."

"She did?" he sounded surprised.

"Her superior attitude made me angry," Katrine lied. "Why did you bring her over here? To impress me with your lack of taste in women?"

"She insisted on meeting you," Trey answered coldly. "Linda is stubborn at times. Immature, spoiled, shallow. I thought the two of you would hit it off."

His insult erased any guilt Katrine felt over purposely misleading Linda. "Such flattery, and coming from a man who mud-wrestles midgets, pukes tequila, abuses Cornish hens with his bare hands and grunts like a pig at the slop trough while doing it. I could see where Linda would be interested in stoking the flames of passion between the two of you again. I'm going home before I become ill."

"Good idea," he snapped. "If you'd taken more care with your appearance before leaving the house this morning, Linda wouldn't have had quite so much to work with while insulting you."

"What?" she gasped. "You hypocrite! Berating me for using perfectly-formed characters in my novels then flaunting that gushy, empty-headed Barbie Doll in front of me. I'm sorry if my appearance ruined your chance to give that... that—"

"Cupcake," Cynthia offered.

"That cupcake a reason to be jealous over her *Darling* doing a feature with Kat Summers. I wouldn't worry about it, Trey. She seemed perfectly willing to jump your bones right here in front of God and everyone! Manipulation isn't necessary to get her into the sack with you."

Strong fingers clamped down on the hand Katrine unconsciously fastened around her fork. "I've never had to use cheap tactics to get a woman into bed with me." Trey brought his face within an inch of hers. "And if you try to stab me with that fork, I won't be held accountable for my actions. I don't think Elise Pennington's lurking anywhere in the shadows to give us another cover picture. Is that why you provoked me last night? To give yourself more publicity? That damned photo could have been torn right off the front cover of one of your novels. Did you set me up?"

"Me?" Katrine choked. "You were the one who provoked me!"

"You're a smart lady. You probably assumed I'd do something to make you take a swing at me before the evening ended."

She snorted softly. "It wouldn't take a genius

to figure that out. It wouldn't take anyone five minutes in your company to realize how competitive you are, either. I knew if I said the right thing, pushed the right buttons, expressed just enough doubt in your manly abilities, you'd let those cowboys goad you into getting on that mechanical bull."

"Let's talk about manipulation," he said angrily. "Linda was right. Pulling strings to make your puppets dance, is, after all, what you do for a living."

"You've been pulling a few strings yourself!" she reminded. "It's your scheming that's turned all our dates into disasters."

His smile took her off guard and made her heart skip a nervous beat. "Which reminds me, I get to choose the next one."

Frightening as Katrine found the prospect, she refused to cower. "You couldn't possibly come up with anything more unromantic than you already have," she challenged.

"I've got a week to think about it." His lips almost brushed hers. "I promise not to disappoint you… again."

Their eyes locked. Katrine's heart sped up a measure. His mouth inched closer.

"Hey, you two, break it up." Cynthia began fanning her face profusely with a menu. "Another second and we'll have the fire marshall in here citing us for overheated circuits. Trey, that cut-out's still standing outside. If her lips get any tighter, her face is gonna crack."

Trey immediately straightened, wondering what the hell had just come over him. How could he want to strangle Katrine one minute, and kiss her the next? He glanced through the glass windows at Linda. He'd only wanted to strangle his ex-wife, and not nearly so badly.

"I should tell Shelly good-bye," he muttered. "I might have hurt her feelings earlier."

"Trey!"

Both he and Katrine jumped. Linda stood inside the doorway of the restaurant, her lips trembling with anger. She flushed a red that matched her lipstick, when she obviously realized she'd just bellowed like a cow.

"My rental car is parked over at the paper," she said with more control. "I thought you were going to walk me back."

His head swiveled between the kitchen doors at the rear of the restaurant and Linda.

"Better go, Darling." Katrine smiled sweetly. "It might start sleeting. We wouldn't want Linda to melt, now would we?"

In a gesture of annoyance, he ran his fingers through his hair. "Tell Shelly I'll call her."

"Doubtful," Katrine countered, nodding toward the impatient Linda. "You'd best get moving."

In revenge for her heckling, Trey fixed Katrine with a sultry stare. "I'll see you... later."

He smiled and walked away when she blushed to the roots of her blonde hair. His smile faded as he escorted Linda outside. Trey wished he hadn't made the suggestive remark. It reminded him of what he'd been trying to forget since their disastrous attempt at love making. How much he wanted another chance. How addicted he'd become to catastrophe.

"It would never work," Linda said beside him.

"What wouldn't?"

She nodded over her shoulder. "You and her. If you couldn't satisfy my, I'll admit, rather disproportionate expectations of happily-ever-after, how could you possibly meet hers?"

"I no longer compromise my sanity in an effort to please a woman," he countered coldly. "It isn't rational, neither is renewing a relationship that ended badly six years ago."

"Almost kissing a woman you're supposedly not involved with inside a crowded restaurant in broad daylight isn't logical, either," Linda pointed out. "It didn't look like anything the Trey Westmoreland I know would do. She's changing you. But then, that's how it happens in her novels, isn't it? Doesn't the hero always sacrifice something he feels is important for the heroine's sake? Doesn't he end up altering his beliefs to coincide with hers?"

"I had no idea you knew so much about it, Linda." Trey found her insight unamusing and disturbing. Had Katrine really manipulated him? Did she take this feature more seriously than he suspected? Maybe it wasn't enough for her if he simply pretended to fall under romance's spell. What if his growing feelings for Katrine and Shelly were merely a trick to prove romance really did exist. If their dates were disastrous, they held all the required elements of a good romance.

Adventure. Dilemma. Sexual tension. Sexual tension. Sexual tension. The latter echoed over and over in his head. Damn, she had him tied in a virtual knot of sexual frustration. One long glance into her green eyes tightened the knot, one touch and he came undone—threw caution to the wind, ignored any and every rational bone in his body.

"Trey, you've got to see me again. You know Daddy would be disappointed if I didn't get you to at least consider his offer. I'll stay in town for another week if we could get together this weekend."

"Look, Linda. I'm really not interested. Besides, I told you, I don't have time. I need to start packing to move at some point, and I have my obligation to the feature."

"I suppose *Texas Trash* will have another disgustingly romantic cover next Saturday."

"Not if I can help it," he assured her. "I need to think of an unromantic setting."

"Well, I'm sure you'll come up with something." Linda obviously wanted the subject of Kat Summers dismissed. "You were married to me for six years and won't give me the time of day, but you can't get your mind off her long enough to consider a very wise career move. I swear that romance writer has cast some type of spell over you. The feature, and Kat Summers; that's all you want to think about."

Linda was right. Suddenly, Trey felt foolish for becoming so wrapped up in Katrine and the feature. Katrine was right, too. He was too damned competitive. He'd made a vow to give her hell writing her end of the bargain, and he planned to deliver. This time, he had to do more than take her to an unromantic setting. He needed the most unromantic element a man could introduce into a date.

"Trey!" Linda snapped. "You're not even listening to me. If you could just stop and take a good look at yourself, you'd see why I'm worried about you."

He stopped. Slowly, he turned his head toward the restaurant down the street. A smile stretched his lips.

"How long did you say you could stay, Linda?"

"As long as you want me to, Darling."

Chapter Fifteen

♥   ♥   ♥

The article was packed with fiction, lies and omissions. Katrine stared at the tiny print, frowning one moment over misleading statements from T. West, such as, *Kat Summers plied me with alcohol in the limousine then seemed unreasonably upset when I couldn't handle my eating utensils properly at Chez Fred's,* and smiling the next over her own ingenious drivel. *T. West quoted Scottish verse while ordering drinks, and later, proved himself equally adept at stepping into the role of old-west cowboy.*

Neither, under Jerry Caldwell's direction, mentioned one word about the picture published on the cover of last week's issue of *Texas Trash.*

"Let them wonder," he'd told Katrine over the phone. "A different version of the story being published on the side will inspire more people to keep up with ours. They'll try to read between the lines. It's great for business."

The feature might be great for Jerry's business, lucrative for Trey's and her own career, but it was hell on Katrine's emotions. Her editor, Craig Martin, called two days before with news her older novels were getting another print run. A good thing, since she hadn't concentrated on anything but Trey and the feature lately.

It seemed ages ago, a lifetime since she'd existed in a world ruled mostly by her imagination and her computer. Now, Katrine knew she could never go back. Infuriating as Trey was, he'd forced her to confront issues much more important than her writing.

If not for his intervention, Shelly might have remained the child who quietly kept her needs and expectations bottled inside, believing herself the protector instead of the protected.

"So why do I feel this miserable?" Katrine asked her coffee cup. "For Shelly," she assured herself. Trey hadn't called the girl all week. Winter vacation had ended. School resumed tomorrow. Shelly had been moping around the house since seeing Trey with his ex-wife at Harold's.

"Inconsiderate bastard," Katrine grumbled. What kept him too busy all week to pick up the phone and make a simple call? A petite, brown-eyed, red-lipped Barbie Doll, that's what!

"Mom!" Shelly stormed into her office. "He called!"

Well, Hallelujah!, Katrine wanted to shout sarcastically. Instead, she said, "That's nice, Honey. Thelma has all your new Christmas things pressed. Why don't you go upstairs and decide what you're wearing to school tomorrow."

"Mom?" Shelly sighed impatiently. "Don't you want to know what he said?"

"Why, yes, Shelly!" Katrine exclaimed with mock sincerity. "I'm waiting with baited breath to hear what infinite words of wisdom Trey Westmoreland had to impart upon my impressionable, young daughter this morning."

"Oh." Shelly sobered. "I forgot, you're still mad at him."

"In case you haven't noticed, it seems to be the rule rather than the exception. If you must discuss whatever he said to put roses in your cheeks and the sparkle back in your eyes, go ahead. I'm listening."

Shelly shrugged. "Looks like you're busy. Sorry I barged into your office that way. I can come back later."

"Hold it," Katrine ordered when Shelly turned toward the door. "You know I'm here for you. I'm sorry I seemed a little short. Now, go ahead."

"Really, it's all right," Shelly insisted.

"Tell me what he said!" Her lack of aplomb brought a smile to Shelly's lips.

"Admit it, Mom, you're crazy about him. You've been moping around all week. The thought of him being with that woman bothers you as much as it bothers me."

Heat rose in her cheeks. "Honey, I told you from the beginning, Trey and I are involved in a business venture and nothing more."

"Because you won't make it more," Shelly complained. "And I don't know why. I don't know a lot of things I've been wondering about lately. Why don't I have any grandparents like other kids?"

Katrine was only surprised it took Shelly so long to ask. She knew at some point in time she'd be forced to explain these matters to her daughter. "I wanted to wait until you were older before we had this discussion, but I think you're ready now. The problem is, I'm not ready yet. I'll tell you, Sweetheart. Let's just make it another day, all right?"

After a moment of thoughtful deliberation, Shelly nodded. "Okay, Mom. You shouldn't wait too long to fall in love with Trey, though. I think you might still have a chance with him. He didn't sound different on the phone. You know, all gooey-brained or anything."

Her mother's answer was a derisive snort. "He didn't happen to mention what he'd been doing all week that kept him too busy to call you, did he?"

"No," Shelly admitted. "But I can ask him. He'll be over in about an hour."

"What?" Katrine choked.

"He asked if he could come over and bring me a present. Of course I said yes."

"Of course you did!" Katrine took several calming breaths. "Shelly, you really should check with me before inviting anyone over."

"Oh." Her daughter understood. "You look geeked out. Well, you've got about forty minutes…"

Despising the erratic beat of her heart, Katrine tried to stifle her urge to run upstairs and make herself more than presentable. "Trey's seen me at my worst before. There's no reason to rush around trying to fix myself up. I told you, beauty's only skin deep."

"Yeah," Shelly grumbled. "He's probably been bombarded by surface beauty all week. You'll be a nice change."

A thoughtful pause followed.

"You find me something to wear, I'll take care of this ponytail."

"Right." Her daughter saluted.

♥   ♥   ♥

Thirty minutes later, Katrine smoothed a short cashmere skirt over her hips. "Shelly, don't you think I'm a little overdressed for a Sunday afternoon?"

"You look hot in pink," her daughter assured her. "The sweater and skirt's just the thing. Sweet but sexy."

A frown marred the smooth skin of Katrine's forehead. "Thanks for the vote of confidence, Coco Chanel, but it's cashmere. I look like I'm going somewhere special. Maybe I'd better wear slacks instead."

The bell chimed.

"Too late." Shelly smiled. "If he says anything, pretend you have a date. You've got great legs, Mom. You should show them off more."

"A date?" Katrine puzzled. "Why would I tell him I have a date when I don't?"

"Ugh," Shelly groaned. "To show him two can play his game. For the same reason Bridget told Stephen she was engaged in *Act of Love*. To make yourself more interesting. Hello, is anyone in there?" Shelly asked when Katrine stood, staring at nothing.

"I see what you're getting at, but honesty is always the best policy in any relationship. I intend to be polite and in control for a change, and fight the usual urge I feel to kill him within five minutes after he's walked through the door. I'd appreciate a few moments of privacy with Trey."

"Sure, Mom. But don't forget, he's bringing me a present so I don't want to wait too long to see what it is."

"Only ten minutes or so," Katrine requested. "Just long enough to see if he's acting gooey-brained."

She winked at Shelly while striding from the bedroom.

Vowing to hide the horrible jealousy eating away at her if Trey did act suddenly disinterested, Katrine walked down the stairs and to the door. As she reached for the knob, she wondered why she'd let Shelly talk her into the pink cashmere sweater set.

True, the short skirt complimented her long legs and the cashmere hugged her slender frame, accenting her womanly curves, but what if Trey thought she made a fuss expressly for his benefit? A date? She couldn't purposely lie if he commented on her appearance.

Katrine took a deep breath and opened the door. Her gaze only locked with Trey's for a second when the attack came. She felt pressure on her shoulders and hot breath on her face. Her knees went weak as wet kisses rained over her neck. A scream of outrage left her lips when she hit the floor with a thud. "Get it off of me!"

"Bad dog!" Trey scolded.

"Make it stop!" Katrine choked, fighting a huge tongue intent on washing every inch of her perfectly made-up face.

"Oh my," Shelly panted with excitement from the top of the landing. "It's a dog!"

"It's a horse!" Katrine shouted as a beefy paw raked across her cashmere sweater.

"It's Beauregard," Trey clarified, taking the dog by the collar to pull him from Katrine's squirming body.

She sat up, puffing every bit as loud as the animal. "What is it doing here?"

"Well," Trey began.

"He's for me!" Shelly shouted, running down the stairs. "He's my present, isn't he, Trey?"

"No," Katrine whispered.

"Yes."

"Oh, Trey!" Shelly flung herself into his arms. "I love him. I've always wanted a dog."

"We can't have a dog," Katrine squawked. "That beast doesn't even qualify as one!"

"He's a purebred Old English Sheep Dog," Trey defended. "His owners are moving to another city and have to rent an apartment until they find a house. They can't take him with them, so…"

"Is he mine for keeps?" Shelly whispered hopefully.

"For keeps." Trey tugged a strand of her long hair. "That is, if you promise to take good care of him."

"I will." She twisted away from Trey to throw her arms around Beauregard's neck. He rewarded her with a sloppy lick to the cheek.

"W—Wait just a m—minute," Katrine stammered, glaring up at Trey. "Did it ever occur to you to ask me if Shelly could have a dog?"

"It occurred," he admitted. "I figured you'd say no."

"She would," Shelly said with a nod. "But, Mom, you can't say no, now. Please? I'll take care of him. I promise!"

"Shelly, he's huge. It will cost a fortune to feed him. Where will we put him?"

"You make lots of money," Shelly argued, her arms tightening around the dog's neck. "We've got a backyard."

"A graveled backyard," Katrine reminded.

"Honey, we can't—"

"Every kid in my class has a dog!" Shelly interrupted rebelliously. "Why can't I have just one thing everyone else has?" Shelly's eyes filled with tears and rather than wait for further argument from her mother, she tore herself from Beauregard with a cry and raced up the stairs.

"Now look what you've done," Trey said. "You've just broken her heart!"

"Look what I've done?" Katrine blustered, her breath coming in short gasps. "Look what that beast did to my sweater! This is cashmere, the finest wool money can buy! He's ruined my outfit!"

Beauregard responded with a loud whine before plopping down on the floor, huge paws outstretched, bushy eyebrows cocked.

"Just what are you doing in the finest wool money can buy at three o'clock in the afternoon?"

Katrine straightened to as tall a height as possible while sitting. "I... I have a date."

The muscle in his jaw twitched. "Is that right?"

"That's absolutely correct," she insisted haughtily. "Do you think I'm lying?"

He smiled. "You're acting defensive. Are you?"

"Most certainly not." Katrine wondered if lightning was about to strike her dead. "Now, get that hairy beast out of here so I can change."

"I thought you liked hairy men," he quipped. "Hairy, dull men."

He appeared to be jealous. Katrine was momentarily speechless. Why had he made that comment? She only knew one hairy, dull man. "Carl?" she said absently.

"Are you seeing him again?"

Her heartbeat increased as his face turned an angry shade of red. "Maybe, maybe not. It's none of your business."

The color in his cheeks darkened. "No," he agreed. "It's none of my business."

His words hung between them, made more ridiculous as Trey's heated stare roamed her features and lingered over her lips. Impossibly, Katrine's skin began to tingle. Her breathing became labored.

Beauregard whined loudly, breaking the spell.

"You've placed me in an awkward position," Katrine said. "I'm going to be the bad guy if I don't let Shelly keep this monster. Why couldn't you have at least called me so we could discuss it?"

An outstretched hand accompanied his sigh of annoyance. "It was an impulse, okay? Besides, I knew you'd say no unless you saw Beauregard. Every kid should have a dog. I could tell Shelly wanted one that day at the skating rink. When the owners asked me if I knew anyone, I thought of her."

Once Katrine gained her feet, the closeness of their bodies almost derailed her train of thought. He smelled wonderful, wore a bright flannel shirt, Levis, and hiking boots. A lumberjack, she decided, envisioning him swinging an ax with his powerful arms.

"Kind of you to find time in your busy week to think of Shelly. Why haven't you called her?"

"An unexpected development came up," he answered distractedly, brushing a stray lock of hair from Katrine's eyes. "I've been packing all week."

The hot blood rushing through her veins suddenly froze. "Packing?"

"Yeah, I'm moving." His fingers lightly stroked her cheek.

"Oh." Katrine took a step backwards, almost as if she'd been dealt a physical blow. Afraid the sudden devastation his casual words delivered would show on her face, she quickly turned her back on him.

"Anyway, I figured Shelly would understand once I explained what I'd been doing. I had some time this afternoon and I remembered about Beauregard, so—"

"So you thought you'd just pop over and give my daughter a trade off?" Katrine asked, wheeling around. Trey's ex-wife appears out of nowhere, and now he was packing to move. As he'd said that day in Harold's, Katrine was a smart lady. It didn't take a genius to piece this pre-school puzzle together.

"Shelly's a rational kid. Once I explain—"

"Just leave!" Katrine interrupted. Her voice shook slightly. How easily those two words 'I'm moving' had unravelled her. Moving as in leaving. Leaving as in abandonment. Deep down, Katrine

knew she had no valid right to feel injured by
Trey's dismissal of both her and Shelly. But she
did hurt.

Trey eyed her strangely. He looked confused.
"I'd at least like to speak with Shelly. Someone
should soften the blow. You're obviously not gifted
in that area."

"Go on up. But hurry. I want you out of here."

"So you can get ready for your *date?* Heaven
forbid if Shelly's feelings interfere with what you
want!"

"You're a fine one to talk. You hurt her, and
for what? That empty-headed, plastic-coated
woman you used to be married to!"

"Linda?" he questioned in confusion. "I don't
see why my ex-wife would be any threat to
Shelly. And," he added with a smile. "I don't see
where she's any of your business."

Katrine opened her mouth, then quickly closed
it. She felt precariously perched on the edge of
sanity. She wanted to kill him, she wanted to beg
him to stay, if not for her sake, because Shelly had
given her heart to him. Katrine did neither. "You're
right," she agreed flatly. "It's none of my business. Say your good-byes to Shelly and get out."

The look of anticipation etched on his face
ebbed. She almost swore he'd been preparing
himself for a good fight and now battled disappointment.

"Fine." He moved toward the stairs.

"Fine," she whispered at his back, despair

seeping slowly into her soul.

Whatever Trey said to Shelly, it didn't take him long. Katrine heard his feet coming down the stairs shortly after he went up. His wonderful scent reached her as he moved toward the door.

"What about the feature?" she asked, not turning to face him.

"What about it?"

"Do you plan to finish the article?"

Silence. Katrine supposed he contemplated the consequences if he didn't.

"Why wouldn't I? Hell, I signed the agreement the same as you did."

That meant he'd be staying at least two more weeks. Two weeks, so what, she deflated the sudden lift in her spirits. "What night are we going?"

"Friday night, about seven, if it doesn't interfere with your schedule." He sounded odd. As if he forced the polite words past his lips.

"You're the one with the busy schedule," she reminded. "I suppose it's some compensation to know we're at least getting paid to date one another."

"Not enough."

"Definitely, not enough," she agreed.

"Until then," he said stiffly. "Come on, Boy."

"Don't touch that dog." Katrine turned to face him. "I've decided Beauregard stays."

An expression of disbelief crossed his rugged features. "Will miracles never cease? You do have a heart."

Unfortunately, yes, she mentally answered. "Before you leave me at the mercy of this monster, I'd like to know where we're going Friday night so I can prepare for battle."

Trey smiled. "A hockey game."

Her brow lifted. "Well, you've certainly chosen an unromantic setting. Still, it doesn't sound too bad, and you could have lied so I'd get all dressed up. No calf fries? No mud-wrestling midgets? I'm almost disappointed."

He slid a heated gaze down her snagged clothing and ruined hose. "I can see where you would be, but then, a washing machine's a tough act to follow. Don't worry, I've come up with a little added bonus I think will impress you. As I said before, I hate to leave a woman disappointed. Good night."

The door slammed. Katrine moved to the wooden obstruction, opened it and slammed it again for good measure. "No, you wouldn't leave a woman disappointed. You'll just leave!"

A sob escaped her throat as she slid to the floor. She'd finally found the nerve to try love again, and now this happened. Trey had to prove her fearful heart right. He had to prove she couldn't trust in him, or in a second chance at love.

Beauregard came to his feet with a hearty grunt. He ambled toward her, then hesitated, cocking his head from side to side as the tears ran down her cheeks.

"What are you looking at? Stupid dog," she

muttered. "How would you know how I feel? You can't understand how it feels to be abandoned... Oh," she said softly, "but you do understand, don't you?"

The dog lowered his head.

"Hey, it's not your fault." At the sound of her soft tone, Beauregard ventured closer. Unthinking, Katrine reached out to smooth his shaggy coat. "Shelly will take good care of you. She'll love you, and if you let yourself love her back, the pain you feel will gradually fade. God never takes something away without giving you something in return."

A sudden dawning found her. It took years of resentment, of fear, of pain, but Katrine understood the truth behind her own words of consolation. Love could heal her wounds. Shelly had mended her heart, but only believing in another man would release her from the past. "Too late," she whispered, throwing her arms around Beauregard's neck to bury her face in his soft hair. "It's too late."

"Mom? What's wrong, and why is Beauregard still here?"

Katrine looked up. Shelly stood poised on the stairs. "I decided you can keep him," she answered in a shaky voice. "Honey, I know how upset you must feel right—"

"For real? He's mine?"

"Well, yes. Now, Honey, I know how hurt you're feeling—"

A loud squeal of delight cut her off as Shelly bounded down the stairs. Beauregard barked with excitement, joining her daughter in jumping bliss.

"Shelly!" Katrine shouted. Both enthusiastic jumpers came to an immediate stand still.

"Sorry, Mom," Shelly apologized. "I got so excited. This is great. Trey said he'd keep him since I couldn't. He said I could come over to his house and play with him anytime, but it's not the same as having a dog all to myself."

"To his house?" Katrine puzzled. "He lives in an apartment and besides, he's moving."

"Duh," Shelly said. "He's moving to a house. He's been packing all week. Trey said he has this huge backyard, and I can come over and play whenever I want."

"He's not leaving, he's moving?"

"Yeah. He said the paperwork got done faster than he thought it would, and he had to rush around and pack. That's what he's been doing all week."

Katrine caught herself just before plummeting over the edge of despair. "Maybe it's not too late," she whispered.

"Trey said his new house has five bedrooms," Shelly rambled on. "Can you imagine one guy having all that room? Why do you suppose he needs a house that big unless he wants to settle down and have a family?"

The relief Katrine felt over discovering Trey's innocent activities fizzled at an alarming rate.

He's been seeing his ex-wife, and now he's bought a huge house. Five rooms? Great, a house full of little Barbies and Kens. He couldn't have bought a house since last weekend, rationality intruded. Maybe last weekend wasn't the first time he'd seen Linda since their divorce. Maybe they saw each other on a regular basis.

Jealousy, the likes of which she'd never experienced, engulfed Katrine. Her feelings for Trey ran deeper than physical attraction. How he'd managed to get under her skin and crawl into her heart, she couldn't begin to understand, not after the disastrous dates they'd shared. But they had also shared wonderful moments—humorous moments—tender moments....

"It's not too late for what?" Shelly seemed to have just registered her remark.

"To 'catch' him, as Cynthia put it," she answered distractedly, then realized what she'd admitted. When her startled gaze landed on her daughter, a huge grin spread over Shelly's lips.

"You're going for it, aren't you, Mom?"

She was tired of lying to herself. Katrine was crazy about Trey Westmoreland... or maybe just plain crazy. "Call me a hopeless romantic, but I'm getting ready to take a deep breath and jump off the deep end."

Shelly squealed her delight, Beauregard barked his confusion, and Katrine wondered what the hell she could possibly be thinking. She didn't know how to swim.

Chapter Sixteen

♥ ♥ ♥

"Honey, have you seen my brown loafers?" Katrine shouted while digging around her closet floor. For some reason, most of her shoes seemed to be missing. "Shelly!" she called again.

"Ah, these brown shoes?"

Shelly stood at the door, her Siamese twin, Beauregard, attached to her hip. In her daughter's hands were a pair of brown loafers, or what once were shoes, but now resembled two large pieces of chewed beef jerky.

"What in the world…" Her gaze settled on a shaggy face. "Beauregard, did you do that?"

He whined guiltily.

"I'm sure he didn't mean to, Mom," Shelly hastened to the dog's defense. "He probably wandered into your closet and mistook it for a trash heap. You know, like anything dumped in there wasn't any good?"

Katrine nodded toward the evidence. "Where did you find those?"

"Under my bed… along with your black flats,

your silver heels, a pair of tennis shoes, your navy belt, and your camel-colored purse."

"Ugh," Katrine groaned. "Has he chewed on all of them?"

Shelly bit her lip for a moment. "I'll put it this way, the loafers look the best."

"Bad dog!" Katrine scolded, moving on her hands and knees from the closet.

The accused lowered his head in shame. Shelly gave him a reassuring pat.

"Well." Katrine struggled to her feet. "I guess I need to get him some of those chew bones. Even though the landscaper I contacted can't plant grass until this spring, Beauregard can still go outside. He'll just have to romp around in the dirt for a while."

"But, it's cold out there," Shelly complained. "Beauregard might freeze, and besides, he's used to sleeping with me now."

"He won't freeze," Katrine assured her. "He's got enough hair to keep all of Dallas warm. Hair, I might add, that seems to be on everything in this house."

When she paused before the mirror to straighten her sweater, Katrine noted Shelly's worried expression reflected in the glass.

"Beauregard is part of our family," she said softly. "I complain about him, but don't worry, Honey. He's here to stay."

Her daughter's thankful smile made the dog a lot less annoying. Katrine hated to admit it, but she'd grown fond of the beast in just one short week.

"Jeans and a sweater, huh?" Shelly asked. "Where's Trey taking you tonight?"

"A hockey game."

"For real? I'd love to see one. I wish I could go with you."

"Maybe Trey will take you another time," her mother offered. "He's done his best to see that we go somewhere unromantic as it is. Having you along would pretty much insure yet another impossible writing assignment. Besides, the shoe monster hasn't been with us long. He might feel abandoned again if we leave him here alone."

After nodding her agreement, Shelly gave Beauregard another reassuring pat on the head. "So, what strategy are you planning to use tonight?"

"Strategy?"

A loud sigh followed. Shelly rolled her eyes. "Surely you've plotted out something to win Trey's heart."

"No more reading my novels," Katrine warned. "My plan is simple. I'm going to be myself."

Shelly groaned. "I guess I can kiss my dreams of being a family good-bye. Mom, face it, you're boring. The only time I've ever seen you act a little crazy is when Trey's done something to make you mad."

"I'm not going to get mad," Katrine assured her, as if she'd practiced the line over and over. "I act out of character when I allow Trey to anger me. Run along now, he'll be here any minute and I need to find a decent pair of shoes."

Wearing a frown that indicated Shelly found her mother's decision disappointing, the girl did as instructed, Beauregard tagging along behind her obediently.

Katrine turned back to the mirror and practiced appearing serene. She planned to be in control of her emotions tonight. She planned on having a nice time. Whether the hockey game bored her or not, she would act interested. There wouldn't be one single thing Trey could do to make her angry. *Nothing,* was going to spoil this date.

The sound of his car pulling into the drive set her heart racing. The fact that she wasn't wearing any shoes sent her racing around the room in search. She spotted a pair of tan flats and barely got them on before the doorbell rang.

Repeating, *I will not get mad,* over and over in her head, Katrine hurried downstairs, walked to the front door and opened it. She breathed a sigh of relief. Trey wasn't wearing a tux. Jeans, a striped Oxford shirt, a light-weight jacket and tennis shoes completed his ensemble. By all appearances, they were going to a hockey game.

"How's Beauregard?"

No hello, nice to see you, or how's Shelly? How's the damned dog? I will not get mad. "He's still alive... for now." She left him standing in the doorway. "Let me grab my coat off the sofa and I'm ready."

"You have something all over the back of your sweater. It looks like... dog hair."

"Great." Katrine moved to the secretarial and began rummaging. She held up the tape. "Would you mind helping me remove it?"

She heard the door close softly, then felt his warm hand close over hers. "The hair, or the sweater?"

Despite the teasing tone of his voice, a shiver raced up Katrine's spine. "The hair," she specified. "Shelly's obviously taken the beast outside and will probably be back any second. Besides, Thelma's in the kitchen."

"Does that mean the answer might have been different without any threat of interruption?"

When she turned her head, Trey's lips nearly brushed her ear. Should she tell the truth? Honesty is the best policy, she reminded herself. "Maybe," Katrine compromised.

"Maybe?" he repeated, surprised. "You'd better watch your step, Kat Summers. Sean McNeil would have taken a maybe for a yes."

She laughed softly. "You're not Sean McNeil."

"No. But sometimes, in spite of myself, I wish I were."

The husky admission sent heat racing to Katrine's face, not to mention her private regions. "I take it the 'date' hasn't officially begun. That sounded almost romantic by my standards."

His breath, so warm against her ear, released itself in a small sigh that might have passed for regret. "I forgot. The game's in progress. We'd better hurry. Fair Park Coliseum is a good drive from here."

It isn't a game anymore, Katrine wanted to say, but didn't get an opportunity. Shelly and Beauregard came charging in, her daughter chattering wildly while the dog barked. Trey finished removing the hair from her sweater, then ushered Katrine outside into the cold. On to the game.

The red Jag purred in the drive and Katrine hurried to the car, shivering in the chilly night. No limo drivers—no cabbies—just her and Trey—all alone. Privacy. Seduction. She shook her head, trying to dislodge the tempting thoughts surfacing. No games, she reminded herself. As her date politely opened the car door, Katrine slipped inside. "Eeek," she squawked when her bottom settled against something moving.

"Oh, good grief!" a feminine voice complained. "Trey, Darling, I told you there wasn't enough room for the three of us in this itsy car of yours."

"Linda?" Katrine whispered in shock. Her head swung from the brunette's red lips up to Trey, who waited to close the door. "Linda?" she repeated incredulously.

Trey shrugged. "I told you I wouldn't let you down." He smiled, the dimples deepening in his cheeks. "It doesn't get more romantic than this, does it?"

I will not get mad.

"Trey, Darling, the console is cutting into my,

well, it's very uncomfortable, and it's getting cold in here. Close the door."

I won't get mad. The door slammed painfully against her hip, forcing Katrine closer to the source of annoyance who had obviously drenched herself in perfume. She thought she recognized the fragrance, then the need to sneeze verified her findings. It was 'Passion', and Katrine was allergic to it. She sneezed.

"Ugh," Linda groaned. "You're not sick, are you? In this cramped space, germs would have a field day with my delicate immune system. Maybe you should stay home."

"I'm fine," Katrine choked out. "I'm not in the least mad, I mean sick," she quickly corrected. "Something in the car is bothering my allergies."

"Oh, you have allergies?" Linda made a clucking sound. "I hope your eyes don't get all puffy and your nose doesn't start running. You'd be miserable before the evening ends."

I will not get mad! "I'm sure whatever's bothering me will stop once I leave the car," Katrine assured her.

The driver side door opened. Trey climbed inside and settled behind the wheel. "You girls all set?"

Linda giggled. "Trey Darling, you're so silly, calling us girls. Isn't he cute?"

I won't, no way, will I get mad! "Cute as a rattlesnake," she muttered.

"What was that, Katrine?" Trey shifted the Jag

into reverse and eased from the drive.

She heard the smile in his voice. "I said, cute as a little ol' button," Katrine mimicked Linda's gooey tone.

"That's what I thought you said," he countered with enough sarcasm to suggest the opposite.

"Now, Trey Darling, I want you to tell me all about hockey so I'll understand what's happening. I wish we'd met before you graduated, then I could have watched you play. I think two people having common backgrounds and common interests are so important in a relationship. Don't you agree, Kat?"

Such as journalism? Katrine mentally counted to ten, pretending to ponder the question. "I suppose it's important to respect each other's interests, but in my books, and I mean that literally, 'opposites attract' has always been a favorite theme of romance. It makes a relationship much more interesting."

"Mmmm," Linda contemplated. "Still, I'd think attraction would only last so long. In reality, a constant clash of wills would wear itself thin. I mean, after the sex wore off, where would you be?"

"Hopefully, too old to care," Katrine answered dryly.

Trey laughed, winning himself a dark look from his ex-wife. "I believe you wanted me to explain the rules of hockey," he reminded Linda, seemingly in an attempt to defuse what promised to be a heated discussion.

"Oh yes, please do," Linda gushed. "This is so exciting. Just like old times. Well, almost." She glanced quickly at Katrine, then turned her attention back on Trey.

I won't get mad, but I never said I wouldn't kill her. Ten ways. Time only allotted Katrine ten gruesome ways to take her revenge on Linda before they reached the coliseum. She ignored Trey's explanation of how the sport of hockey originated, the rules, etcetera, and concentrated instead on her most ingenious form of torture. Linda at the world's largest shopping mall, forced to wander aimlessly from shop to shop without a credit card to her name, tangles in her hair, fingernail polish chipped—and Katrine's favorite, with her ruby-red lipstick smeared all the way up to her pert little nose.

Katrine giggled softly at the thought. She didn't like the sound of her own voice. It smacked of madness. Not insanity really, but something very close. Trey Syndrome, she redefined the term. A temporary condition that oddly disappeared when he did, and understandably returned, when he did.

"Here we are." Trey darted into a parking place, receiving a loud horn blast from a Toyota vying for the same spot.

When the Toyota's headlights glared into the passenger side window, Katrine did something she'd never done before. Subtly, she expressed her view thus far of the evening with a vulgar gesture. Afterwards, she felt wickedly wonderful, and then it dawned on Katrine. She seemed headed toward the edge of insanity and her brakes were being controlled by a Barbie Doll and the man she strongly suspected she'd fallen in love with—a man who just happened to be the cupcake's ex-husband. A fall seemed inevitable.

♥　♥　♥

There had been the irritating wait in line to exchange tickets for entrance; the tiring walk around the coliseum to find their section. Then the nauseous press of bodies as they filed through the doors and down the steps leading to their seats, and finally, the unromantic seating arrangement that ended up with Trey, Linda and herself, seated in just that order.

The safety rope of Katrine's sanity began to unravel. Linda's perfume was about to gag her and the man sitting directly behind Katrine kept belching loudly. I'll ignore Linda and Trey, she decided, pretending an interest in the players skating around the ice. *I won't get mad.*

"Would either of you care for a Coke, some popcorn or a hot dog?"

Trey's question penetrated the wall Katrine built around herself. "I'll have a Coke and popcorn," she decided.

"A diet soda for me," Linda specified. "And no popcorn. I've got to watch my figure. I'm still the same size as when we got married, Trey. I haven't changed a bit."

"No, you haven't."

Katrine unconsciously lifted a brow. His muttered agreement hadn't sounded too flattering. She must have mistaken the sarcastic tone of his voice. Men probably found little to complain about regarding Linda. So she was a little dim-witted and a lot annoying, both faults could be ignored if she kept her mouth shut and just sat around being gorgeous.

She'd make the perfect heroine, appearance wise anyway. Linda had dark, shiny, brown hair cut in a style that never appeared mussed. Her skin was china doll flawless, her eyes a soft velvet brown. She had a petite frame, a generous bust line, and a tiny waist that flared into nicely rounded hips.

It was sickening that someone so vain had been blessed with so much. Katrine had walked behind Trey and Linda a couple of times, hoping the woman's clinging stretch slacks would reveal a too big butt or some other compensation—no such fault had been found. As Trey squeezed past her, she noted the two made a perfect pair. A perfect pair of asses.

"Nice, wasn't it?" Linda questioned beside her.

"Very nice," Katrine answered distractedly, then felt a burst of heat blaze a trail across her cheeks. Surely Linda hadn't made reference to Trey's....

"What was nice?" she asked.

"It was nice of Trey to get us front row seats. I believe this is your first hockey game, too?"

"Oh, yes it was considerate," Katrine admitted. "I can at least write some drivel about him seeing that I got a close-up view."

"You sound as if your dates haven't been all that romantic," Linda speculated. "Of course, I've kept up with the articles, but one can't help but read between the lines when that dirty little gossip rag flashes those vulgar covers of the two of you. Trey said I totally misunderstood the conversation at the restaurant last weekend, but tell me, just between us girls, are you sleeping with him?"

Linda had just revealed a major character flaw in Katrine's opinion. The woman lacked tact. "I believe that would be *just between* Trey and me."

"I don't think you are," Linda said with a satisfied smirk. "I guess he told me the truth about the feature."

"Which is?"

"That it's strictly business. He assured me the two of you don't have a relationship going on the side, but, well, I had my doubts. I suppose I felt a moment of insecurity."

"You poor thing," Katrine drawled sarcastically. "You were jealous of little ol' me?"

"Not really." Linda laughed. "You know how men are? They don't know what they want until a woman takes them in hand and tells them. Sometimes they even want the wrong thing. I feared Trey might be confused about his feelings for you, but now I see there's nothing to concern myself about."

Tiny red dots appeared before Katrine's eyes. Trey's ex-wife was a bitch with a capital 'B'. Nothing to be concerned over? No relationship between them? Trey might be confused? "I wouldn't recommend trying to take him in hand just yet," she said softly.

"What was that?"

Katrine jumped, then glanced up to find Trey extending her a Coke and a box of popcorn. *How much had he heard?* "I said the ice looks a little thin," she answered.

"Does it?" He smiled slightly.

"I told her not to worry herself over it," Linda commented stiffly. "It appears solid enough to me." Her gaze slid Katrine's direction and narrowed. War had been declared.

A loud blast of organ music, followed by a cheer and strains of the National Anthem began the game. Once Katrine reseated herself, she tried to concentrate on the uniformed men positioning themselves on the ice and forget about the combatant seated next to her. After the, what had Trey called it? Oh well, after the little black thing fell to the floor, all hell broke loose.

Trey, along with most of the coliseum's occupants, came to his feet. Linda, who stood beside him, clapped her hands with fake exuberance and managed to rub her breasts against his arm by *accident* a few times. Katrine wanted to twist her empty little head off by accident!

"Go Dallas, go Dallas," the annoying man behind her began to chant.

Turning, Katrine cast the overweight, bald man a dirty look. He failed to heed her warning.

"Kick butt, Boys!" he bellowed. "Send the Thunder back to Wichita without any noise left in 'em!"

It seemed unfair so many people were cheering for the Dallas team when the Wichita team had few supporters present. Besides, the visiting team was obviously loosing. The Dallas team had knocked the little black thing in a net three times, and the visitors hadn't done the same even once. Katrine thought the Wichita team's uniforms were prettier, and she liked an underdog.

"Kick butt, Thunder!" she shouted with gusto.

"Katrine!"

She would have turned to see why Trey had called her name, but two men came slamming into the wall directly in front of her. In horror, Katrine watched as either sweat or spit, she wasn't sure which, flew from the combatants' bodies and sprinkled her sweater, and her refreshments.

"Oouh!" Linda squealed, shielding her drink with her hand.

"Give him a taste of your fists, Dallas!" the annoying man behind Katrine shouted.

A loud smack sounded. Gloves were thrown to the ice. Where there were only two men swinging at each other a second prior, now there were six. Katrine heard the grunts of pain as punches were exchanged, smelled the blood from broken noses and slipped right over the edge of sanity.

"Kill them, Thunder!" she exploded.

"Katrine!"

This time she glanced past a pale Linda toward Trey. She felt an urge to giggle. His face was bright red.

"You're yelling for the wrong team!"

She widened her eyes in mock distress. "I am? But I like the other team's colors better," she explained.

"Hey, Blondie, your boys are getting red all over their pretty uniforms," the bald man guffawed.

"Stick a sock in it, Baldie!" she turned to shout, past the limits of her patience with the man. Katrine felt a measure of satisfaction when his eyes bugged and his mouth fell open.

He pointed a shaky finger at her. "Hey, I saw you in the parking lot. You flipped me off!"

"Hold on a minute, Buster!" Trey squeezed around Linda, whose velvet-brown eyes had grown quite large. "Katrine has more class than that!"

"You must be the idiot driving the red Jag," the man accused.

Trey seemed momentarily confused, then he smiled. "You must be the too slow Toyota horn-blaster."

The man snorted. "You jocks are all alike. Just because you can afford a fancy sports car you think every driver on the road should bow down and kiss your feet."

"At least I can see my feet," Trey countered dryly. "I'd like you to apologize to Katrine."

"Are you saying I'm fat?"

Trey lowered his gaze to the man's bulging belly. "No, I didn't say it. Now, if you'll apologize to Blondie, I mean, Katrine," he quickly corrected. "We'll drop the matter."

"And what if I don't?" the man goaded. "What are you going to do about it?"

"Trey," Linda said. "Maybe she did, you know, do something with her hand. Why don't you just forget this nonsense and watch the game."

"Yeah, Pretty Boy, why don't you mind the little woman and leave this argument to me and Blondie?"

"You're asking for trouble," Trey warned. "This isn't my little woman and if she were, I damn sure wouldn't take orders from her. Why don't you do what Blondie suggested and stuff a sock in it!"

"All right, I'll stuff a sock in it," the man sneered, and punched Trey square in the jaw.

When Trey stumbled back a step, Katrine gasped, "Oh my God, are you okay?"

With a nod, he said, "You and Linda get out of the way." He lunged for the man behind him. The intended victim moved and Trey's fist connected with a tall cowboy who'd been watching the exchange with amusement.

The cowboy wasn't amused.

After Trey came stumbling back again, reeling from another blow, Linda stomped her foot.

"Just look what you've done!" she screamed at Katrine. "I've never seen Trey get in a fight. He's not behaving rationally!"

Katrine wasn't listening. She was too busy watching a chain reaction take place. Trey's blunder caused a snowball effect. When the cowboy had drawn back his fist to hit Trey, he'd elbowed the man behind him in the stomach. The man in turn shoved the cowboy, who shoved him back into another man... she lost track at that point, but fists were flying all around them.

"Oooh, I've never been so embarrassed in my life!" Linda fumed. "Trey Westmoreland, stop it this instant!"

"Better listen to her, Pretty Boy," the bald man taunted. "Otherwise, you ain't gonna be so pretty anymore."

A fist in the face was the man's answer.

"Hit him again, Trey!" Katrine encouraged, caught up in blood lust.

"You, you hussy," Linda sputtered. "How dare you cheer him on! Don't you realize how humiliated I am?"

"Will you shut up!" Katrine ground out.

Seconds thereafter, she received a slap to the cheek. Linda's eyes were wide as saucers. She brought a hand to her mouth, obviously stunned by her actions.

Katrine's gaze narrowed on her. She balled her fists at her sides, telling herself Katrine Summerville would not involve herself in a cat fight. Kat Summers, maybe, but only on paper. "Say you're sorry," she suggested softly.

The brunette's lips tightened. "I will not."

"Hey, gorgeous, are you gonna take that from her?"

Glancing toward the ice, Katrine noted the players were no longer fighting, but appeared to be enjoying watching the spectators scuffle amongst themselves. She realized the question had been addressed to her. One glance at Linda, who stood with her perfect chin tilted snootily toward the ceiling, and Katrine sighed. It was a tough job being a real-life heroine, but someone had to do it.

♥   ♥   ♥

"Jerry? It's Trey. I've got a problem… I'm not mumbling, I have a swollen lip. Well, yeah, that's what I'm calling about. Could you come down to the police station and bail me, Katrine and my ex-wife out of jail?"

He held the phone from his ear when Jerry began shouting. "Caldwell, I'm not in the mood for this. No, I didn't see Elise Pennington at the hockey game. No, I don't think we've been recognized. Jerry, just come get us out. I don't have enough cash on me to pay the fine on all of us.

Oh, that. Disturbing the peace."

When he heard the phone click and a dial tone, Trey assumed Jerry was on the way. After all, his two hottest commodities had landed themselves in the slammer.

"Come with me, sir," the officer ordered.

Trey followed the policeman down a hall and into the processing room. Katrine and Linda sat on a long bench against the wall. Of the two, his ex-wife looked the worse for wear. A small scratch stood out starkly against her pale cheek, and the expensive blouse she wore had one sleeve ripped clean from the shoulder. One corner of Katrine's mouth showed a small cut, but other than that, she looked sound enough. Sound in body, he corrected, if not in mind.

What possessed her to act the way she had? The ingenuity of inviting his ex-wife on a date with them would understandably upset her, only because he'd met her challenge. But pouncing on Linda? My God, Katrine had been a spitting she-cat. It almost appeared as if she was... jealous. His heartbeat increased. Did Katrine care for him, the way every logical bone in his body resisted the feelings he'd developed for her?

"Well? Did he say he'd come get us out?" Linda demanded.

Grateful for an intrusion into his damning thoughts, Trey nodded. "He'll be here."

"Thank goodness," she sighed. "I swear Trey Westmoreland, I've never known you to act so irresponsibly. Getting yourself in a fist fight over a strumpet. Why did you have to insist that man apologize to her? Why didn't you just drop it and watch the game? You were so—"

"Impulsive?" he interrupted. "Illogical? Unpredictable? Spontaneous? I thought you liked those qualities in a man, Linda."

"I–I do," she stammered. "I mean, I believed I did. Now, I've decided I liked you better before. At least you were safe to be around."

"I'm not the same man you married, after all," he said softly. "If a person can't change, he can't grow. There are certain things in life logic can't explain away and rationality can't battle. Safe?" He laughed. "No one is safe."

Linda thrust out her bottom lip. "Why, Trey Darling, that was almost literary. Next thing I know, you'll be writing fiction."

Her barb went wasted on Trey. He'd glanced at Katrine and was captured. Her stare held question, confusion, hope? Damn, why had he revealed so much of himself to Linda? Did Katrine understand the change in his life was because of her? More importantly, did the soft glow in her eyes reflect a shared desire to give love a second chance?

"I don't care for this new you," Linda decided. "I'm sorry, Trey, but I can't see the two of us becoming involved with each other again."

Unconsciously, he smiled. Linda finally understood there would be no reconciliation between them. Odd as it seemed to him, his ex-wife resurfacing in his life was the best thing that could have happened. Trey now realized he hadn't failed at their marriage, he'd only married the wrong woman. Linda was the type who would always want the opposite of what she had.

He also knew, whoever Katrine Summerville really was; protective mother, sultry seductress or spitting she-cat; she wasn't in the least like Linda. Katrine was a well, deep and mysterious. He suddenly longed to see beneath the water's surface—to know about her life, her loves, her dreams.

"Hey, I just recognized the two of you!" The bald man who'd started the trouble leaned forward in his seat.

Trey glanced down the row of people waiting to answer for their part in the disturbance. The cowboy, boasting a shiner the size of silver dollar, also leaned forward, obviously curious to hear what his pot-bellied cohort had to say.

"You're T. West and Blondie there is Kat Summers. Hot damn, if I'd known it was T. West I was pulverizing, I'd have shook your hand instead. I hate that romance crap. My wife reads that trash morning, noon and night."

"Maybe you should read a few yourself," Trey suggested sarcastically. "You didn't pulverize me, and you never apologized to Kat for wrongly accusing her."

"He didn't wrongly accuse me."

His head swiveled toward her so fast his neck

popped. Trey noted the flush to her cheeks and the shameful lowering of her eyes. "What?"

Katrine took a deep breath. "I did, you know, do something with my hand."

"You did?"

She nodded. "I–I felt a little out of sorts. I think it was an allergic reaction."

"An allergic reaction?" he repeated. "To what?"

Her gaze slid subtly to Linda. "Passion."

"A romance writer who's allergic to passion?" the cowboy asked in a disbelieving tone.

"The perfume, 'Passion'," Katrine explained.

"That's a relief," Trey injected softly.

When Katrine looked at him, he smiled, a mischievous light dancing in his eyes. Warmth flooded her. He wasn't angry. His expression was blatantly sexual.

"Maybe I'm allergic to passion, too. I've been out of sorts since the night I first laid eyes on you."

"Oh pa-lease, Trey," Linda said. "If you have to flirt with her, save it until later. In case you've forgotten, we're in jail."

"Hey, I guess Blondie's the one who owes me an apology," the bald man said.

"No she doesn't," Trey muttered. "You're a jerk."

"Amen," the cowboy agreed.

"Oh no, not again," Linda whined.

The bald man got to his feet. "You called me a jerk."

Trey sighed, turning to Katrine. He lifted a brow. "Later?"

Indecision warred within her for a moment. Did she dare believe the warmth reflected in his eyes spoke of commitment, of a beginning for them? Trey had fought for her tonight. He'd made it plain there wasn't anything left between him and Linda. Could she trust him? Did she dare give her heart again, only to have it broken? She fought the insecurities that had kept her a prisoner for years, lifted her chin and met his stare without shame or fear.

"Later," she promised.

Chapter Seventeen

♥   ♥   ♥

As Trey eased the Jag into a covered parking space, Katrine questioned her brave decision. She'd agreed to go to his old apartment for a 'drink', knowing full well his offer had only been a polite way of setting the stage for what would follow. Keeping their hands off each other until Jerry Caldwell could bail them out had been difficult enough. Now that they were alone, Katrine was scared to death.

"Here we are." Trey also sounded nervous. "I'll warn you ahead of time, the place is a mess. Half my stuff's at my new house, and the rest is in boxes over here. About the only furniture left in the apartment is in the bedroom."

Suggestive silence.

Katrine swallowed loudly. "I don't mind sitting on the floor."

"Well, let's do it." Trey opened his car door. His face flushed slightly. "I mean, let's go."

While Katrine waited for him to open her door, 'do it' echoed around her head and increased her worries. Would Trey expect her to be experienced the way Carl had? Would he be disappointed in her lack of creativity in bed the way Carl had? Would he—

"Katrine?"

She glanced up. The door stood open. Trey waited. Fighting her fear of inadequacy, she bravely left the safety of the car. When he took her cold hand in his warm one and squeezed lightly, she immediately felt better. She knew Trey wasn't the type to pounce on her the moment they entered his lair.

The condition of his apartment hadn't been understated. It was a mess. Katrine found the clutter somehow relaxing, less threatening than if she'd stepped into a swinging bachelor's pad. Regardless of the living area's untidiness, the plush carpet, the few pieces of art left on the walls and a cherrywood table on which an expensive lamp sat, were a testament to Trey Westmoreland's impeccable taste.

"All I can scrounge up is a bottle of white wine. Is that all right?" he called from another room.

"Although something stronger might have been more fitting to the occasion, white wine will do," she answered. "I've never been arrested before." She heard him laugh.

"I thought you were going to take a swing at the security guard who pulled you off Linda," he said, reentering the living area with two paper cups in hand. "Sorry, all my glasses are packed."

She felt her color rise while accepting the cup he offered. "I guess the violence on the ice got to me."

"Was that what got to you?"

His grin made her knees weak. Should she lie? No, Katrine had vowed to be honest. "Linda got to me. I was jealous. Of you and her."

The smile on his lips faded. "You have no reason to be. I didn't invite her along in hopes of making you jealous."

"Why did you, then?"

He shrugged. "I didn't figure there was anything less romantic than bringing your ex-wife on a date with you."

"Very ingenious," she agreed dryly. "Why did you marry her?"

For a moment, she thought he wouldn't answer. Trey seemed to suddenly find one of the few remaining pictures on his wall of interest.

"I'm not sure," he confessed, running a hand through his thick hair. "I guess I felt flattered. Linda Tate, of the journalistic Tates, wanted a poor boy like me. I assumed her childish behavior would stop once we married—once we settled in the daily routine of living. I assumed too much."

"And yet, you stayed with her. She left you, isn't that right?"

"Yeah." Trey turned around. "It never occurred to me to leave. I wasn't raised to be a quitter. My dad always said, once you make your bed, you lie in it. I kept hoping Linda would change. I wanted children, she didn't. I guess I saw it as my own failure when I couldn't make my priorities hers, as well."

Katrine hadn't meant to stir up old resentments. She wanted to ease the tension discussing his marriage had created between them. "Are you sure you did a wise thing? Throwing Caldwell to the wolves, a she-wolf in particular?"

He smiled. "To be honest, I can't think of two people who deserve each other more. I knew Jerry couldn't resist a woman who looks like Linda, especially when her father just happens to own the largest paper in Philadelphia. In turn, I told her Caldwell had a very respected name in the business, a cushy job that let him goof off most of the time and make a lot of money."

"He's disgusting." Katrine shivered slightly.

"And if Linda decides she wants him, he's as good as caught."

"*If* Linda decides she wants him, she'll be your editor's wife. Have you thought about that?"

She laughed at his horrified expression.

"I wonder if it's too late to get out of my mortgage loan? I'd have to quit, then I couldn't afford the payments on my house."

"I'm sure after the feature ends you'll be flooded with offers," Katrine assured him.

"Probably," he agreed. "I've been thinking about doing something else with my life.

Curious, Katrine asked, "Such as?"

A tinge of red surfaced beneath his dark complexion. "I've been thinking of writing a novel."

"T. West stooping to fiction?" She flashed him a skeptical look.

"Murder mysteries," he specified, then took her cup, placing both his and hers on the cherry-wood table. "For some reason, I keep thinking about killing someone."

Her lips twitched. "Anyone I know?"

The heat in his eyes when he pulled her in his arms, melted any misgivings Katrine might have had about becoming intimate with him.

"Someone I'd like to know... better."

"Know in what way?" she teased.

One finger traced a slow path down the front of her sweater. "I want to know you inside and out." His lips brushed her ear. "Backward and frontward and every way in between."

His husky whisper turned the blood in Katrine's veins to molten lava. The feel of his breath against her neck drove her crazy. His body pressed closer, and she felt his arousal. There were no more doubts, no fears to hold her back. She wanted Trey, had wanted him since her imagination first created him—a hero of her own to love during the dark hours between dusk and dawn.

"Take me, I'm yours," she whispered passionately.

The faceless 'specter' who'd haunted her dreams for years drew back to look down at her.

He lifted a dark brow. "Take me, I'm yours?"

"Oh." Katrine cringed. "Overused, huh? Sorry,

I–I'm a little nervous."

In response, he took her hand and placed it against the hard desire she'd felt pressed against her a moment earlier. Slowly, he brought her palm up the flat planes of his stomach to his chest. His heart beat strong and erratic.

"I'm nervous, too. Part of me desperately wants you, but the other part, the part you feel beneath your palm, is scared to death of loving you."

"Afraid? Of me?"

Trey nodded. "I'm not sure I can give you one part, without giving you the other. I want to know who you are before I know what making love to you feels like. Separate the waters and let me see inside your soul before I drown in mere desire. Tell me about yourself, about your past, your family, your dreams."

What he asked sounded so simple, but it was too painful. Tears formed behind her eyes. Her body could be his without protest, but he wanted more. Never had she created a hero who would demand so much when a woman could be his for so little. Katrine wasn't ready to tell him about her past. "What if I can't share that with you right now?"

"Then we have no business going into the bedroom together. That's what makes the twentieth century unromantic, Katrine. A society comfortable enough to go to bed with someone they don't really know. Is sex all you want from me?"

"No," she answered, outraged. "I'm not that type of person. I–I'm not experienced. After John, there was only Carl, and that was only one night. John and I were both virgins. We didn't get a chance to experiment much before he left me."

"You mean, before he died," Trey corrected.

"I mean before he left me!" She pulled away. "I think John's accident was no accident. He'd lost his parents shortly before we met. I guess he was in denial until after we married, then suddenly the impact hit him, and along with it, the responsibility of a wife. A wife who'd just told him she was pregnant. He left after I broke the happy news, and he never came back. What could I assume, but that John would rather die than spend the rest of his life tied to me?"

"Assumptions can get a person into trouble," Trey said quietly. "You were both young. I'm sure John was feeling overwhelmed when he left, and because he wasn't paying attention, lost control of the car. Did you meet him in high school?"

Katrine shook her head, spilling teardrops down her cheeks. "His parents were killed in a boating accident shortly before he turned eighteen. Because he had no living relatives, he ended up in a foster home. That's where I met him."

"Your parents fostered children?" Trey asked in surprise.

"No."

"But…"

The past had been bottled inside Katrine for so

long, she couldn't stop the flow of words, the release of her pain. "I don't remember having a father. I suppose I'm illegitimate. My mother pinned a note to my dress and left me on the steps of the social service building when I was five. I can't recall her face, but I remember what she said to me. 'I'll be back soon, Honey. I won't be gone long. Mommy can't take care of you right now. Don't ever forget... I love you'."

It amazed Katrine she could even remember that day. How clearly the picture had been imprinted on her young mind. Recalling the panic she'd felt, the fear, caused pain to rip through her, then Trey's arms pulled her close.

"I'm sorry, Katrine," he whispered, thinking of all the times he'd imagined her a spoiled, coddled child. "I'm so sorry."

She drew strength from his touch, allowing pent up emotions to seep from her soul. Unashamed, she wept, accepting the comfort denied her when she'd been a five-year-old child, lost and alone in a world where no one took the time to explain.

How long Katrine stood there, clinging to his solid frame in desperation, might have been a minute or an hour, she wasn't certain. Slowly, she lifted her tear-stained face to Trey's. Tenderness shone in his eyes, so pure, her fear of loving, of losing, drowned within a need to share more than pain.

Cleansed of the darkness, her gaze sought the

light shining in his eyes. She ran her fingers over the solid shape of his lips, down his neck, and paused at the top button of his shirt. Trey's hand closed over hers.

"Maybe now is not the time," he said. "You're vulnerable, upset and probably not thinking straight. I don't want you to have regrets later."

Rationality was the last thing Katrine wanted from him. "I gave you what you asked for. Don't try to back out of your end of the bargain. Dammit, Trey, you know as well as I do why we're here tonight!"

He sighed. "Katrine, you're still a virgin by twentieth century standards. I just want you to be sure."

Frustrated, fearful Trey wouldn't allow her to express with her body what she couldn't yet say with words, Katrine gathered the material of his shirt between her fingers and ripped it open. *"I'm sure!"*

His eyes widened slightly. Trey glanced down at his gaping shirt. "I suppose you sew about as well as you cook and do laundry?"

"Worse," she admitted, then leaned forward to taste his skin. When she ran her tongue around the copper circle of his nipple, he groaned and pulled her away. Trey tilted her head back. Slowly, he lowered his mouth to hers.

He took her lips gently, tenderly exploring the moist recesses of her mouth until the urgency of their hands on each other, turned gentleness into throbbing, uncontrollable desire. Roughly, Trey pulled her against his hardness.

The deep thrust of his tongue in Katrine's mouth brought a longing for comparative pleasures. She pressed closer, moaning his name between wine-flavored kisses.

"I can't stand anymore," she broke from him to whisper. "I want to feel your skin against mine. I want—"

"Wait," he said, sweeping her up in his arms. "Wait until I unveil your beautiful body inch by inch. Until my hands are on you, my mouth, then tell me what you want."

Wait? The door Katrine supposed led to his bedroom appeared a long distance away. Scooping her up in his arms had certainly been romantic. Still, they'd have made faster time if Trey had let her walk, or more to Katrine's impassioned way of thinking 'run'! "Hurry, Trey," she pleaded against his neck. "Hurry."

In his haste to obey, Trey tripped over a box. His shoulder made a popping sound as he landed against the door frame. "Damn," he muttered.

"You didn't break anything, did you?" Katrine asked fearfully.

"Nothing we'll need," he assured her, then charged onward. Once inside the darkened bedroom, he tripped over a second obstacle. Thankfully, the bed broke their fall.

"Trey," Katrine snapped. "How is it a man who can balance himself on two thin blades and race around an ice rink, can't seem to walk and chew gum at the same time if he's trying to make love to me?"

"Maybe he's *trying* to be romantic so he doesn't get a bad review," he answered through clenched teeth.

"Maybe he's *trying* too hard." Katrine wiggled uncomfortably beneath his weight.

The feel of her body wiggling seductively beneath him reminded Trey the last thing he wanted to do with Katrine was argue. "Katrine, let's not talk to one another. When we talk, we get in trouble."

A thoughtful pause followed.

"All right," she agreed. "We won't talk."

"Unless," he stipulated. "It's passion-related."

"What do you mean?"

In answer, he moved down her body, gathering the sweater over her stomach to trace a lazy circle on the flat surface of her abdomen. "Do you like that?"

"Yes," she sighed.

"That's what I mean." He trailed kisses up her stomach, inching the sweater up as he went. When his mouth met with the lacy fabric of her bra, Trey steeled himself for battle.

"I consider this passion related," Katrine said softly. "I took your advice. It hooks in the front."

To Trey's surprise the bra offered no resistance when he undid the clasp. He pulled Katrine's sweater over her head, peeled back the lace of her bra and worshiped her perfect breasts—a perfection that filled his hands nicely, if he couldn't see her in the darkness.

"I'm going to pull the drapes on the balcony door. There's a full moon tonight. I want to look at you."

Katrine grabbed him by the collar. "Don't go out there."

He paused in his attempt to rise. "I'm just going over to the balcony. I'll be right back."

"Trey, if you hurt yourself," she started, then said nothing.

"Are you suggesting I can't walk across my bedroom without doing myself bodily harm?"

"We're talking," she reminded.

"Oh, right." Trey eased his weight from her and cautiously approached the far side of the room. When he banged his knee against something, he held the curse word between his teeth and limped the rest of the way.

He'd opened these particular drapes countless times over the past six years. Tonight, he couldn't find the damn draw cord. Trey fumbled around for several seconds before locating the nuisance. With a swish of cloth, pale moonlight filtered into the room.

His gaze travelled over boxes to find Katrine, a marble work of art sprawled across his bed. How many times had he imagined her there, waiting for him to love her? And he suspected he did love her, despite a rational vow he'd made to never give his heart again, he had. Twice over the past few weeks.

"Come here," Katrine whispered to him. "But… take your time. Don't hurry."

Slowly, he moved toward her, his eyes feasting on the flat indention of her stomach and the full rise of her breasts. He heard Katrine giggle when he stubbed his toe on a box. Luckily, he still had his shoes on.

"Do you think that was funny?" he asked, staring down at her.

"That wasn't a passion-related question," she answered. "But if you must know, it was a relieved reaction to your making it all the way across the room and back without damaging anything we, ah, need."

Trey took her hand and pulled her up. "Maybe you'd better check me for injuries."

Katrine rose off the bed to stand before him; all traces of humor vanished. Bravely, she pushed the shirt from his shoulders and reveled in the warm, smooth texture of his skin. The sleeves proved bothersome, she'd forgotten to undo the cuffs and couldn't get the shirt past his hands.

"I've noticed Kat Summers doesn't devote much detail to undressing her characters. In the space of seconds, they end up conveniently naked. Why is that?"

His teasing tone brought a smile to her lips. "Maybe because Kat Summers doesn't have much experience at undressing men. Why don't you give me a few pointers."

He shrugged. "What's two more buttons. Rip it off."

"The bodice ripping days are over," she informed him flatly. "But I guess it's all right to rip the hero's shirt off."

With two or three good tugs, Katrine managed to remove his shirt. Her hands strayed to the fastening of his jeans.

"Shoes," he said softly.

"What?"

"Shoes next or we'll have the same problem, only worse."

Removing a man's shoes and socks wasn't in the least romantic, but Katrine viewed the task as a means to an end. When she rose from her chores, she took a steadying breath.

"Now?"

"You can have the button, but I'm not trusting the zipper to a novice. Especially not under current conditions."

She laughed. "This conversation doesn't sound passion-related."

"It's very passion-related," he insisted. "That zipper stands between you and me and something we need. A very uncomfortable something. Undo the button, Katrine."

With trembling hands, she obeyed. Trey took over, carefully unzipping his jeans, then pushing them down the length of his legs.

Katrine swallowed loudly. "My God," she

whispered. "You're beautiful." As she ran a heated survey over his muscular thighs and corded hamstrings, she circled him, unaware that she did so. His backside was nice. Damned nice indeed.

"I have a scar on my knee," he informed her proudly. "All us hero types are supposed to be scarred, aren't we?"

"I'm surprised you don't have more than one." She touched the smooth skin on his back, trailing her nails down the center before tracing the muscled curve of his tight hindquarters. He sucked in his breath sharply.

"I'm not clumsy by nature," Trey said. "For some reason, when I'm around you, I become a bumbling idiot. And, the least you can do is not insult me while I'm standing here buck naked. You clearly have me at a disadvantage."

"Maybe you should even the odds," Katrine suggested, walking around to face him.

An expression of anticipation accompanied his smile. "For an almost virgin, you're a brazen wench."

♥ ♥ ♥

Flat on her back a short time later, Katrine acknowledged that Trey knew her nature far better than she. With the tool of his tongue, he'd reduced her to a panting, clawing, she-cat. Her fingers twisted in the thick silkiness of his hair. Her thighs were trembling. He'd kissed every inch of her while removing her jeans, then turned his attention toward a taboo Kat Summers persistently avoided while writing sex scenes; mostly because having never experienced such, she could only imagine the act as repulsive and embarrassing.

She closed her eyes and let the strangeness wash over her, the gathering sensation that had gripped her the night she and Trey almost made love in the basement. Her fingers tightened on his scalp as the first spasm took her. She gasped, then arched, floating up to a place she'd never been. A place of death, but not death—of life, but not life—another world in itself. She hovered there, brought down to earth by the feel of Trey's mouth on hers, the taste of herself on his lips.

"Katrine," he groaned. "You're so beautiful. You're beautiful everywhere."

"I'm dead," she whispered.

"I know how to bring you back. Let me take you there again."

"Can you?" she asked skeptically. "My bones have dissolved. I'm limp as a dish rag."

His lips travelled to her ear. "I have the opposite problem. Touch me, Katrine."

Suddenly shy, she willed her hand to move, her fingers to close around his arousal. Her pulse quickened at the feel of steel wrapped in hot velvet. His fingers found her wet, willing, receptive to his touch and when Katrine arched against his hand, the ache began to build again.

"I want you inside me," she whispered.

Trey groaned in answer, wedging her knees farther apart before grasping her hips. Katrine held her breath, waiting for his hard length to appease the ache. Instead, poised upon the brink of completion, he swore loudly and released her.

"Dammit. You drive me so crazy, I almost forgot."

"Forgot what?" she panted.

"Protection. It won't take but a minute."

"Hurry, Trey," she bit out.

He rose in all his godly splendor, glanced around the room and cussed again.

"Now, what's wrong?" she asked.

"I packed the damned things."

"Just unpack them," she suggested rationally.

His gaze lifted to the ceiling, she supposed in appeal. "I don't know which box they're in."

Katrine groaned. "Didn't you label them?"

"Oh sure, I wrote 'neckties and condoms' in big letters for the movers to snicker over. Which, come to think of it, would be fitting. They both strangle a man."

"Don't get short with me, Trey," Katrine warned. "I've had my 'burst of ecstacy'. You haven't. Now, where did you keep them?"

Moonlight allowed her to witness the sarcastic twist to his mouth. "Getting short with you is what I'm desperately trying to avoid. I had them in the top of my closet, which means, they could be in any of the six boxes marked 'closet'."

She sighed. "I guess we can always wait until

you move."

After Trey ran a lengthy survey over her naked curves, he said, "I'll get a knife."

A knife? Katrine wondered, for the briefest of moments, if he'd succumbed to his earlier confessed desire to kill her.

"For the tape," he specified, as if reading her thoughts. "I'll be right back."

Watching him walk away was bliss. Katrine snuggled deeper into the soft comforter on his bed, already missing his warmth. He returned a moment later, made an animal sound and set to work. The sight of his muscles rippling as he tore into the first box set her blood on fire. Clothes flew, shoes, belts, and unfortunately, something that made a shattering noise when he flung it against the wall. Katrine began to squirm after two more boxes met their doom.

"Hurry, Trey," she whispered huskily.

He paused, glanced her direction, then renewed his efforts with greater vigor, slashing into the fourth. "Hell, I've scattered the contents of four boxes with no relief in sight." He rose and kicked an empty box from his path.

"Trey?" Katrine thought to question. "That night in the cab, and then in my basement, what were you planning to do about protection?"

Knife raised, he froze. "I keep a couple in my wallet."

"Oh." Silence. "Then—"

"Don't," he warned softly. "Don't ask me why

I didn't think to get my wallet from my jeans and save myself the hell I've just inflicted on this room. That would have been too easy, too—"

"Why don't you get one, now," Katrine suggested, strangely impassioned by his sacrifice. Watching a man raid and pillage was a definite turn on. "And why don't you hurry."

Violently, he buried the knife in a box and strode toward her. Trey bent, retrieved his jeans then pinned her with a hot stare. "I don't intend to hurry."

Obviously not, Katrine realized shortly after he settled beside her, touching, stroking, kindling a smoldering fire into a blazing inferno of mindless desire. Katrine moaned and writhed beneath his skilled torture, bravely exploring him as he explored her. Every inch of him was magnificent.

The slope of his back, the muscled contours of his buttocks, and the flatness of his stomach. When her hand closed around the hard, hot, length of him, he groaned in either agony or ecstasy.

"Holding back is killing me," he said hoarsely. "Don't touch me, Katrine. I want you to want me as much as I want you."

"I do," she whispered, releasing him to press against his throbbing member with urgency. "Please," Katrine panted, twisting her head from side to side. "Please give yourself to me."

She found her face tenderly clasped between his hands. In his eyes, the light of victory shone, frightening in its sureness and compelling in its promise of pleasure. He entered her slowly, stretching the tight confines of her passage. Her body accepted his thickness, welcomed the unfamiliar feel of his generous offering and strained to receive all he had to give.

His lips fastened on hers, tenderly tasting before the kiss deepened, until his tongue began to thrust and his body took up the rhythm. A tide of pleasure rose in Katrine as Trey labored above her. He held her captive with his eyes, burning coals of desire in the moonlit room, penetrating her soul as deeply as he penetrated her flesh.

Instinctively, her hips matched his movements. She'd been with John in inexperienced innocence, with Carl in acceptance that a relationship lasting that long would inevitably end with sex, but never had she been so willing to give herself, so desperate to find release.

Trey pounded her defenses, demanding surrender. When her breath caught, when her back arched and her eyes widened with wonder, he thought her the most beautiful creature God had ever created. Conscious observation ceased as his own release exploded. Pleasure, agonizing in its intensity tore her name from his lips to merge with the sound of his own. He gathered Katrine close, both trembling in the wake of the storm, both awed by a force that tossed them into a sea of wondrous emotion. Gradually, their hearts slowed, their breathing returned to normal.

"I've never felt like that before," Katrine said.

"I never really believed anyone could feel like that. Was it… different for you?"

Drained of strength and past defense, Trey pulled back to look into her eyes. "Yes," he answered honestly. "With you, it was special. What you just made me feel was beyond pleasure, beyond expectation or duty. It was beyond passion."

Her overexerted heart lurched in her chest, then swelled with love when he kissed her softly. "Mmmm," she sighed. "Do you think you can make love to me again?"

"I'll see what I can do," he said against her lips. "Once more by the grace of my wallet, greedy wench. Then, if you're still hungry, I'll have to go on the hunt."

Katrine felt certain two more boxes would meet their doom before morning.

Chapter Eighteen

♥   ♥   ♥

"Mom," Shelly repeated, sounding annoyed. "I'm talking to you."

"Oh." Katrine shook her head. "Sorry, Honey. What were you saying?"

"My P.E. coach thinks I should try out for spring soccer. What do you think?"

Katrine lifted a brow. "Soccer? I didn't know you were interested in sports. That is, unless Trey happened to be coaching."

Shelly distractedly stirred pencils in a cup stationed on Katrine's desk. "Trey likes sports. He's very athletic, isn't he?"

"Very," Katrine sighed.

"You didn't say much about the hockey game. Did you enjoy it?"

"Immensely. Trey was wonderful, I mean, it was wonderful." She straightened in her chair. "Honey, if you want to participate in sports, I think you should. I'll see that you get to practices and games."

"In a cab?" Shelly snorted softly. "I wish we

could get a fancy sports car like Trey's."

"You know I don't drive," Katrine scolded gently. "Although, it seems silly if you're going to need to be constantly chauffeured around, not to invest in a car. Tell you what, I'll think about taking driving lessons and getting my license. But a Jag is out of the question. I read somewhere that a Volvo's one of the safest cars on the road. Maybe a station wagon."

"Yuck." Shelly curled her lip. "Only old women with a bunch of screaming kids drive station wagons."

The phone interrupted Shelly's discontent. Deeming herself secretary, the child quickly snatched up the receiver. "Trey?" she said with surprise. "Why didn't you call on my private line? Oh, you want to talk to her? All right, but call me later." Smiling, Shelly handed the phone to her mother. "Would you like me to leave?"

"If you'd be so kind." Katrine's hand shook when she took the receiver from Shelly. Once her office door closed, she tried to sound calm. "Hello." The rich texture of his voice rose goose bumps beneath her skin. "I'm fine," she answered stiffly. "Oh, you've been moving the last couple of days?" *Is that why you haven't called?* "The phone was disconnected the day after our, ah, date?"

What about work? Isn't there a phone in your office? "Jerry gave you a couple of days off to get moved? That was considerate of him. So, did you

get settled in? Boxes everywhere, huh?" She
fanned her cheeks and squirmed in her chair.
"I've been thinking about you, too.

"What's wearing your shirt tail out got to do
with thinking about me? Oh," she said when he
explained. She dropped the pencil she'd been
toying with. "Where are you calling from? The
office? I hope you're alone. Does Jerry know he's
paying you to make obscene phone calls? He's
avoiding you? What's up? I–I mean, what do you
think is going on?" she quickly corrected.

"Maybe he's still mad about having to bail us
out of jail," Katrine offered. "Yes, I know how
difficult this week's feature will be, thank you
very much. As a matter of fact, that's what I've
been working on all morning." Hurriedly, she
shuffled paper around on her desk to make noise.

"I know, only one more. Why should I let you
pick the date? It's my turn. Your house? What?
Will Linda be there measuring for drapes?" She
laughed at his answer. "All right, I'm curious.
Wednesday? But that's the day after tomorrow.
We're supposed to wait until the weekend." She
smiled. "No, I can't wait that long, either. Later."

Katrine hung up the phone. She sat quite calmly
for a few seconds before reaching for another pencil
and a note pad. In big block letters she wrote,
YES!

♥   ♥   ♥

"Yes, what?" Jerry Caldwell asked, sticking his head inside Trey's office.

Trey felt his face grow warm. He didn't know Jerry stood outside his door when he'd hung up the phone and said 'yes' rather enthusiastically. *"Yes, We Have No Bananas,"* he quoted dryly.

Caldwell scratched his head, resembling a monkey. "What the hell is that supposed to mean?"

"Exactly," Trey agreed. "It's silly when you think about it. *Yes, We Have No Bananas.* Why not, no, we don't have any bananas? Or, bananas? No, we have none."

His editor approached him, a frown marring his unappealing features. "Is this what I pay you a salary for? To sit around and rewrite stupid songs?"

"This is passion-related, ah, I mean, work-related," Trey corrected, feeling the heat in his face increase. "I thought I might do a feature on grammatically incorrect songs. There's a ton of them out there, you know?"

Jerry cast him a dark look. "If you'll recall, you already have a feature to write, and by the looks of things, it isn't going too well."

After glancing down at his clean desk, Trey shrugged. "What is there to write about? You said I couldn't mention the fight or getting thrown in jail. That doesn't leave me much to work with."

"Then lie for God's sake. Kat Summers does!"

"Katrine doesn't exactly lie," Trey defended. "She sugar-coats the truth. It's called creative writing."

"Humph." Jerry eyed him curiously. "You've been charging to her rescue with regularity lately. You got in a fight because some mouthy spectator insulted her. In fact, you've been acting irrational since the feature began. Your ex-wife seems to believe you've fallen for Kat Summers. Is it true? Has she convinced you that romance still exists in the twentieth century?"

Uncomfortable with the conversation, Trey made a pretense of scrounging up materials to begin the feature. He wasn't certain how or when he began to fall in love with Katrine, but he knew their relationship wasn't anything he wanted to discuss with Jerry. "Speaking of Linda," he artfully changed the subject. "Has she gone home?"

It was Jerry's turn to appear uncomfortable. "Well, ah, no, she hasn't." He glanced up sheepishly. "Actually, I asked her to stay a while longer. Linda is a fascinating woman. I hope it won't cause problems between us if I continue to see her."

Linda fascinating? Trey tried not to laugh out loud. "No, it won't cause problems," he lied. *Only my resignation if the courtship becomes serious.* "Linda and I are old news."

Caldwell visibly relaxed. "She says her daddy is thinking of retiring soon…" Jerry let the statement trail.

Sam retire? Maybe when he was six feet under. Trey kept his suspicions to himself. It hadn't taken Linda long to find Caldwell's weakness. "That would be a cushy position to walk into."

Jerry's eyes took on a glazed look. He shook his head as if to bring his lust under control. "It wouldn't hurt my reputation any if you kept me at number one for a while longer, either. After this feature, you can't simply return to book review. We'll have to come up with another feature run, and then another, and then another. Play your cards right, and you might be my replacement when, I mean, if, I end up in Philadelphia."

The prospect wasn't appealing to Trey, which was the most irrational thought he'd had to date, or to be more precise, since he and Katrine's first date. Wasn't the editorship what he'd been working toward? Stuffy offices, deadlines, headaches, the rating game... suddenly it wasn't what Trey wanted at all.

"I'm considering a different field," he said quietly. "Fiction."

His editor laughed, then sobered at Trey's serious expression. "Novels? Good God, Trey. She has turned your brain to mush. You're a professional, not some novelist spinning yarns. You owe it to me to stay for a while. I gave you this feature knowing full well it would make you a hot commodity!"

"You didn't give me the feature. I gave it to you, and then you shoved it down my throat," Trey reminded in a deadly voice. "You don't own me, Caldwell. I won't accept another offer in the journalistic field for a while, but what I do with my future is my business. There's more to life than busting your butt at a job for the sake of security. I owe you this feature, after that, I'll decide what I can or can't do."

"You'd starve if you tried to write fiction," Jerry scoffed. "I doubt that you could handle the rejection. If you feel like creating, create me a feature article for Sunday's edition, and remember, you've got to give the readers a little romance this time."

"I'll deliver," Trey said. "But for future reference, I just wanted you to know I'm considering a career move."

"You'll talk yourself out of it," the editor assured him. "You're a rational man. Once you get Kat Summers out of your life, and your blood, you'll see the logic in staying right where you are." Jerry started toward the door. "I want that feature on my desk by tomorrow morning."

Trey didn't like the desperate look in Jerry's eyes, or the worry lines creasing his forehead. Caldwell made him uneasy. He swiveled his chair and switched on his computer. The feature was the last thing on Trey's mind. All he could think of was Katrine. Katrine and boxes. Katrine in a pair of red-sequined heels and nothing else, sitting bare-bottomed on his immaculate dresser top.

Unconsciously, he smiled. Romantic? Insane seemed a more appropriate word. He couldn't get enough of her. Even after having her four times in his apartment, he'd made love to Katrine in front of her house, in his Jag of all impossible places.

She made him want her like no other woman. They'd talked between love-making sessions—talked about her past and her fears. Trey had confessed his own fear of failure, told her about his huge family and felt his heart break at her envious expression. Katrine, he now realized, enjoyed a fantasy world so much because real life had sorely mistreated her. Trey wanted to show her reality could live up to fantasy. He felt driven to give her candlelight, to let her see a side of himself he didn't know existed until she brought it forth.

Resentfully, he opened his word processing program on his computer. What he felt for Katrine wasn't a game anymore. It wasn't a story he wanted aired for all the world to read. He was simply a man in love, and scared to death the dreams taking shape in his mind might remain only fantasy. Trey wasn't sure he believed in happily-ever-after, but then, he was no longer certain he didn't.

One thing he knew without question, was that come Wednesday night, Trey Westmoreland planned to do exactly what his editor once suggested. He planned to romance Katrine Summerville right out of her clothes.

♥   ♥   ♥

The house, what Katrine could see of it, was a huge Victorian number with a large front lawn and neatly trimmed hedges. When she'd been in the market for a house five years ago, she remembered the realtor driving around this prestigious subdivision. At the time, she thought the lawns would prove too bothersome, the rooms too numerous for only her and Shelly; and the number of children roaming the neighborhood too staggering to insure she received quiet while she wrote.

Now, pulling into the drive where a soft glow showed behind the bay window, Katrine felt, strangely, as if she'd come home. The limo's headlights outlined the red Jag in the drive. Katrine's pulse quickened. There was something erotic about making love in a cramped space. Especially, if that cramped space wasn't exactly private. The fear of being caught made the kisses more urgent, the fumbling to remove clothes more frantic, the climax all the more intense.

"Mr. Westmoreland said he'd be taking you home," Bob informed her from the front seat. "Would you like me to escort you to the door?"

"No, if you'd just wait until I get inside the house, I'd appreciate it."

Bob climbed from the limo to get the door for her. The scent of wood smoke hung pleasantly in the air as Katrine's heels, not the sequined ones Trey refused to let her take home, made a soft clicking noise on the cobbled sidewalk.

'A smart man would hold on to these for a while longer,' Trey had said jokingly. 'This way, if you want your shoes back, you'll have to venture into my territory and face ravishment to get them.'

His remark hadn't been funny to her. Trey knew too much about pleasing a woman. Not that she minded while he proved himself so adept, but later, after he'd brought her to climax for the third time, she wanted to know how he'd gotten so experienced. He openly discussed his past sex life, much to her annoyance, and assured her he'd abstained more than his body wanted to, but in cases where he hadn't, had been very careful. Katrine supposed she should be thankful Trey was a rational-thinking man.

The protection he demanded they use was mostly because she didn't take birth control pills. Still, he'd warned her never to trust a man's word when it came to sex. Men would say anything. She smiled unconsciously, recalling that after giving her the advice, he'd acted mad over the possibility she'd need it for future reference, and made love to her again.

Her smile faded when Trey opened the door. Wanting him became immediate. The clean scent of his cologne engulfed her. The heat in his eyes sent tiny shocks of anticipation racing through her bloodstream. Without a word, he opened the door wider. *Step into my parlor,* she thought.

Trey wore a tight-fitting pair of black jeans and a white shirt open at the neck. The sleeves were full and pushed up to mid-forearm. Katrine quirked a brow, thinking it wasn't the sort of shirt Trey Westmoreland would wear. He looked like a pirate. A very roguish pirate.

She started to speak, then held her tongue, realizing the silence between them felt right. It added an allure to seeing him again. When last they met, it had been a night of whispered worship, of labored breaths and skin against skin.

He took her hand, leading her in silence down the gleaming tile of the entry hall. They stepped into a room, and the breath caught in Katrine's throat. She'd walked into another era. The vaulted ceiling made the spacious living area appear all the larger. A fire burned cozily in the grate, and the hardwood floors gleamed from the light of what must have been a hundred candles stationed in various places around the room.

Everywhere she looked, were vases of freshly-cut roses. The room was void of furniture, but a huge Persian rug spread on the floor beckoned her to sit among rose petals and dine from silver covered dishes. A bottle of wine chilled in a cooler nearby, waiting to be poured into gleaming crystal goblets.

"It's beautiful," she whispered.

"No." He turned her to face him. "You're beautiful. Inside and out."

Seemingly from mid-air, Trey produced a perfect red rose, although Katrine realized he must have retrieved it while she stood in awe surveying her surroundings. Instead of handing it to her, he ran the smooth petals down the bridge of her nose, chin, throat and into the deep vee of her neckline. It rested there, a sensuous caress as he lowered his lips to hers.

His kiss bespoke hunger, passion stored, and lust too long denied. She moaned against his mouth, clinging to his strength. When her knees buckled, Trey lifted her into his arms and carried her to the rug.

Gently, he lowered Katrine to the floor, never releasing her lips. As her arms encircled his neck, she felt a pin prick of pain between the valley of her breasts. Trey released her lips as if he, too, felt the sensation. Glancing down, she noticed a small bubble of blood. The rose had thorns.

"Look," he instructed huskily.

An identical wound marked his chest. A double-sided thorn had pricked them both.

"Does it symbolize something?" Katrine asked in an over-dramatized whisper.

His smile was lazy, sensuous. "It must be an omen."

"But, what could it mean?" she fretted.

The smile he wore stretched over her acting abilities. He turned thoughtful, brooding, and looked all the more roguish in the role. "Though a rose is gentle on the eye, soft to the touch and pleasing to smell, to embrace its splendor, one must suffer the consequence. In all things living, within the beauty of perfection, lies the ability to deliver pain. A natural defense."

Her humor fled. How true were his mock findings, and how ironic the thorn had pricked the skin above her heart. "And you said you weren't creative." She glanced down with the intention of wiping the blood away.

His hand stilled the motion. "And in all suffering," he added. "Lies the beauty of love, when the pain is shared." He leaned forward and removed the small bubble of blood with his tongue.

When he lifted his head, his expression challenged her to do the same. Her tongue touched his skin, tasted the saltiness of his blood and lingered against the warmth of his flesh.

"Maybe we should eat," he said hoarsely.

"I wanted to see the house…" her voice trailed as she glanced around.

"I have every intention of showing you the house. *Every single room.* Later."

Katrine's gaze returned to his. Heat settled in her face, her neck and private regions. "Every single room?"

"Even the pantry in the kitchen," he answered with a wicked twist to his lips.

"How many rooms are there? I–I mean total?"

"Eleven."

"I doubt you could show me eleven rooms," she said, her smile as wicked as his.

"I forgot to count the staircase. Make it twelve. Back it up with a fifty, and you've got a bet."

She laughed at his daring. "Haven't you learned your lesson about gambling?"

"In this instance, the rewards to be reaped will be much sweeter."

Having thrown down the gauntlet, Trey removed the silver covers from their plates. Steam rose, and the smell of lobster mingled with the scent of roses and candle wax. Katrine glanced up at him with inquiry.

"Surely you didn't prepare this?"

"No." He uncorked the wine. "I ruined your last meal at Chez Fred's. I hope this makes up for it."

Chez Fred's, to her speculation, didn't offer a take out service. His thoughtful indulgence must have cost a small fortune, not to mention a room full of roses. She took the goblet of sparkling wine he handed her, waiting until he filled his own before bringing the glass to her lips.

"Wait. I want to make a toast."

Curious, she lowered the goblet.

"To the end."

Katrine's heart twisted painfully. Her goblet remained untouched.

"Of the beginning," he finished.

Slowly the frozen blood in her veins thawed. His smile reassured her. The future lay ahead, time needed to explore her feelings for him and the ones his heated regard said he felt for her. Katrine clinked her glass to his, sealing a promise to herself. The world waited. She felt strong enough to gamble on Trey, to believe in happily-ever-after. They began the meal in silence. Trey's manners were impeccable, even if the hot stare he directed her way could only be labeled obscene.

Stimulated to the point of discomfort, Katrine recalled the aspect of his barbaric mannerisms inside the restaurant that had heated her blood. She wondered if she could do the same to him.

Setting her fork aside, she tore a chunk of tender lobster from the shell. She allowed the buttery juice to run down her fingers before bringing the morsel to her lips. Greedily, she sucked at the meat, popped it into her mouth, then lapped the juice from her fingers. Trey swallowed loudly. She smiled.

After the third repeat, his fork dropped to his plate. Not that Katrine had seen him eat a bite since the seduction began. The fourth time she lifted her fingers, he snatched her hand.

Firelight flickering in the blue depths of his eyes, Trey attended to the task for her. He licked the juice from her hand, sucked on her fingers and brought her breathing to a volley of soft pants. His mouth travelled up her sleeve, bit at the material of her jumpsuit, nuzzled her neck and hungrily lapped the juice from her lips. When she moaned, he stole inside, boldly caressing her tongue with his.

Dishes rattled and wine spilled as he shoved the expensive meal aside with the sweep of his arm, gently lowering Katrine to the rug. When his hands moved to the buttons on her jumpsuit, she tugged the shirt tail from his jeans. The speed with which he undid the long row of buttons caused her a moment's annoyance. Pulling the shirt over his head, she sighed with bliss when his heated flesh touched hers.

Trey drew back to run his gaze down her body. "Shit, you don't have anything on underneath your clothes."

"You can't say the 'S' word," she scolded softly. "Not in romance."

"Can I say damn?" he wanted to know.

"I don't see why not," she reasoned.

He lowered his mouth to her breasts. "Damn."

As his lips fastened greedily on one passion-filled bud, Katrine arched her back and moaned his name. His hands clasped the material at her shoulders, and as his tongue traced a path down her body, Trey took the jumpsuit with him.

When he pulled Katrine to her feet, she hurriedly kicked off her shoes and stepped out of her clothes. While Trey's heated gaze hungrily roamed her naked curves, she reached for the fastenings of his jeans.

"Not taking any chances with zippers, huh?" she asked with a smile. "I see you're wearing button downs."

"Button downs about to lose their buttons. Let's go upstairs."

"What's wrong with right here?" Katrine managed to undo the buttons and he stepped out of his jeans in almost one fluid motion. Her fingers closed around him.

He sucked in his breath sharply. "Don't, Katrine," he warned. "There's something upstairs we need and the bedroom's too far away as it is."

"You should have scattered them in with the rose petals," she teased, refusing to release him. "Mmmm, you're so hard, so hot, so… generously endowed."

"If you don't stop that, you'll find out just how generous I am. I thought about scattering them in with the rose petals, but then, that would look pretty presumptuous, and not at all romantic."

"Let's go then," she whispered huskily.

This time, Trey didn't scoop her up romantically in his arms. He took hold of her hand and practically dragged her from the room. In their haste to reach the bedroom, they tripped on the stairs. Katrine landed on top. Warm need encountered strained control. She moaned softly, unable to end the delicious contact.

"Katrine," Trey warned again, then sighed. "To hell with it. One time won't matter."

Roughly, he grasped her hips, plunging into her with force. Katrine gasped with shock, then groaned with pleasure. His hands on her hips guided her movements until she understood the rhythm. Panting above him, the glow from a light upstairs outlining the rugged contours of his face, the first taste of her own power slid down Katrine's throat. She rode him mercilessly, inflamed by the passionate words she stole from his lips, maddened by the building sensation she knew ended in release, and when he thought to slow her movements, she clasped his wrists and held them above his head. In retaliation, Trey licked and sucked at her breasts when they were within sampling distance. His teasing caused her to grind frantically against him, and when she felt the first shudder of surrender, Katrine threw her head back. An inhuman sound escaped her throat to merge with his growl of release.

Trey thrust deep, giving his heart, giving all of himself, then held her when she collapsed against him. After his breathing slowed, an admission slipped past his defenses. "I could stand that for the rest of my life," he said in a voice laced with tenderness. "Katrine, I realize we haven't known each other that long, but I've developed feelings for you. I t–think I—"

"I think I smell smoke," Katrine sat up abruptly. She'd been only half listening to him while her brain tried to identify the faint odor.

"It's probably just from the fireplace." He pulled her back down.

"Oh." Katrine snuggled next to his warmth. "Now, what were you saying?"

He cleared his throat. "I said, I… smell smoke, too. I'm sure the screen on the fireplace was closed. "Christ," he groaned. "The candles!"

Chapter Nineteen

♥   ♥   ♥

"That's it?" Cynthia Lane asked, obviously disappointed. "You managed to gook up a hockey game but good and he only wrote one line?"

"Ah, but that one line says a lot," Katrine said, refilling her friend's coffee cup."

"*'This hardened realist is reconsidering the extinction of romance and questioning his belief in un-happily-ever-after,'*" Cynthia quoted, then smiled herself. "Sounds like our boy has fallen in love."

"I hope so." Katrine's expression became worried. "I have."

"I know," the spunky brunette reminded. "I told you, remember?"

Katrine brought Cynthia's coffee, pulled out a chair and quickly seated herself. "No, I really love him," she stressed. "I mean, I'm not afraid to love him anymore. Now that the feature has ended, all we have to do is write our last article and we're free."

"Free?" Cynthia repeated, confused.

"Free to have a relationship of our own without the nation looking on. Hopefully, without Elise Pennington hiding in the bushes, waiting to catch us at some embarrassment. We've agreed not to see or speak to each other until after the feature ends in this Sunday's edition. Then we'll celebrate."

"So." Cynthia leaned closer. "How was the last date?"

"Up until the fire, it was as romantic as it gets."

"The fire?"

"A slight mishap with a burning candle." *So much for my black jumpsuit.* "Once Trey and I emptied the rose vases and poured water over the flames, you could hardly tell the Persian rug had a burnt corner."

"I guess that left the evening on an exciting note." Cynthia chuckled softly.

"Actually, the evening didn't end." Katrine's eyes took on a glazed look. "Trey showed me the house. Every single room."

Cynthia appeared to be puzzling over what could be so exciting about that, then she shrugged. "I gotta go, kid." She rose from the table. "I told you there was a Prince Charming out there for every woman. Mine just happens to look like a frog. Yours? Well, his picture's probably next to the word 'gorgeous' in the dictionary."

"Bye, Cynthia." Katrine got to her feet and walked Cynthia to the front door. "Thanks for all the advice. You were right, the thought of a real flesh and blood man in my life scared me. But now, I can't imagine existing without Trey. I just hope he feels the same." Katrine worried her bottom lip.

"You hope? Can't you see it in his eyes?"

"I think I do. But then, maybe I just want to."

"Don't worry, kid." Cynthia patted her arm. "If it's meant to be, it'll work out. Now, go write that feature while I tell Shelly good-bye. I barely had time to say hello after she got off the bus."

Nodding distractedly, Katrine closed the door. "It has to work out," she whispered. "I'll die if it doesn't." *Stop it!* Katrine squared her shoulders. "I believe in love. I believe in happily-ever-after. I believe in Trey."

♥　　♥　　♥

"Well, Westmoreland, we've squeezed the orange until the juice is almost gone." Jerry sighed. "We're number one. Kat's editor called me this morning. He hopes you do better on the last feature. One damn sentence. Care to explain your strategy?"

Pushing away from his computer, Trey reluctantly faced Jerry Caldwell. "There was no strategy. I wrote the truth."

Jerry rolled his gaze upward. "Oh, man. Did she do a number on you. Kat Summers managed to get exactly what she wanted without forcing you into anything. Like a lamb to the slaughter,

Westmoreland."

"I'm not in the mood to listen to your snide comments about Katrine this morning. Maybe you'd better go."

His editor waved a hand. "I'm going," he assured, moving toward the door. "I should call her and thank her for making this easier than I anticipated." Jerry paused. "Tell me, did you romance her on the last date? Did you give her roses and candlelight? Has she made you into one of her silly, love-besotted heroes?"

"Get out." The order was given as Trey rose from his chair. "You're ugly enough, Caldwell. Don't tempt me to add further aggravation to an already sad situation."

"You did give her roses and candlelight, didn't you?" Jerry asked, then shook his head. "You wanted her to feel special. Well, here's a bulletin for you, Westmoreland, you're not special to her. That babe could have any man she looked at twice. She probably *has* had any man who looked at her twice. Knowing how to pull all the right strings has gotten her exactly what she wanted, what her readers expect. You're a fool, Westmoreland. A fool for love."

In the blink of an eye, Jerry found himself shoved against the wall, an angry columnist in his face.

"Don't talk about Katrine as if she were a whore! You don't know her! She's not that kind of woman!"

"H–Hey, calm down," Jerry stammered. "I got out of line, I'm sorry. I only have your best interest at heart. I think you've forgotten it's all a game, only a story. I'm afraid she's led you to believe there's more to the feature than ratings and careers. Face it, Kat Summers would enjoy making you eat crow after the review you did on her three years ago. Although we've agreed you'll shed a romantic light on the last article, I don't want you to go overboard. Don't give her more than is necessary, in case she pulls a fast one."

"What do you mean, 'a fast one'?" Trey demanded, releasing Jerry's shoulders.

Tugging at his collar, Jerry explained, "You humiliated her three years ago. Hasn't the thought occurred to you that she might be seeking revenge? Frankly, if she did decide to string you up and gut you in front of the whole nation, there'd be nothing I could do to stop her. Our readers will be waiting for her half of the last article. What could I do but publish whatever she hands over? Kat Summers would have me over a barrel, and she knows it."

Trey turned away from the disturbing possibilities. He walked to his desk. "Katrine wouldn't publicly humiliate me. Not now." He hated the insecurity in his voice. "I've done some rotten things to her. I've taken her on one hell of a ride over the past few weeks, but she knows my feelings for her have changed along the way. My opinion of what she does has changed. I respect her. I lov—" Trey abruptly cut himself off.

"I rest my case," Jerry finished. He sighed. "Trey, there's nothing I'd like more than a fairy-tale ending to the feature. There is nothing our readers would like more, but fairy-tales are a fantasy, and the Trey Westmoreland I know lives in the real world. Give her some gush, but don't lay your heart on the line. You've been charging to her rescue, fighting battles for her, defending her honor. You've become a perfect hero. Think about it."

The door closed. For six years Trey had wanted to punch Jerry Caldwell in the face, and for six years, he'd refrained. A moment ago, he'd almost given in to the irrational urge. And he would have, not for his own personal pleasure, but for Katrine. She wouldn't lie to him, would she? The whole affair hadn't been a game to her, had it? A game she intended to win by humiliating him in the end.

Stop it! Trey straightened his shoulders and moved back behind his desk. "I believe," he said, seating himself. He turned to the blank monitor. "I believe in Katrine," he vowed, then began to type.

For centuries, flowers and candlelight have topped the list of romantic ways to win a woman's heart. Although a beautiful setting enhances the mood for love, without the proper chemistry

between a man and a woman, they go wasted. I have, on occasion, been asked to define romance, or more precisely, what I consider romantic.

Once upon a time, I based my opinion on old movies, on the classics, on everything but personal experience. A date with reality taught me to look beyond the obvious. If when you speak, he listens, if when you cry, he holds you, if when—

The phone's shrill ring interrupted Katrine's writing. With an irritated sigh, she snatched up the receiver and muttered a hello.

"Katrine? Hi, this is Jerry Caldwell."

"Oh, hi," she said, surprised.

"Listen, I know you're probably busy working on the article, but it just occurred to me, I've never really thanked you for agreeing to do the feature. I realize the project has taken up your valuable writing time."

"That's true." Katrine felt a prick of guilt. She'd sorely neglected the novel she'd been working on before she met Trey. "But I consider it time well spent, Mr. Caldwell."

"Please, call me Jerry." The editor laughed into the phone. "Mr. Caldwell sounds so stuffy, especially since I feel as if I've come to know you well over the past few weeks. If Trey's been rather sketchy in his portion of the articles, he's kept me well informed on what's been happening between the two of you."

"He has?" Katrine asked weakly.

"Oh, yes, I know what he's put you through,

and frankly, I'm surprised you've been such a good sport about it all. Of course, I fully expected he'd try to get his jabs in where he could. He knew from the beginning a certain criteria had to be met by the third date."

"Criteria?"

"Surely Craig Martin filled you in on the details?"

"No," she answered. "He didn't."

Jerry laughed again. "Probably because he didn't believe Trey would deliver his part of the goods. Personally, I never doubted him. Trey's a professional. He knew from the beginning what was expected of him, or I should say, what our female readership expected from him."

Katrine's stomach twisted. She took a deep breath. "Exactly what was expected of him?"

"What else would please your readers and ours, but a fairy-tale ending? He wasn't too happy about pretending to fall under the spell of romance, but I'm sure he'll play out the role to perfection. Trey enjoys a good challenge."

"Yes, he does," she agreed softly.

There was a slight pause on the other end, then Jerry said, "I shouldn't have expressed my doubts that he could possibly compete with your well-loved heroes," he admitted. "Trey's the sort who'd take the challenge simply because I goaded him with it. I told him not to bother. That, after all, would call for creativity, plotting beyond the scope of a journalist's imagination. I doubt Trey could grasp the concept."

Katrine didn't doubt it one bit.

"Anyway, I just wanted you to know how much I appreciate your cooperation. Our readers will find satisfaction in a fairy-tale wrap up. You leave the public eye smelling like a rose, and we get our female following back. End of story."

"End of story," she whispered, clutching a pencil in her fingers so tightly it snapped.

"Well, I guess I should let you get back to your writing," Jerry said politely. "Trey indicated this last one should be a piece of cake. He said something about living up to all your expectations. I assume he gave you the standard ingredients to write a romantic feature—roses and candlelight?"

Katrine didn't answer. She felt her old fears gathering around her like a pack of hungry wolves, waiting to pounce the moment they smelled insecurity. A dose of reassurance would keep them at bay. "Is Trey in his office?"

"Ah, no, he isn't. He's already at work on another feature. Busy boy, our Trey. I imagine he's out gathering research material. You know how he is, such a perfectionist. Of course, that's what makes him a great journalist. Sometimes, however, he goes too far out on a limb and I end up taking the fall. You sound strange. He hasn't done anything to cause us more trouble, has he?"

Katrine's whole body began to shake. "He did everything perfectly. *Everything.*" Without another word, she gently replaced the receiver. She sat in stunned denial for a moment. Trey wouldn't do this to her, she tried to assure herself. The capture of her heart hadn't been a carefully-plotted scheme. The feature had ceased to be a war game the night they made love, the night she bared her soul to him.

Besides, she reasoned, if he'd been trying to seduce her from the start, he'd gone about it strangely. Trey had been a total jerk, arrogant, annoying... as were all heroes in the beginning. Gradually, she'd seen another side to him, the vulnerable side, the side she couldn't resist.

Conflict, sexual tension, bonding with a family member, jealousy, seduction—what elements smacked more of romance than those? None, she reluctantly answered herself. In his review three years prior, he'd suggested it didn't take a high degree of intelligence to plot a romance novel, any grandmother could do it—any columnist could do it if he dissected the formula spelled out so clearly in her own novels.

"But why?" she whispered. "Why would he bother?" Revenge seemed the only answer. How better to get back at her for the trouble she caused him three years ago? Imagine, making a romance writer believe in her own romance? The gushy article she'd been working on was all the proof he needed of success. Then what? He'd reap his sweet rewards by burying a knife in her heart. He'd tell her it was all a game—a game he'd won. Katrine fought the horrible accusations her mind created, but her childhood scars went deep.

"Damn him," she said, tears brimming in her eyes. "Damn him." The curse came out a sob as the nightmares of past loss settled like a dark cloak around her once more.

♥ ♥ ♥

Finally, Sunday arrived. Trey, dressed in jeans and a sweat shirt, sat at his desk with the morning edition folded before him. True, he could have read today's feature from the comfort of his new home, but somehow it felt right to be at the office, reading a happy ending to what started as a very rocky beginning.

His separation from Katrine had been hell. There wasn't a room in his new home he walked into without thinking of her, smelling her scent, wanting her. He knew what the huge house he bought for the sole purpose of accommodating his family was missing; a family of his own. Children to run screaming through the halls on a day-to-day basis, instead of only when his relatives came to visit. He'd resigned himself to never having what he wanted most in life; now, the future seemed too bleak without them.

Katrine, Shelly, one or two dark haired, blue-eyed Westmorelands to call him Dad instead of Uncle—that was his dream. Putting his heart on the line, telling Katrine he loved her, needed her with him always, that was his nimbus.

What if she didn't want the same things he wanted? What if she didn't love him?

It was the twentieth century, after all. Just because a woman slept with a man, gave herself totally to him in passion, didn't mean she expected more. But deep down, Trey knew Katrine wasn't the type to want sex without commitment. When they made love, it seemed right, more so than he'd felt with another woman before her. Trey wasn't sure he'd ever truly loved Linda. He knew one thing for certain, had it been Katrine who left him, he would have gone after her, fought for her love, begged, whatever it took to get her back.

Linda had hurt him six years ago, but it was a selfish emotion, pain that dealt a blow to his pride, rather than to his heart. His feelings for her hadn't compared to what he felt for Katrine. He'd found that one special person, that once-in-a-life-time love everyone, male or female, dreamed of finding.

His hands shook when he poured himself a cup of coffee. Maybe he expected too much from her half of the feature today. He didn't believe Katrine would feel any more comfortable revealing her true emotions for the nation than he had. Later, when they were alone, Shelly and Beauregard romping around outside on actual grass, he'd talk with her seriously, tell her he loved her and wanted to spend what time they had left in life together. Still, he needed a sign, an admission, at least one sentence that reflected what she felt for him.

Assurances to strengthen his new-found faith in everlasting love, his faith in her. His hands shook with anticipation as Trey spread the paper in front of him. He turned to the article. The headline read; *The Truth About Romance*. First, Trey scanned his own entry.

A good journalist will admit to being wrong when he is, or in my case, assuming there is anything rational, or logical about love. Within the hustle and grind of our everyday lives, there are unforeseen forces at work. One of which is called attraction. The unconscious pull of one mass toward the other. A shifting of two separate entities, merging until they become one, yet able to separate themselves again and again, only to return.

Who can explain how it happens or what it really is? This force that brings male and female together? A talented author once called this compulsion to connect, 'a state of mind', or to go a step further and add my own opinion, 'a state of being', being in love.

A hero lives in every man, a heroine in every woman, and when the two meet, when they defy logic and redefine rationality, the phenomenon is called romance. I owe Kat Summers an apology. What she gives us with the gift of words is a commodity precious in its rarity. The hope to believe love still exists in the twentieth century, and the courage to dream we, too, will fall under its spell and find happily-ever-after.

Well, there it was, his assignment, a lesson in

reality Kat Summers had taught him. Trey took a deep breath and lowered his gaze to Katrine's feature.

Into every romance writer's life, a little reality must fall. These past few weeks have taught this author the differences between fiction and fact are indeed far apart. More than ever, I understand the lure that first led me to dream of dashing heroes and brave heroines, of adventures in a bygone era where in the end, love conquers all. Our modern times are not only lacking in heroes and heroines, but in creativity, as well.

Put simply, romance in the twentieth century plots itself with all the ingenuity of a badly written novel. The characters are most times immature and one dimensional, the relationship between them, about as warm as a business arrangement. The greatest conflict seems to be which character is best at the age-old game of deceit, or who delivered the last jab when the battle between them ends. The only gratification derived from the conclusion is relief that the story is finally over.

When the disappointment of reality pits itself against the fulfillment of imagination, Kat Summers will take fantasy every time, despite how entertaining I found a date with reality; regardless of the valuable research I gained from my experiences.

And with those findings, I renew my efforts at providing women with an escape into fantasy

when Prince Charming turns into a frog. A safe
harbor against the ravages of modern-day love,
and a few hours of romance in a day and age
where little can be found. Happy reading.

Numbness stole over Trey. For a moment, he
felt no pain, no knife plunging into his heart,
cutting away his dreams, his expectations, only
shock. Sluggishly, a *business arrangement* filtered
through his consciousness. *The age-old game of*
deceit? Relief that the story is finally over?

Katrine had delivered the last jab. Had she
seduced him for the sole purpose of getting
revenge for the review he wrote on her three years
ago? Had she used the unfortunate circumstances
of her past to lower his defenses, to gain access to
his heart?

He didn't want to believe her capable, couldn't
let go of his faith easily, but why else would she
have written those cruel words? "Damn her." The
curse left his throat in a hoarse whisper.

Trey waited for the rage to come, the angry
feelings that accompanied being made a fool of.
Neither did. Instead, his eyes began to burn. Up
until that moment, he didn't realize how desperately he wanted to believe in Katrine Summerville
and the purity of true love. She had extracted the
best revenge, turning a hardened realist into a
love-besotted idiot, and still, he couldn't quite
resign himself to her deceit.

"Trey?"

His heart lurched traitorously at the sound of

his name. He glanced up. Linda stood framed inside his doorway—not Katrine come to explain, but Linda.

"What are you doing here?"

Undaunted by Trey's lack of enthusiasm to see her, his ex-wife stepped into the office. "Glad to see you, too," she said sarcastically. "Jerry and I were down the hall in his office. I went to the ladies' room to check my lipstick and saw you in here." Her gaze lowered to the paper spread out on his desk. "Are you all right?"

"Fine." He shrugged, wishing she'd get out of his office. "Why are you and Jerry here?"

She moved closer. "He wanted to read this morning's edition in his office. I think he's getting a power rush. Most all of Dallas is sitting down to breakfast this morning with a cup of coffee in one hand, and his newspaper in the other. Jerry is wonderfully corrupt. He reminds me of Daddy."

"Sounds like love," he said as dryly as he could manage.

Linda lifted a brow. "I thought you believed in love and happily-ever-after. Once I read your feature this morning, I realized something about you I never knew. You're a hopeless romantic."

"Yeah, hopeless," Trey muttered darkly. "Look, I'd like to be alone."

The brunette seemed undaunted by his blunt declaration. "I don't think so," she argued. "I don't know why I feel compelled to tell you this, but Kat Summers didn't mean what she wrote in her feature. She's in love with you, Trey. She loves you with a depth I'm not capable of feeling. I see it in her eyes when she looks at you. Jerry suspects she's fallen for you, too, and vice versa. He's been acting smug for two days. He likes being number one. He needs you to keep him there. Think about it."

Trey reluctantly met her gaze. "Are you suggesting Jerry somehow influenced her article?"

"Did he try to influence yours?"

He hated the sudden pounding of his heart. "Yeah, he did, but I wouldn't let him. I had faith in Katrine. If she let him influence her, it doesn't say much for her depth."

The brunette shrugged. "Maybe not." She turned toward the door. "Don't you imagine believing comes harder for some people than it does for others? Maybe her faith has been battered around more than yours. I was impressed by your article, but you didn't really confess. You never said *you* found true love in the twentieth century."

"What? For all the world to read?" he defended at her back. "Katrine wouldn't have expected me to do that!"

His ex-wife paused at the door. "Do you know what I think is romantic? When a man gives a woman more than she expects. You told me love is unpredictable. Jerry is living proof. He's ruthless, greedy, and he's perfect for me. I think I might have just found my Prince Charming."

"In Jerry Caldwell?" Trey asked incredulously.

She turned her head to look at him and smiled. "Go figure. Good-bye, Trey. Really, good-bye." Her soft velvet eyes held sincerity. "You told me you don't make the same mistakes twice. Fight for her. Don't disappoint your readers… and me, by leaving this feature unfinished. Give her the unexpected."

As Trey watched Linda leave his life, he felt a measure of comfort at her words. She had redeemed herself in a moment of weakness, proving that everyone wanted to believe in romance, and happy endings. He and Linda's love hadn't been strong enough to last forever, but what he felt for Katrine could withstand the ravages of time. A lifetime. He was still angry she hadn't confronted him with her doubts, but like Linda said, believing came harder to some people than it did to others.

He snatched up the phone, then set the receiver back in its cradle. Calling seemed too easy, and heaven knew, nothing about their relationship had gone smoothly. Linda was right. He wanted to give Katrine something she wouldn't expect. He refolded the newspaper spread across his desk, reached over and turned on his computer.

The feature wasn't complete. He had one last matter of unfinished business to clear up, then Jerry Caldwell would be receiving a punch in the nose and his resignation. Trey Westmoreland intended to write murder mysteries, and the victims would always be long-legged blondes.

Chapter Twenty

♥   ♥   ♥

For a solid week Shelly tiptoed around the house, allowing her mother the privacy she wanted, listening to her sobs late into the night. Her mom refused to talk about Trey.

Shelly didn't understand what had happened. Trey didn't do anything wrong as far as she could tell. Her only hope was that he'd fix whatever mistake he'd made. She consoled herself with assurances Trey would save her mother from retreating into her computer. A fear that had not yet come to pass. Her mom didn't seem interested in writing, in anything, until this morning.

Emerging from the shrine of her bedroom with red-rimmed eyes, her mom had come downstairs, fixed a perfectly awful breakfast and said she was going to organize her closet. Obviously, she'd gone insane.

"Where'd all this stuff come from?" Shelly perched herself on the edge of her mother's bed, surveying the clutter.

"I have trouble parting with things," Katrine

answered from the closet's interior. "Shelly, hand me that shoe rack and a hammer—no wait, you might get hurt."

She appeared at the doorway, scanned the messy room and spotted the hammer on her dresser top. "Make yourself useful, Honey." Katrine carefully stepped over a pile of twisted belts in her path. "See if you can match up all those shoes lying in the middle of my bed."

"There must be twenty pairs here," Shelly grumbled.

"Look for a tan flat in particular." Her mother glanced down at her feet. She wore only one tan shoe. "I couldn't find it earlier. Maybe it's under the bed."

Dutifully, Shelly slid down, got on her knees and lifted the comforter. She came face to face with Beauregard. "There you are."

"Did you find it?" Katrine asked hopefully, hammer in hand.

"Afraid so." Her daughter held up a the missing flat covered in slobber.

"That dog is nothing but trouble," Katrine scolded softly, then smiled. "But, for better or worse, he's our problem."

"What about Trey?" Shelly blurted. "If you can still love Beau when he screws up, why can't you forgive Trey, too?"

Katrine sighed. "I don't want to discuss this—" she cut herself off. Shelly couldn't be kept in the dark forever. "Honey, you've asked about your father, and about your grandparents. The time has come to tell you."

"But, what do they have to do with Trey?" Shelly asked in confusion.

"Nothing," her mother answered. "And everything. You see, I learned very early in life that sometimes the people who are supposed to love you the most, hurt you the worst. Do you know what abandonment is?"

"I think so." The little blonde's brows crinkled. "Isn't that what Janie Reardon's mother did? She just left."

"Sort of," Katrine answered, distractedly brushing Shelly's bangs from her eyes. "Janie's mom didn't run off without telling anyone where she was going. She went to a place to get help, and Janie knows her mother will come home when she feels better. Abandonment is when a person leaves a child alone by herself, or often in the care of people she doesn't know, for an extended period of time, or in my case, for many years."

"My grandma did that?" Shelly whispered. "She just left you somewhere without ever coming back?"

"Yes. But I don't want you to be angry with her. I've been angry for a long time, and it didn't change anything, well, not anything but me. Deep down, I thought I was somehow to blame. I believed there must be something wrong with me, either that, or maybe I didn't deserve to be loved."

Shelly's brown eyes filled with tears. "You're

wrong, Mom. I love you more than anyone in the whole world."

"I know you do," Katrine quickly assured, pulling Shelly into her arms. "But once those fears took root inside of me, they kept growing. Your father understood how it felt to be suddenly left alone. People can be drawn to each other out of mutual pain. When he died, I began to feel the anger again. It took me until this week to realize I can't hold a grudge against your father for leaving me, leaving us," she corrected.

"Fate brought us together, and fate separated us. Your father didn't leave me alone. He gave me you. When you let yourself care for someone there are risks, but even if you lose at love, there are rewards to be gained."

"You mean, something good can come from something bad?"

"That's right." Katrine hugged Shelly tightly. "I have a beautiful daughter, and every time I look into your eyes, I see John again. So, you see, he never left at all."

Shelly's expression grew thoughtful. "I still don't understand what Trey has to do with this."

Her mother worried her bottom lip for a moment, then took a deep breath. "Trey taught me to stop avoiding what I can't control. Because of him, I've learned important things about you and about myself. I hurt inside right now, but I'm not afraid anymore. I understand that pain is part of loving, and I'm strong enough to survive and go on with my life. In time, what I feel will fade, but I'll still have the important lessons learned from our relationship."

"I don't want your feelings to fade," Shelly declared passionately. "I want—"

The ringing of Shelly's private phone interrupted them.

"Go on," Katrine urged, gaining her feet and helping Shelly up. "Maybe it's Melissa. You should get out of the house for a while. This," she indicated her room with a sweep of her hand, "will take hours, maybe weeks."

Reluctant to leave the matter unresolved, Shelly glanced between her mother and the doorway leading into the hallway. "Can we talk about Trey later?"

"Yes," Katrine answered, although she hoped Shelly would give her heart a reprieve. "Later," the word left her lips in a whisper. "Take Beauregard with you," she roused herself to instruct.

She managed to maintain a facade of strength until Shelly and Beauregard disappeared, then Katrine rose and walked to the dresser. With trembling hands, she picked up the hammer and studied it without interest. She hadn't lied to Shelly about her ability to survive the heartbreak of love—she simply failed to mention how desperately she wanted Trey back in her life. A week without him seemed like an eternity, and yet she'd had time to think, to examine all the good and bad his intrusion brought, and to regret writing her last feature while under the influence of angry hurt.

Although Katrine hadn't forgiven Trey for tromping on her emotions for the sake of ratings, or for revenge, she tried to convince herself that she wished him success. Mostly, she failed at it. When she thought about his tactics, how he seduced her, how he made a fool of her, she honestly wanted to do him bodily injury. Noting the hammer in her hand, she suddenly felt the need to pound something.

♥   ♥   ♥

Trey pounded on the horn. "Move it, buddy!" he yelled, annoyed at the Sunday driver in front of him. His gaze darted to a newspaper in the seat beside him. Waiting a week to release the article had nearly driven him insane. More times than he cared to count, he'd been tempted to forget about giving Katrine a public declaration. Storming her house, throwing her over his shoulder and carrying her to his cave seemed more in line with his emotions.

Shelly would be his accomplice today. The little vixen sounded more than eager to help him gain entrance to Katrine's fortress when he called earlier. Ignoring Shelly all week ate at his conscience, but Trey didn't want Katrine to anticipate his intentions. Nothing told the truth more than an unguarded reaction. Besides, he deserved com-

pensation for the blow she delivered last Sunday.
Shelly said her mother had cried most of the
week. Horrible as it was, Trey smiled. His heart
sped up when he turned on her street. The front
door eased open to his soft knock.

"You didn't ask who it was," Trey said before
stepping inside.

"I knew it was you," Shelly countered.

"And you." He pointed a finger at Beauregard.
"Didn't make a sound. Some watch dog."

"He wasn't supposed to," Shelly defended. "I
told him to keep quiet."

Trey smiled and ruffled her hair. "Where is
she?"

Shelly nodded toward the stairs. "Up there.
Cleaning out her closet, so be careful when you
go in, and, Trey," she sighed, "try to say the right
thing."

His smile widened. "I'll try. I even wrote it
down."

She eyed the newspaper he removed from
beneath his arm skeptically. "Isn't that what got
you into trouble with her to begin with?"

"I guess it is," he agreed. "Let's see if it can
get me out of trouble for a change."

"If it doesn't, chew on her shoes and look real
sad about if afterward. It works for Beauregard."

He laughed softly at her suggestion, then
sobered. "Shelly, you're special to me. You always
will be. You know that, don't you?"

Her pink cheeks turned pinker. "Yeah, I know.

Better go win my mom."

Trey took a deep breath and forged ahead. A small voice floated up to him as he mounted the stairs.

"I love you, too, Trey."

He turned, but Shelly had disappeared. A door closed downstairs and he assumed Beauregard had been taken outside. A warm feeling settled in the pit of his stomach. Someday, he wanted to hear that little blonde minx call him dad. He knew which bedroom belonged to Katrine because of the night he sat out front and admired her silhouette against the shades, but finding her wouldn't have been difficult. The sound of banging drew him to her open doorway. His gaze roamed the clutter. He wondered how she'd fit all that into her closet to begin with.

"Dammit!" The banging ceased.

Trey stepped over a large bundle of clothes and stared across the room into Katrine's closet. A shoe rack stood propped against the wall. Katrine had a hammer in one hand and her thumb in her mouth. As if sensing his presence, she wheeled around. Her eyes widened and something incoherent escaped her lips.

"What?" Trey asked.

The thumb left her mouth. "What are you doing here and how did you get in?"

"Shelly opened the door for me," he answered the last part of her question. "And, by the way, didn't bother to verify it was me before doing so."

"She's definitely in for a lecture on that mistake," Katrine assured him. "You didn't say what you're doing here."

He smiled. "I wanted to read you my feature."

"I read it," she said stiffly. "It was garbage, but I'm sure Jerry is pleased."

Caldwell was the last person Trey wanted to discuss. His thoughts leaned more toward surrender. Hers. He'd been fighting the need to touch Katrine from the moment he saw her standing in the closet with her thumb in her mouth.

"This is a new feature, and Jerry's on his way to Philly with Linda. She's taking him home to meet Papa."

"Well, Mr. Hot Commodity, I suppose you'll be filling his shoes?"

Trey shrugged. "Only until I make a few sales in fiction. That's what this article is about. Since you're such an expert, I wanted your opinion."

When a dark tinge of color crept up her neck, his smile widened. She was getting mad as hell.

"You've got nerve," Katrine bit out. "Next, I suppose you'll be asking me to read your manuscripts or speak with a publisher on your behalf?"

"Would you?" he asked innocently.

She glanced toward the hammer in her hand. "No," Katrine answered strongly.

"Then, would you listen to this one? I think you might find it of interest." Without waiting for her permission, Trey removed the paper clutched beneath his arm and snapped it open. "It's another special, entitled, *The Real Story."*

He waited for her to react. When her brow lifted in a gesture of curiosity, Trey cleared his throat, embarrassed when the paper quivered in his hands.

"She walked into my life and rationality ceased to exist. Was it the length of her legs that first caught my attention?" Trey paused to glance at her legs. Katrine's slacks were covered in lint and dog hair. "To say no, would be a lie. Could I have ignored the fullness of her lips, the slant of her eyes, the silkiness of her hair, and instead, thought she seemed intelligent—a woman I'd like to know better on a intellectual level?" His gaze lifted. "To say yes would also be a lie. It began as it often does, with a physical attraction, but ended as it often doesn't, within the heart."

The hammer in Katrine's hand made a loud thud as it hit the floor. He watched her walk out of the closet to stand directly across from him. Trey didn't need to read the rest, he knew the words.

"I'm not a story-book hero. I'm only a man, flesh and blood—one who makes mistakes. There are no real dragons, Katrine, but the demons that torture our minds, our hearts, are often worse."

When her eyes filled with tears, it took all his resolve not to go to her, but he couldn't. Not yet.

"I can't slay them all for you, but I'll stand by your side in battle. I will promise you forever, but I can't promise to be with you forever. Life delivers death. Love delivers pain. Time is short. There's nothing predictable about true love. It writes its own story and leaves the proof of its heaven and hell in the lines on our faces, in the children that follow behind us. And without struggle, there are no victories, no rewards. Dare to dream beyond the scope of your imagination. Share life's joys and sorrows by my side. I did find love in the twentieth century. I found you, Katrine Summerville. Give me a happy ending. Marry me."

Katrine's heart pounded loudly inside her chest. Tears ran unchecked down her cheeks. Love, she supposed, was meant to be a private emotion shared between two people, but Trey's public proposal reached deep and plucked at the strings of her heart. She couldn't think of anything more romantic, and knew she would never doubt him again. He was her hero.

When he held out his arms in appeal, she rushed forward. Her feet got tangled in a twisted wad of belts on the floor and she felt herself falling. A panicked glance at Trey allowed her to witness his heroic leap over a pile of clothes. She lunged, fell on the bed and into his waiting arms.

"Ouch." Trey dislodged a black pump from beneath his back, then tossed the shoe aside. His lips brushed Katrine's. "I love you, Katrine. Give me an answer."

She smiled. "You'll have to wait and read my response in tomorrow's edition. I have an 'in' with the new editor."

His mouth grazed her ear. "I know ways to make you talk."

"Mmnn," she sighed as his tongue traced a path down her neck. "I love… that," she admitted.

"How about this?" His hand slid slowly up her thigh.

"I love… that, too."

When he gently nipped at her breasts through the material of her blouse, Katrine moaned softly. "I do love you, Trey. I'll always love you."

"You'll always love me and…" he prodded, unfastening the top button on her blouse with his teeth.

"I'll always love you and… Shelly!"

Both Katrine and Trey sat up abruptly.

"It got awfully quiet up here," her daughter said from the open doorway. "Me and Beauregard were wondering what was taking so long." She glanced between the two of them, then winked at Trey. "Looks like you said the right thing."

Katrine saw him blush. Trey would have to adjust to the fact that they couldn't always throw caution to the wind and surrender to passion when the mood struck them.

"Ah, I haven't managed to get a full-fledged 'yes' out of your mother, but with your help, I believe we can convince her to say the right thing."

Katrine's gaze darted nervously between her daughter and her prince, who sometimes wasn't in the least charming. Her heart was full to bursting with joy. Trey had given her a special gift today. He'd proven one special hero existed for every woman.

"How do we get her to say it?" Shelly asked curiously.

"We can tickle it out of her."

"Trey," Katrine warned.

Shelly's grin stretched. With a squeal of delight, she made a dash for the bed, a muddy-pawed, drooling Beauregard fast on her heels. After the dog managed to decorate not only the bedspread, but everyone's clothes, as well, Trey pinned Katrine to the bed so Shelly could tickle her feet. The light of desire still shone brightly in his eyes when he leaned close to whisper, "Later?"

Noting the soiled condition of his shirt, Katrine smiled wickedly. "I'll meet you at the washing machine," she whispered back.

THE END

Dear Reader,

We hope you enjoyed this LionHearted novel. You may have already noticed some differences between our books and many others, beginning with our covers. I was always embarrassed to read books with 'bodice-ripping' covers in public, so I had our team of artists create covers I wouldn't even hesitate to recommend to my male friends.

You may also notice that any necessary violent scenes in our novels have been toned down or take place out of view of the reader. I personally enjoy empowered heroines and heroes who show that integrity, persistence and love will ultimately triumph over adversity.

It takes authors with talent and imagination and a diligent and caring editorial staff to produce entertaining and memorable stories. But it also takes you! Please write and let me know what you like, and don't like, so we may continue to provide quality and entertaining stories. And, don't forget to tell a friend about us.

Thank you for choosing a LionHearted book.

Mary Ann Heathman
President & CEO
LionHearted Publishing, Inc.

About LionHearted

When forming LionHearted we discovered many things about the publishing industry that we felt could be improved. For example, due to excessively large print runs, and less than hoped for sales, over half of the paperbacks printed today are now being dumped into our landfills and oceans as waste. Yet, publishers continue to release more books each month than there is room for on store shelves.

An overabundance of titles and a shortage of display space has led to a shorter shelf life for most titles. Many books may come and go before the reader even has an opportunity to see them. If you only visit a bookstore once a month, you've probably missed seeing hundreds of paperbacks. The result is fewer sales per title and correspondingly lower author royalties. Also, many books being released today are not new titles but re-prints of old titles avid consumers have already read.

There appeared to be a need for an alternative approach to the marketing and distribution of novels. How often have you recommended a great movie, an excellent restaurant, a good book, or even a brand name you liked? All the time! But has any movie theater, restaurant, or book store ever reimbursed you for the highly effective "advertising" you did on their behalf?

LionHearted does! We allow our customers to earn free books or extra cash as a referral fee for introducing new customers to LionHearted. Now, telling friends about books you love can truly be rewarding.

The feedback we receive from our customers is most encouraging. They have come to trust the LionHearted logo to offer a quality entertaining read that won't disappoint, and our authors tell us they love having creative writing freedom.

We publish many sub-genres of romance including contemporary, historical, time-travel, Regency, comedy, suspense, intrigue, futuristic, fantasy, westerns and more.

LionHearted is a reader and author friendly company, so if you would enjoy some new blending of romance sub-genres let us know.

We also encourage you to support your local and national literacy programs. One out of five adults in this country can't read, and illiteracy has been found to be the biggest link to crime. Unfortunately, many adults won't attend public reading programs because they don't want others to know they can't read. In an effort to solve this dilemma we are working on a literacy video that will teach people how to read in the privacy of their home. Your ideas and support are appreciated.

LionHearted Publishing, Inc.
P.O. Box 618
Zephyr Cove, NV 89448
702-588-1388, 702-588-1386 Fax
admin@LionHearted.com
http://www.LionHearted.com

A Fun LionHearted Contest

Answer the following questions and you could win a romantic prize from LionHearted. Each calendar quarter (Mar, Jun, Sep, Dec) we will draw a winner from the submissions received.

In the story you just read, what award was T. West presented at the writers awards banquet?

_____

What is the name and address of your favorite book store that carries romance titles:

Name_____

Addrs_____

_____

Phone_____

What is your name and address:

Name_____

Addrs_____

_____

Phone_____

Email_____

Send, fax or email this information to us at

LionHearted Publishing, Inc.
P.O. Box 618
Zephyr Cove, NV 89448

702-588-1388, 702-588-1386 Fax

admin@LionHearted.com

(This contest may be terminated at any time by publisher)

Your Opinion Counts

LionHearted will give you a **free gift** for filling out this questionnaire (or a copy of it) and sending it to us.

1. Where did you get this book?
❏ Bookstore   ❏ Online bookstore _____
❏ LionHearted   ❏ Friend
❏ Other _____

2. Tell us what you liked about this book?
❏ Overall story   ❏ Easy to read type size
❏ Characters   ❏ Good value for the money
❏ Other _____

3. Would you enjoy similar books? ❏ Yes   ❏ No

4. Tell us if you disliked something about this book.

_____

5. Would you buy another LionHearted book?
❏ Yes ❏ No ❏ If _____

6. What other romance genres do you enjoy reading?
❏ Historical   ❏ Regency   ❏ Medieval
❏ Contemporary   ❏ Futuristic/Fantasy/Paranormal

7. How many books do you read per Wk___ Mo___

8. Which magazines do you read?
a. _____
b. _____
c. _____

9. What is your age group?
❏ Under 25 ❏ 25-34 ❏ 35-44 ❏ 45-54 ❏ 55+